W9-BYG-488

The Happy Valley

Also by Max Brand ™
in Large Print:

Sixteen in Nome
Outlaws All: A Western Trio
The Lightning Warrior
The Wolf Strain: A Western Trio
The Stone that Shines
Men Beyond the Law: A Western Trio
Beyond the Outposts
The Fugitive's Mission: A Western Trio
In the Hills of Monterey
The Lost Valley: A Western Trio
Chinook
The Gauntlet: A Western Trio
The Survival of Juan Oro
Stolen Gold: A Western Trio
Timber Line: A Western Trio

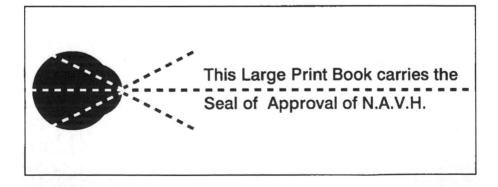

This Large Print Book carries the
Seal of Approval of N.A.V.H.

MAX BRAND ™

The Happy Valley

G.K. Hall & Co. • Thorndike, Maine

1682 2049

Published in 2001 by arrangement with Golden West Literary Agency.

G.K. Hall Large Print Western Series.

The text of this edition is unabridged.

Set in 16 pt. Plantin by Al Chase.

Printed in the United States on permanent paper.

Library of Congress Cataloging in Publication Data
Brand, Max, 1892–1944.
    The happy valley / by Max Brand.
      p.   cm.
    ISBN 0-7838-9354-X (lg. print : hc : alk. paper)
    1. Ex-convicts — Fiction.   2. Revenge — Fiction.   3. Large type books.   I. Title.
    PS3511.A87 H39 2001
    813′.52—dc21   00-053846

The Happy Valley

CHAPTER ONE

Little Danny Green brought the news into Burned Hill. Danny had been out looking for strays, and when he came plunging back, he was riding his pinto to death. He made a little detour and paused at the house of the Dollars. He dipped down from the saddle and looked through the front door.

"Where's Tom? Where's Tom?" he screeched.

"Back in the smokehouse cutting up a hog," said Lew Dollar.

"Then you go and tell him! The Phantom's back! The Phantom's back! I seen him with my own eyes, comin', and I cut for it. You tell Tom to clear out!"

There was much confusion in the Dollar house. Some of them put together a pack of food. Others rolled blankets inside a slicker. Tom himself, hastily summoned from the smokehouse, rushed for the corral, but his hands were so uncertain that he could not succeed in putting the rope on the long-legged chestnut that he wanted. He had to get the help of his brother, Dick, who daubed the rope properly, though he was as white-faced as Tom, well-nigh.

Together they dragged the saddle onto the back of the chestnut, and in another moment Tom Dollar was off across country, flattening himself along the back of his gelding, and looking back with frightened eyes until the willows at the first slough were passed and he was screened from observation. Even then, he rode hard. The next day, says legend, he pulled up in Stumpy Hollow, which is eighty miles as the crow flies and more than a hundred by trail.

The good chestnut gelding was not worth a dime, by that time. He hardly could hobble into a corral, with one man leading and one beating him behind. That evening, he died; but Tom Dollar was safe for the moment, and the ride was considered worth while.

Danny Green had not waited to see all of these developments. He drove straight on toward Burned Hill with the foam flying from the mouth of his pinto and spotting Danny himself. But he knew that this was a great day for him. Not another boy in that town had achieved so much of the public eye as he was about to gain!

So he stormed up the main street.

As he came to the crossing in the center of town, he was delayed by an eight-horse team which was making the turn, and, while he squeezed past, Danny screamed to a line of idlers whose chairs were tilted back on the veranda of Bertram's saloon: "The Phantom's comin'! I seen him! I seen him with my own eyes!"

Every man in the line stood up, agape; and then, suddenly, they grinned evilly, as some men cannot help smiling when they see a great headline in a newspaper, telling of disaster about to fall upon others.

Danny Green got down the street like a small cyclone. He pulled up at the office from which Sheriff Bud Cross ruled the town and the countryside, equitably and fearlessly. Bud now leaned his length against the side of his front door, with his big hands in his pockets and his feet crossed, while he started at the pattern of black and white beneath the mulberry tree in his front yard.

"Hey, Sheriff!" screamed Danny. "The Phantom! I seen him comin' up Fuller's Draw —"

And Danny was gone.

The sheriff gulped. He almost swallowed the large quid of tobacco which was stowed in one cheek, then he lunged back into his office and reached for his guns.

Danny had gone on in a puff of white dust which dissolved about him as he reached the Phelan home. Mrs. Phelan was in the front yard, picking the dead flowers and the young pods off her hedge of sweet peas.

"Hey, Mrs. Phelan! Is Larry to home?"

"He's in the back yard diggin' up the potato patch," said Mrs. Phelan. "Hello, young feller! Are you gone crazy?"

For Danny had ridden through the open gate and was digging up the garden path as he rushed his horse to the rear of the house. There he saw the powerful shoulders of Larry Phelan stooped above his spade. He was in the very act of turning a great black slice of the soil.

"Larry, Larry!" shouted the boy. "The Phantom's comin'! The Phantom! I seen him in Fuller's Draw!"

The spade fell from the hands of Larry Phelan. His eyes turned toward the corral, where he could see the fine head of a brown mare, the pride of his life. But then he remembered another head which was appearing over the board fence at the side of the yard. Pretty Josephine Dolan was standing on a box to watch him work and exchange the time of day. The thought of her stiffened the back of Larry Phelan. He said with a snarl:

"Don't come jumpin' at a man's back and givin' him a start, because what do I care about The Phantom? To — Well, let him watch out for himself, if he's comin' back! Besides," he went on, gathering heat and color as he went on, "it's a lie! He couldn't come back this soon!"

"Maybe he's busted loose from the penitentiary," said the boy. "Or maybe he's had his term shortened up for bein' good!"

"Good? Him?" grunted Phelan.

Nevertheless his rising color faded again, and he looked very sick.

Danny Green turned his horse around, disappointed at the effect of his news.

"Well," he said gloomily, "I've told you. That's all I gotta do with it! Maybe he'll go after *me* for tellin'!"

The thought made him shudder, and he switched the tired pinto into a laboring gallop that took him back through the front yard and past the outraged screech of Mrs. Phelan.

"Whose phantom?" asked Josephine Dolan.

Young Larry Phelan gripped the handle of the spade and shrugged his shoulders.

"Why, *the* phantom, of course," said he. "Jimmy Fantom. You've heard about him, I guess."

"Never a word. We only been in town six months, or less," said she.

"Well — it's a funny thing — that you ain't heard. Even if he's been five years away."

"Five years in the penitentiary?"

"Yes."

"It's a long time, Larry! Why should he have it in for you?"

"Him?" said Larry, talking more loudly than necessary, so that he might raise his own courage. "Why, they ain't no reason! Except that he's a devil! That's all!"

He went on, breathing hard, still gripping his hands to nerve himself up to a part.

"Kids are fools, Jo. You oughta know that! I'll tell you what. I was as bad a fool as the next one, when I was a kid. Well, this here Jim Fantom, he got me and Tom Dollar into a mess of trouble. He got us to go out with him and hold up the Fullertown stage!"

"Larry!" cried the girl.

He looked curiously at her, but she did not really look horrified. Instead, her face was shining with curiosity and interest.

11

"There was shootin'," said Larry Phelan hoarsely. He looked earnestly at the girl again.

"How awful!" said she.

"You seem to think it was a joke, maybe?" said he.

"A joke? Of course I don't!"

"Well, they was *three* men guardin' that stage. And they was all shot down. Well, it was Jim Fantom that done the shootin'. I mean, it was him that dropped 'em all. That was proved afterward. He had an old-fashioned forty-four, and that was how everything was proved ag'in him!"

"Did he kill the three men?"

"He'd a hung, wouldn't he, if he'd a *killed* 'em?" asked Phelan peevishly. "Nope. But he sunk a slug in the thigh of Steve Morgan, and another through the shoulder of Bill Lorris, and he drove a third slug into the hip of Jack Keene. I never forget how Jack hollered. It hurt him terrible bad!"

"What were the three guards doin'?" asked the girl greedily. "Just settin' up like babies, waitin' to be shot down?"

"Them? I should say not! Why was they hired except that they was good gunmen, and that they was a lot of gold dust in the boot of that stage? You betcha we was takin' our chances when we stepped out and lit into the three of 'em!"

"Weren't any of you hurt?"

"Aw, nobody but Fantom. He got a couple of scratches."

"What kind of scratches?"

12

"Why, one that ripped up his left forearm, and one that drilled through the thigh of his right leg."

"D'you call that scratches?"

"I mean, Jim was tough as leather. It didn't bother him none. Why, he rode ten mile, with them wounds."

"While he was shot through the thigh?"

"Yeah. He's kind of an Indian, for standing pain!"

"And then what happened?"

"Why —" said Larry Phelan, and paused. But he looked hungrily at the girl. She was very pretty. Twice, already, she had gone with him to dances and made him the most envied man in the town; besides, she was sure to hear the story in an uglier guise from someone else.

"It was this way. They run down me and Dollar. They found some of the stuff on us. Mind you, we hadn't figgered on stealin'. But it was like a kind of a lark. Fantom, he got us into it all!"

"Go on," said Josephine Dolan, her eyes narrowing a little.

"Well, they wanted to know which of us had done the shootin', and had the forty-four caliber gun. Well, it would of meant pretty near life, if we was caught. We said we hadn't done it, and so they said all they wanted was the man that had done the shootin'. They let us tell the truth—"

"You turned state's evidence?" asked Jo Dolan.

The face of Phelan wrinkled.

13

"You say that in a funny way," said he.

"Well," said the girl, "anyways, they couldn't get him. He must of been cached away in the hills?"

"Well, Tom Dollar told where he was," muttered Phelan, and suddenly his eyes were weighed down to the ground.

He heard a stifled gasp. Then:

"If he's coming back, I suppose that it means he'll try to get you? Ain't you terribly scared, Larry?"

"Scared?" shouted Phelan with unnecessary force. "I'm gunna go down the street and meet him comin' in!"

CHAPTER TWO

Larry Phelan watched the girl disappear, and his heart beat fast. He never had been so frightened in his life, but after all, he was not a coward. He was a fighting man, he knew guns, and the one blot on his fair fame was the turning of state's evidence in that unlucky affair. He had not wanted to betray his companion. As a matter of fact, it was only the grim, steady pressure of the sheriff in an all-night conversation that first had broken the nerve of Tom Dollar. And when Tom began to talk, Phelan had talked also. There was no reason why Tom Dollar should have the pleasure of going free while two men went to jail!

Besides, the third man was the one they wanted. Sheriff Bud Cross had said:

"I don't wanta bother you boys. You've had your lesson. But I wanta get that other young skyrocket, whoever he might be. He shoots too straight, and he's got too much in the bean. He needs a rest, and a doggone long rest. I'm the man to supply him with a free bed and free board!"

There was a touch of grim humor, always, in the sheriff!

But Larry Phelan, on this day of dreadful trial, prepared to do battle for his life. And for Josephine Dolan! Whenever he thought of her blue

15

eyes, his heart quaked with something like homesickness, and also like the dip of a car on a rollercoaster. He decided that he would fight.

He had another good reason. For five long, mortal years, Jim Fantom had been behind the walls of a penitentiary, turning big ones into little ones. And in that time it seemed most probable that he must have lost the inhuman cunning of his hand when the butt of a revolver was inside it. He must have lost the edge of his spirit, also. Men got such things as the "prison shakes" in a penitentiary. They could walk bravely enough up to a crisis, but, when the pinch came, they melted away like creatures of sand in a strong wind. Perhaps this would be the case with The Phantom!

It will be seen that Phelan was a reasoning man, and he finished adding up one fact to another, and to the facts the probabilities, until he was ready for the battle, since battle there must be. If he left town, he was disgraced forever, and would have to go to the ends of the earth and there try to find a new life, with a new name to wear on it.

He did not select a rifle or a revolver. Instead, he took a sawed-off shotgun. Even with five years of absence from gunplay, it was hardly conceivable that Jim Fantom could not beat him to the draw. But he must bet that Jim's shot would go wild, and in reply, he would send a double charge of buckshot into the breast of the ex-gunman!

16

So he loaded that gun with care, and, with it slung over the hollow of his left arm, he walked slowly down the street. He passed a good many people, and every one of them had heard the news.

When they saw him coming with that gun, and marked the slow, deliberate step with which he proceeded, most of them turned straight around and began to drift behind him. One or two even hurried on ahead and passed the news along, so that a good many faces appeared at windows, and other forms hurried into doorways to look at him.

In this manner, Larry Phelan was put upon a stage, and his somewhat mean and bitter nature felt the stimulus and enlarged itself with the sun of public attention. He could not turn back. Presently he began to rejoice in the prominence of his place. And he could feel beneath the curve of his trigger finger the power which would quite wipe out the stain of that state's evidence which he had given five years before!

Suddenly a mustang cantered out of a side street, and he halted, mid-stride, heart thundering.

No, it was only the sheriff! He drew rein beside Phelan.

"Larry," said he, "you better go home, and stay home!"

"What for?" demanded Phelan huskily. Then his voice came to him. "I gotta right to go where I please in this here town, and I'm gunna go!" said he.

The sheriff looked him up and down in an

oddly thoughtful manner.

"Well," said he, "the word is that he's comin' up from Fuller's Draw, and I'm gunna go down to that end of the town and try to stop him on the way up."

"You don't need to do it for my sake," said Phelan. "I'll take care of myself — and him too, maybe!"

The sheriff remained quietly thoughtful.

"You're your own boss," he said at last. "I've told you what you'd better do!"

With that, he turned his horse and rode off, and the very heart of Phelan was thrilled by a murmur of applause. Up to his side came little Sam Kruger, and touched his arm.

"That's the stuff, Larry," said he. "You're a man to make the town proud of you, all right! You wouldn't take water from nobody, not even The Phantom!"

Larry Phelan looked down at Kruger with mingled astonishment and disgust. He knew that Kruger had hated him passionately since a time when Phelan had referred to him as a "dancing rat." For Kruger distinguished himself neither on a cowhorse nor in a hayfield, but only on a dance floor. That remark Phelan had made in the presence of many witnesses, among whom was pretty Jo Dolan; and Kruger had taken it so much to heart that, so said rumor, he had vowed he would have the heart blood of Phelan for the insult! But here he was, muttering praise and encouragement!

"Thanks," grunted Phelan. "I'm gunna blow the skunk's liver right in two. You stick along, kid, and you'll see me do it!"

"Aw, I'll be there, all right!" said Kruger, and he rubbed his hands together, and laughed almost hysterically.

Phelan went on until he came to Bertram's saloon, and there a long line of idlers rose as though to salute him. He paused easily on the steps. He looked up and down the line and recognized many old companions. Some of them were men whom he had accepted as equals or superiors before this day, but now he was conscious of a great superiority.

"Come in and liquor, boys," said he, airily, and he waved toward the saloon entrance.

He waited until they had crowded in before him, all except one elderly man with a long, almost patriarchal gray beard.

"Ain't you gunna have a taste, old timer?" said Larry Phelan.

"I've passed my drinking days," said the other. He looked with bright, steady eyes at Larry Phelan. "When we get on in years, we have to keep our wits about us, you know!"

Larry laughed.

"Half a brain is good enough for any job," said he, "and the other half for red-eye!"

He went on into the saloon. The smell of the wet sawdust on the floor, the sour-sweet of beer and whisky fumes in the air, the coolness, all were helping to relax the tenseness of his nerves.

19

He stood up to the bar and drew out his wallet.

"Let's have a taste all around, Bertram," said he.

And, for the first time in his life, he felt that Bertram was looking at him with a grave and almost covert respect, as he dexterously spun the long line of glasses down the bar, so that each whirled and jingled to a stop before its appropriate customer. Then, with equal speed, he produced four bottles, and spun them, likewise, into position. They made a small thunder as they walked down the thin boards of the bar.

"Here's to you, boys," said Phelan grandly.

"Here's to the bravest man in Burned Hill," croaked a shrill voice in answer.

It was little Kruger, standing at the farther end of the bar and holding the glass straight and high above his head.

"Aw, quit yer kiddin'," said Phelan in pleased embarrassment. "Here's how."

"Here's to the boy with the guts!" exclaimed another.

And down went the whisky in a single, reddish-brown flash.

"Another!" squeaked Kruger. "Liquor up, boys! Liquor up, and give our friend good luck!"

Once more the glasses were filled. The second shot followed the first, and Phelan winked the tears out of his eyes. The sweet fire had burned his throat, but almost immediately he craved another.

He treated again, and again. Then he could

feel all of his muscles at ease. He was sure of himself, at last. All of these good fellows were wishing him luck. That was good! Furthermore, they believed in him! Anyone could see by the melting brightness of their eyes that they were for him!

Still the whisky bottles were rumbling up and down the bar, and his mind gave only a partial attention to the subject of The Phantom.

"After all," said Kruger suddenly, "what did The Phantom ever do?"

"Them two that he killed in Tombstone, they was both greasers," said one.

"It was an Indian that he shot in Chihuahua!"

"Harry Lord was gettin' to be an old man when the kid blew the front of his face in."

"And Lynch wasn't lookin'. He wasn't expectin' nothin' when The Phantom sashayed in and shot him through the heart. He didn't even give him time to fill his hand."

"Naw. That ain't right. I was there, buddies, an' he called out to Lynch to fill his hand, all right. Naw, give the devil his due!"

"Well," said Phelan, "I'll tell all of you what *I'm* gunna do to him, and if I don't, you call me a liar!"

"What are you gunna do, kid?"

"I'm gunna give him one barrel in the belly!"

"That'll make him show what's in him!"

They guffawed at the brutal thought.

"Then," continued Phelan, "I'm gunna step up and blow his face off with the second barrel.

21

That's what I'm gunna do, in case that you wanta ask me!"

"Good kid!"

They cheered him.

"You'll do it, too!"

The front door of the saloon was dashed open.

It was little Danny Green standing before him.

"Hey, hey!" he gasped. "He's double crossed the sheriff and come in from the other end of the town and — he — he's almost here now! He ain't a block away!"

CHAPTER THREE

No matter how prepared for battle, when Larry Phelan heard this announcement, he felt very much like the hunter of bears, when a bear starts up at the roadside under the nose of his gun. In other words, he felt a sudden desire to run.

But instantly he remembered himself. The kindly whisky remembered him, too. It threw a rosy cloud of confusion into his brain and sent warmth all through his arteries with each stroke of his heart.

He laughed in an instant, and looked bravely around him, as the noise of a horse came trotting down the street and stopped in front of the saloon. But when he looked around him, he saw that the men were instinctively shrinking away from him, and all of them were looking toward him with faces from which the whisky flush gradually was dying out. There was neither compassion nor confidence in their eyes, but rather a touch of cold curiosity, as men look at a prize fighter about to step into the ring for combat.

He did not like that. Two thirds of his purchased confidence shrank from him. He had to snatch up the shotgun and hold it at the ready before a little of his courage reasserted itself. He said aloud:

"You wait and see. I'm gunna rip him in two

and then blow his face in for him!"

In repetition and in boasting there is also a strength. And in this manner he reassured himself while a brisk step came up onto the veranda outside.

He heard a clear voice hail:

"You've had a dusty trip, young man!"

"Yeah," said a voice deeper and calmer than he remembered the voice of Jim Fantom, "I've had to slope through a good deal of dust. Will you come in and have something, stranger? I hate to drink alone."

"Thanks," said the other, and it was undoubtedly that same clear-eyed, elderly fellow who was speaking. "I guess I won't. I'm past those days, thank you. But you'll find a crowd inside."

"Praying?" asked Jim Fantom, with a short laugh.

And suddenly it reminded Larry Phelan that, as a matter of fact, not a glass, not a hand, not a foot was stirring in Bertram's saloon. The brisk step drew nearer, the door was flung open, and Jim Fantom stood before them.

He never could have been recognized! He had gone away a boy of eighteen, he came back a man, and more than a man of twenty-three. His face was much thinner, so that it looked rather long. Over each temple appeared a tuft of gray hair that gave him the look of thirty-five, at least; but two things remained to him that had been true of the boy who was taken away those years before — the lightly arched nose, thin and sensitive about the nostrils, and the unusually blue eyes. They seemed bluer and younger than ever, perhaps because his face was now pale, and his hair touched with gray.

Something had happened to young Jim Fantom. He had received a heating and a hammering such as turns iron into steel, more strong, more supple. So that, into the mind of watchful Larry Phelan there came a recollection. He had traveled as far as Denver, on a day, and there in a museum he had seen a slender sword blade of a curiously mottled bluish look.

"Damascus steel," said the label. "The secret of making this fine steel is now lost. The edge was so delicate that it would cut silk without drawing a thread; yet it could be struck through heavy armor and the edge remained true. The Oriental armorers carried the secret of its composition with them, to the grave."

Larry Phelan remembered that caption, now, and he felt that the secret had been rediscovered, at last. He moistened his dry lips.

These observations had been possible during the half second that the newcomer lingered in the doorway. In that instant, his glance turned rapidly over the faces in the crowd — not a sweeping look, but one that seemed to rest studiously on every man, so that each felt it had been a mere casual survey of the others, but a particular considering of himself.

Larry Phelan was surer than the rest! He gripped the heavy shotgun until it trembled in his grasp. If there had been so much as a gesture toward him, he would have leveled the weapon and pulled both triggers. For, after all, there was not the ice water of cowardice in his veins.

He took note of other things, too. There were gauntlet gloves upon the hands of Jim Fantom; and gloves never made for a fast draw; but the leather of these was a mere film over the fingers — "thin as a weevil's skin!"

He decided that he would wait. After all, it was not up to him to make the first aggressive step; he was not the man who had been wronged and must demand vengeance.

James Fantom turned his back upon that crowd, upon that trembling shotgun. He stepped to the bar and stretched out his hand.

"Hello, Bertram," said he.

"Why, hullo," said the bartender in a wavering voice, as he touched the hand of the gunman. "I'm — we're — it's fine to have you back with us!"

"Give me a glass of beer," said Fantom. "My throat's lined with dust. And have something yourself."

He added, with a gesture over his shoulder, as Bertram poured out the foaming beer, and then filled for himself a brimming glass of his best whisky:

"I don't see any other men in here to drink with, Bertram!"

He raised his glass and made with it a gesture of salutation to the bartender, who was gaping with fear as he watched the semicircle of his customers.

Then he turned. The whiplash of that insult had been drawn across every face alike, and now the blue eyes of The Phantom followed, and repeated the blow. He had at this moment a glass of beer in his right hand, sipping slowly from it. In his left hand, he grasped the glove which he had just drawn off the right. With both hands occupied, what a temptation to draw or to pull down on him now!

The red temptation burst into the brain of Larry Phelan. The foretaste of murder made him grin like a wolf, with wide-stretched lips. Yet something held him back, something like contemptuous knowledge in the eyes of this man, something unconcerned, and aloof, and pitying.

"You'd oughta try to drum up a better trade, Bertram," went on Jim Fantom. "If I had the makin' of the laws of this here state, I'd forbid saloons to let in children — an' half-wits' — an' yaller-livered, sneakin' boobies that ain't got the pride of a barnyard duck or the manners of a rootin' pig. I'd sweep this here sort of trash out and keep 'em out."

He made a slow gesture, beer glass in hand, and the whole line shrank before him.

There were in that crowd fellows who would have died a thousand deaths rather than submit to such insults, had they been alone. But they were not alone. Each had been subtly welded into the mass of the crowd, and, losing his indi-

27

viduality, had taken on the psychology of the mob, which is braver than any one man; and more cowardly than any coward. They were abashed. When one eye turned to a neighbor, it saw shrinking and horror there. Some of them even were trying to smile, as though they struggled to consider this a jest, which amused them at the expense of their companions. But it was a weak, a sickly pretense, from which they could gain no real comfort.

Jim Fantom finished drinking his beer. He turned fully around and rested his elbows on the upper edge of the varnished bar. Again he surveyed that crew, as a sheep dog surveys sheep. They were beginning to stir and shift uneasily, like fallen leaves when the wind just touches the surface of the ground.

"I came here lookin' for two men," said he. "Tom Dollar wasn't at home. He had heard that I was comin' to pay a little call on him."

His blue eyes flashed suddenly upon the face of Larry Phelan. There they stopped and sipped the very life blood of poor Larry.

"The other was Phelan, and I've found him here."

He nodded at Phelan.

"D'you know why I've come, Phelan?" he asked.

For grim action, Larry was prepared, but he was not prepared for talk. He had foreseen this affair as a sudden flashing of weapons and a roar of guns. His nerves were not attuned for a different test. So he opened his lips, but it seemed as though he only drew in icy air that chilled all his blood. He could not speak; with all his soul, he wanted another drink!

"You don't know?" said Fantom. "I'm kind of surprised and hurt by that, Phelan. I'd thought that you would of knowed that the main reason why I'd made this here long trip was in honor of you, and chiefly for the sake of havin' a little chat with you. Yes, sir, you're the main cause of me takin' this ride, just as you're the main reason of my short hair!"

He smiled upon Larry Phelan, and the heart of the latter sank again. He could not endure it any longer. He saw that his soul was running out of his boots and that if he were to strike at all, he must strike now. So he roared suddenly:

"You — Fantom — if you got anything to do, you start it now, will you? Or else, shut your face!"

That sudden roar of his shocked every man in the barroom. It shocked and flushed them with a sudden hope that, after all, they would be championed by one of their number against the overweening manner of the other.

But Fantom did not stir a hand toward his gun. He merely considered his enemy for a moment, and then he said:

"I came back here to kill Larry Phelan, and kill him I will — but not by a damn sight when he's drunk."

He walked leisurely across the floor toward Phelan.

"Now!" said Phelan to his heart. "Now I'll kill him — or now — !"

But he could not stir, as it seemed. He was frozen in place, until the gloved hand of Fantom reached out and plucked the shotgun away from his nerveless grasp.

"You dirty puppy, you can't make your blood red with whisky; so don't try it again. Go home and get your mother to pour some cold water over your head. And then come back!"

Larry Phelan, white and shaking, turned toward the door.

It was far more horrible than a murder, and if the others looked upon this shaming of a grown man, and a brave man, it was because they could not draw their charmed eyes away.

"Here — you!" said Fantom. He reached out the butt of the gun and jabbed Phelan in the back. "Take this home with you. You'll need it later on — for rabbits!"

Phelan took the gun, and fled with a stumbling run, caring for nothing except that the doors of that saloon might swing shut and cut him off from the observance of all who had looked upon his fall!

CHAPTER FOUR

Out of the saloon, behind Phelan, came the remainder of those who had drunk with him. They wanted nothing except to escape from that scene, to wash their memory of the horror they had looked upon, if that might be, and to get to their own homes, where they could fill their minds with familiar objects. There is nothing like the handling of well-known things by the eyes to bring back happiness and steady nerves. And fully half of those fellows were as good as the next man. Only, they had been caught in the slimy current of the crowd.

After they had scattered, the gray-bearded man on the veranda heard the bartender say:

"Have another — have one on me, Jim, and make it something stronger. I got some Old Crow here that's the best stuff you ever laid a lip over!"

"I'll tell you, Bertram," said the calm voice of Fantom; "I drink when I'm thirsty, now. And nobody's thirsty for whisky unless he's been facin' a blizzard. I've been ridin' under a hot sun."

With that, he walked out onto the veranda, and sat down by the stranger. He took out a sack of Bull Durham, a package of brown papers, from which he peeled off one translucent oblong, and then shook in the tobacco.

With his right hand and his teeth he drew up the string of the sack. By the time that was done, his left hand, with a wonderful dexterity, had smoothed the tobacco in the paper and rolled it with one clever twist.

"That's useful on horseback," said the stranger.

Young Jim Fantom turned his head and regarded his companion, not long enough for the stare to become insolent, but long enough to study his man; and he found the first pair of eyes since the penitentiary that could meet his glance with utter steadiness, without confusion, without become startled.

"It's useful on horseback," admitted Fantom. Then he added: "I guess I don't know your name."

"I know yours," said the gray-bearded man, "and mine is Jonathan Quay."

"Quay?" said Fantom. "Quay? Seems to me that I've heard that name, too. Quay?"

"Perhaps you have," said the other. "In some places it's not an unknown name."

"Quay?" murmured Fantom. "Hold on! You're the fellow that takes crooks when they get out of prison and helps them to go straight!"

He looked brazenly into the steady eyes of Quay.

"I've done that, too."

"Well, I'm a case for you," said Fantom. "Straighten me out if you can!"

~ee years in the reform

in prison. And I'm

~ as high as that in

a sneer in his

~ said Quay. "You

~is head around.

~!" he requested.

~t to the reform school," said Quay,

~o the penitentiary. They've done your

~siness for you. They've made you a straight man."

"The law!" said Fantom, and his lips smiled over the gleam of set teeth. "It's done a pile for me, all right. It's given me board and lodging for eight years!"

"It's done more than that. It's given you a straight eye, as well as a straight mind. It's given you a strong hand and steady nerves and a sense of what's right. Otherwise, you would have killed young Phelan, a moment ago."

Fantom smiled again, and again there was no mirth in his smile.

"Whatcha think?" he asked. "That Phelan's better alive or dead, just now?"

"Not for this section of the country, of course. But he can go away with a lesson inside him and start his life in a new place."

"Ay, he could do that. By your look of it, I'm a

kind of a reformer, eh?"

"You've reformed Phelan," sai[d] only he lives long enough to profit[

"Why ain't he apt to live long? [that he'll come back to me for troubl[

"No," said Quay. "He won't do that[be apt to have trouble other places. A[day, there's not a ten-year-old boy that wo[stand up to Phelan. He's taken water, and[the children will laugh in his face! His ner[v broken, and everyone knows it."

"I hadn't thought of it in that way," muttere[d the boy.

"So that you're in real danger, now."

"Danger of what? Of Phelan and Dollar?" He laughed, and there was a snarl in the laughter.

"Danger that the law may do you its first injustice."

"Its *first*, eh?"

"You deserved the reform school," said Quay, without heat but with perfect conviction. "You deserved it, because you called every day wasted that didn't see you in a fight. It was bad enough when you were ten, and gave all the boys of the town black eyes and bloody noses. But at fifteen you were hitting hard. You were breaking bones, now and then. And when you made your little tour down to Tombstone and came back with a few scalps —"

"That was a fair fight."

"No fight is fair that a man puts himself in the way of," said the other almost sternly.

34

Young Fantom looked askance at him, but did not answer.

"You got the reform school. It was good for you. For three years you had to submit to authority. In a way, you really liked it. Is that right?"

Fantom rubbed his chin and a puzzled frown appeared on his face.

"You seem to know a bit about me," said he.

"I was once a young man," said Quay gently. Then he went on: "After reform school, you had only a few months. In those months you killed an Indian in Chihuahua, you killed Lynch, and you killed Harry Lord, both of them famous gunmen."

"They'd asked for trouble."

"And you didn't turn the other cheek. Very well. It wasn't for that that the law sent you to prison. Afterward, you shot down three guards and robbed a stage."

"And got the only punishment! The other two sneaks, who'd persuaded me into the job, and then had got out —"

"Persuaded you into it?"

"Why, they dared me. I wouldn't let a dare go by — not in those days!"

"Then the law sent you to prison. Well, the other pair weren't worth bothering about, but the law has hammered you into good metal, now!"

"If that metal was a steel knife, it would like to be between the ribs of the law!" said the boy. "I've had my hell!"

"Because you insisted on bumping your head against the stone walls, when they first put you in prison. As soon as they thought you had straightened out, they cut down your sentence!"

"It was the warden," said the boy. "There was one man with a heart as big —"

"He was the same warden who made life hell for you at first, I believe."

At this, Fantom was silent for a moment, only to say, afterward:

"Look here! How do you know about these here things? You seem to know the whole book of me!"

"It made interesting reading," said Quay, "and as you know, my business is trying to help boys who have been turned out of the prison gates — trying to help them onto a steady path!"

Fantom frowned.

"Well," said he, "kind of you to take an interest. But I'll paddle my own canoe."

"You'll paddle it into a rapids, unless you get out of this town," answered Quay.

"I will?"

"You will. Dollar's cut and run for it, but if somebody kills your friend Phelan inside of the time you're in town, who'll be blamed for it?"

"You mean me?"

"If you were in the sheriff's place, who else would you suspect?"

"Ah, damn the sheriff!"

"On the contrary, Bud Cross is an excellent man and wants to give everyone a perfectly square deal! But he's liable to human error. Mind you, the law *does* make a few mistakes. So far, not in your case. You can't complain of five years, after shooting down three men and stealing nearly a hundred thousand dollars! But the law will certainly take you by the collar if Phelan is harmed."

The boy set his teeth, and the muscles at the base of his jaw stood out in a white spot.

"Well —" he said at last, but could not find words for the sullen rage that burned within him.

"You'd better go," said Quay again, gently.

"I'm damned if I'll go," said the boy.

"Very well," said Quay. "I knew that you wouldn't."

"Why did you know that?"

"Because gray hairs don't make an old mind!" answered Quay. "God be with you, my boy!"

Fantom turned back and laid a hand on the other's shoulder.

"You're a strange one to me," said he, "but you sound like a straight one. I'm gunna think over what you say. Maybe I'll leave. But — after all —"

He paused and looked up and down the street. The blacksmith shop had been long silent, but now the mellow clangor of hammer faces on yielding hot iron began again. Smoke was rising from many chimneys. The life of the town once more was rippling on after a slight disturbance.

"After all," said the boy huskily, "this here is my town. I know it. For five years, I've been

37

hungerin' after it. I've been lookin' at my picture of it. I've been listenin' — to the barkin' of its dogs, even. Heard 'em in my dreams."

He made a gesture of pain and rage.

"Back I come, and they're all snarlin' at me from the first step. It's — it's sort of hard!"

He sighed.

"I'll look it over, once, and then maybe I'll take your advice!"

"Young man, I'm afraid you're like the wife of Lot. I hope to God that I am wrong. Good-by!"

CHAPTER FIVE

Jonathan Quay left the veranda of the saloon and started down the street, but Jim Fantom remained behind, and there he sat until the sun hung low in the west, and a breath of coolness stirred across the town, raising the dust in little whirlpools, here and there. Then he sauntered away, still thoughtful.

He made the round of the place from familiar spot to spot. He circled back to the old swimming pool, to which the boys used to sprint after school, undressing on the way, hungry for the honor of being first into chilly water.

He had won that honor time and time again. He had discovered, twice, new routes which saved precious seconds of time and brought him in first. Now, as he wandered through the woods and the brush, he saw that his newly discovered ways were well-beaten trails; it made him feel old and time-worn!

At the edge of the pool all was altered. The pool itself had shrunk to a quarter of the size it had seemed to be; the great black rock was dwindled to a little stone; the branch of the willow from which they used to dive was a crooked, bark-worn limb. The very trees, that once had seemed so tall, so dark, so awful, now were spindling second growth!

He left the swimming pool and came back to the town through the Egan pasture, where he had ridden the roan mustang for a bet of fifty cents, and had been thrice thrown, and yet had conquered, and then had gone home and fainted on the doorstep.

He passed next through the woods behind the Lander house, pausing in the open space among the scrub oaks. In that mystic circle, on a moonlight night, he and Chip Lander had fought their famous battle. He was thirteen and Chip fifteen. He had been long king of the smaller boys, with Chip the recognized authority among the older. But at last ambition made him attack even the great Chip.

One dreadful hour they battled here. He had turned the face of Chip into a sheet of crimson, flowing steadily, but at last superior age and strength told. He could remember vividly the finishing punch; he had gone numb, his arms hanging at his sides. It landed on his temple, that driving fist. He fell into darkness and wakened on the knees of Chip, who was saying fine things about him.

"Next year, you'll be able to beat me to a pulp," said Chip.

A fine fellow, Chip Lander. The heart of Fantom warmed as he thought of the boy, who had gone off onto the great range and was heard of no more in Burned Hill.

He climbed to the top of the hill itself, went by the house of the Purchasses — the rich people of the town — and looked down on the huddling lights of the village. In his boyhood he had stood here and thought it was like a sea of illumination. Now it seemed to him that the long main street, with its irregular fringing of lights, was like a ship at night, wandering among the dark hills of the sea.

In the late dusk he passed down again into Burned Hill, starting at the upper end of the town. He passed the cool whisper of sprinklers, spinning on the lawns; the scent of cookery hung drowsily in the air; now and then a breath of garden flowers rose up before him.

He was very sad. Twice he passed men on the street, and when he was close enough to be recognized, they sidestepped, as though they had seen a prowling wild beast.

A youngster, squealing with delighted fear, burst out of a garden gate before him and darted into the street.

"Billy Dolan!" cried a girl's voice. "You come right back here. Dad'll spank you within an inch of your life!"

"*I* don't care!" crowed Billy, from the delicious deep dust of the street.

The girl suddenly emerged in pursuit. Fleet was the boy, and dodged like a rabbit, but the girl was arrowy swift. And as a greyhound swerves gracefully after the rabbit, until at last the little hunted thing will swerve back into the waiting jaws, so the boy swerved into the arms of his sister, at last. He struggled furiously.

"Leave go! It ain't fair to grab me by the ear! I'll hit you, Jo!"

"If you hit me," said Jo Dolan, "I'll turn you over and spank you, right in front of that man who's standing and watching you make a silly thing of yourself!"

"You can't! You dassn't!" protested the lad.

"*Can't* I, though!" said she.

They passed into a shaft of dim lamplight that streamed through the door of the house, and Fantom saw that she was able to do as she threatened. In her round arm there was strength enough to rein a bucking mustang or to swing an ax. She stepped like a deer, lightly and proudly; there was both laughter and sternness of battle in her eyes. So she dragged the culprit to the front gate, and thrust him in.

"You go upstairs and wash yourself in a jiffy," said she, "and get ready for supper, and I won't tell on you. But if you don't, I'll catch you again and do what I promised!"

Billy Dolan sulked up the path, head down, hands in his pockets, dark schemes of revolt and vengeance in his mind.

"*He's* a handful!" panted the girl to Fantom.

"I bet he is," said he.

"Another year and he'll be too much for me."

"Not if you get a good ear-hold."

She laughed.

"He's a rascal," she said affectionately. "You're a stranger in town, I guess?"

"Yeah. I just came in. Looks like a good town to me."

"It's pretty dead, but I guess it's all right. We

been stirred up today, though."

"That so?"

"Sure. Haven't you heard?"

"I just sloped in."

"The Phantom's come back!"

"Who's he?"

"Why, Jim Fantom. You must of heard."

"A long time ago, maybe."

"Yep. He's been in the penitentiary for five years. But now he's come back to get even."

"For what?"

"He got a bad deal, in some ways, I guess. But he's a real mean one, now."

"I hope I don't meet him," said Jim.

"You better not. He's the kind that would just as soon kill a man as take a drink of water. He's a devil, I guess!"

The Phantom was silent, as she continued:

"But I'll bet if I was a man, I wouldn't let him bully me around, the way that he does the others. I'd rather die, first!"

"I bet you would," said The Phantom.

"Well, so long. It's supper time. I hope you like the town!"

She went to the gate, and opened it.

"So long," said he. "What's your name, might I ask?"

"Me? Oh, I'm Josephine Dolan." She added: "Who are you?"

"Me? Oh, I'm Jim Fantom," said he.

He took off his hat and stepped a little closer, so that she could see his lean, hard face, and the gray tuft over each temple.

"My gracious!" she whispered, and shrank away from him. But she came bravely back.

"I guess I've said some pretty hard things to you, Jim Fantom. I'm sorry about that."

"I don't mind," he replied. "Sometimes a bad start makes a good finish!"

"Yes, yes," said she. "I was a fool to talk so free about a man I'd never seen."

"You're going to see me again," said he.

"I hope so."

"If you don't mind people talking about you?"

"I wouldn't mind. Jiminy!" said the girl. "I should say that I wouldn't!" And she laughed.

She had come still a little closer, full of excitement and invitation.

"Drop around tomorrow," said she. "We're goin' up country the next day."

"Thanks," said Fantom.

They shook hands; in hers, he observed a faint tremor.

"Maybe I'll be goin' up country, too," said he.

The pleasure went out of her eyes and her face grew cold; he realized as he turned down the street that he had gone much too fast. But still, though he shook his head, he was hardly sorry. Perhaps it was because he had been put away for the five years, but it seemed to him that he never had seen another like her!

She was fresh as the spring, delicate as a flower, strong as whipcord. What a woman to make a wife in this man's country! Those thoughts opened the mind of Jim Fantom, opened his heart, as well, so that when he heard the half-stifled bark of a revolver, somewhere behind him, he hardly noticed it.

He went on slowly, filled by his thoughts, until he came to the hotel. There he lingered by the troughs, watching a twelve-mule team taking water, thinking idly how differently a thirsty horse drinks. A mule is dainty; a horse will plunge in above the nostrils, eating the water, as it were!

Then he went in. It was supper time. A dozen men sat at the long table in the dining room, and he took the place at the foot, nearest the window. He was rather doubtful of that window, which yawned upon his back. There were men in this town who would think nothing of putting him out of the way with a bullet from behind. However, once seated there, he would not change. He shrugged his shoulders at the danger and settled himself to his food.

They were all afraid. It was as though a sudden cold wind had blown upon them, for they all began to frown and stare at their plates with fixed eyes. They looked not even at one another, except for a traveling salesman at the farther end of the table. His voice was free and easy enough.

He talked with such appreciation of himself that, as he told his stories, he swung from side to side, so as to peer past the big circular-burner lamp and read the expressions of his audience.

Then his nearest neighbor muttered something. At that, the salesman was silent suddenly;

his face turned white, and Jim Fantom sighed gloomily. It would always be like this, and between him and the rest of the world there existed a great wall that towered to the sky.

CHAPTER SIX

Even the waiter was ill at ease. When he offered the stewed prunes to Fantom, and received a curt refusal, he actually jumped, and Fantom lost his patience.

"Great God, man," said he, "I ain't goin' to eat you, am I?"

"I dunno!" stammered the waiter. "I sure hope not, sir. Can I fetch you something else?"

"No," said Fantom, and his voice was a groan of protest.

He gave his attention to his second cup of coffee. It was piping hot, and he had barely sipped of it when he was aware of a jerk of the body and a straightening of the man next to him.

He looked up in turn, and there stood Sheriff Bud Cross in the doorway, with a long Colt in either hand, bearing full upon him.

"Stick 'em up, kid!" he said. "Stick 'em up, and pronto!"

"What's the matter?" asked Jim Fantom.

"A dead man is the matter," said Cross. "You fool, to think you could drop Larry and get away with it! Get up them hands, will you?"

Slowly the hands of Fantom mounted. He was bewildered, amazed, but dimly in his mind he seemed to hear again the boom of the revolver shot as he walked down the street. He thought of other things, too. The girl could swear that, just before, she had seen him leave her, near the house of Phelan. That would make perfect the case against him.

Not penitentiary, this time, but hanging would be the word!

"You there, Clauson," barked the sheriff's voice. "Stand up behind him and lay a gun ag'in the back of his neck!"

Clauson did not move.

"Hurry up," said the sheriff. "What you scared of?"

Clauson, unwillingly, rose.

"This ain't of my choosin', Sheriff," said he, "but I suppose I gotta do what I'm told."

So he arose, drawing his gun; but as he did so, and stepped behind the chair, it seemed to Jim Fantom that he saw a narrow chance through which he might escape. His feet found the cross beam beneath the table, and suddenly he thrust out with all his might.

The table shot over on its farther side, bearing down two men before it. Their yells mingled with the crash of dishes. The lamp was dashed to bits, and the room flooded with darkness just as the sheriff let off both guns.

The sing of one bullet fairly kissed the ear of Fantom, and the window pane behind him crackled. The other shot thudded into the wall. But, in the meantime, that thrust of his feet had hurled him strongly back against Clauson. The man went down, with a groan of fear, but

48

Fantom did not have him in mind.

The sheriff was his danger. He could see the big man sidestep out of the lighted square of the door, and Fantom went for him across the floor, crouched like a cat. Out of the darkness at the sheriff's feet he rose at the tall man, gun in hand. It would have been a simple thing to split the forehead of Bud Cross wide open with a bullet, then, but that was not in the mind of Jim Fantom.

The long barrel of his Colt rang along the head of Cross, and the sheriff went down on both knees. Another man would have been knocked prostrate, but the fighting instinct of the sheriff held him up on his knees, shouting hoarsely to the others to block the way to the door. For his own part, the blow had blinded him, and he dared not shoot into the darkness that covered his eyes.

But no one blocked the door. They would rather have run into the path of a charging tiger, at that moment. They saw the slender form of Jim Fantom slither through the doorway and disappear. The clerk in the lobby dropped with a groan of terror behind his desk, as he saw the gun in the hand of the fighter. Two others, agape, flattened themselves against the wall and thrust their arms stiffly up over their heads.

Jim Fantom went past them, unheeding, but once more it seemed to him that men could be like sheep — pitiable, cringing sheep, who tremble when they see the sheep dog. He darted down the back hallway, burst through the rear

49

door, and sprang to the ground without touching a step.

The stable was just before him. He groaned with his haste as he saw the door closed. It required a long heave and pull before it slid open, the rusty wheels grinding mournfully above his head.

But he was inside. He found the bay pony. By the light of a lantern on the wall, he noted the sweat streak, white along its hips, and wondered how much he had taken out of it during that day's ride! However, he had the saddle on its back before the thought was completed.

Left and right stood sleek speedsters, long-legged, dainty, the very animals for him in this crisis, but to take them would mean what in his eyes was worse than murder — horse-stealing!

He heard the rear screen door of the hotel bang rapidly. They were pouring out after him, and they would guess where he was. He flung himself into the saddle and reined the pony back.

No matter how tired, it had enough hot blood in it to rise to a great moment, and it was gathered under him like a tightened watch spring as he turned its head toward the door.

The passageway behind the stalls was low; the rafters reached down just above his head, but he threw himself along the side of the mustang like an Indian, his revolver thrusting out under the neck of the animal.

In that way, like a storm, he broke out of the door of the stable. He saw men streaking toward him, gun in hand. At sight of him, they stopped and threw themselves to the ground, except for the tall form of the sheriff, who stood erect and dropped his guns on the fugitive.

"I'm gone!" said Fantom to himself, and began to shoot beneath the reaching neck of the pony, not at any target — the jerking of the pony's gallop would have made it impossible, probably, to hit anything — but merely in the air, in the hope that the flashing of his guns might shake the nerves of the others.

They could not shake the nerves of the sheriff, he well knew, but Bud Cross was not half himself. The blow on the head still kept a veil over his aching, burning eyes; sharp pains stabbed his head; he was shooting at a double image, as it were, and, as the rider darted past him and around the corner of the hotel, he cast down his guns with a groan of disgust.

Then his voice rose like a clarion. Fantom, rounding into the street so fast that his horse skidded in the liquid dust, heard the voice:

"Hoss and saddle, every one of you, or Burned Hill is gunna be a laughin' stock!"

Jim Fantom heard no more, except distant shoutings, and the banging of doors, and the noise of windows slammed up. He sped on down the street, with the acrid dust fanning up like moth wings into his face. So the last lights shot past him on either side, and the comfortable darkness of the open country received him into its breast.

51

CHAPTER SEVEN

He kept up full speed until he was between the two hills just east of the town. Then he turned in a wide detour, and galloped furiously to the west.

He was in a draw behind the hills, a hollow which the water filled with a rush during the floods in the spring of the year, when the higher snows were melted by the first rains. The bottom was chiefly sand and small pebbles, such as would not give out the noise of falling hoofs; but here and there the pounding feet of the bay hammered on the surface of a rock and the sound echoed up and down the draw like a rifle shot. However, this was his best way, as it seemed to him.

Finally, he saw before him the woods. He entered them, turned, and looked back at Burned Hill. The very lights of the town seemed to be trembling and winking in excitement. He heard a roar of distant voices; he heard a pounding of hoofs, distinctly, but the whole flood of the sound of men and horses was streaming away to the east.

Now let them burn up their speedsters, their half breeds and their thoroughbreds, the pride of the town. Let them ride them to death on the eastern trail, while he drifted comfortably to the west!

He drew the pony back to a walk. He even leaned and loosened the cinches of the panting little beast, so sure was he of himself. And so the big, dark trees walked past him. Now and again, he saw the bright faces of the stars above him, in glimpses, they too seeming to pulse slowly to the rear as the horse walked on.

His nerves were relaxing. His spirits began to rise. As for the killing of Larry Phelan, it was what was coming that young man's way. His chief regret was that he had *not* accomplished that feat himself. Only, in fair fight, of course!

But it occurred to him, suddenly, that there was hardly such a thing as a fair fight for him, from this time on. He had killed too many; the law had put a mark upon him, and no matter whom his bullets touched, no matter what the provocation, he was from this time forward branded with murder if a man fell before him.

He knew that Bud Cross was a fair and reasonable man, but Bud Cross had not dreamed of doubting that the killing of Larry Phelan lay at the door of Fantom.

So, gradually, he saw the life that lay before him. He could not exist inside the law; he must live outside of it. They trembled before him with a sort of natural detestation. Well, then, let them tremble, not because he was a sheep dog, but because he was a wolf.

Bitterly he made that decision, with a profound sorrow in his heart that he beat back, and would not consider.

There was the girl, at the bottom of it all. Somehow, she seemed to have slipped quietly into his mind, like an idea which he had known long before. She was as familiar to him as the stars are familiar in the face of the sky. The very sound of her voice was like a well-known thing!

He felt that if he could have seen her a second time, the illusion would have vanished, but, as it was, she had stepped into his thoughts along with the cool of the evening, the whisper of the falling water on the lawns, the breath of the gardens. There had been light enough by which to see her beauty, but not the flaws. He had heard her speak. He had heard her laugh. He had seen her eyes shine.

So she remained to him partly real and partly ideal. She was made out of his wishes, like a child's daydream, but also there was about the image of her something which had been made outside of his imagination. Then he told himself again, and cursed aloud as he said it, that this absorption in her was merely the result of his five years of confinement behind stone walls.

He kept the bay pony on at a steady jog, up hill and down dale until he came to a bright-faced lake in the middle of the woods. Into the wood dropped a zigzag stream, lying like a frozen bolt of silver light along the mountainside. He could see that the pony's head was beginning to droop. Therefore he halted and made camp for the night. He found a good strip of pasture for the mustang. He had in his saddlebag a feed of crushed barley for it, and, when he curled himself up for the night, he assured himself that his horse would be fit for another long march on the morrow. As for his own empty stomach, that was a matter of small importance. He drew up his belt a notch when he rolled into his blanket. He took up another notch in the morning, and all was well. For that matter, he had been accustomed from boyhood to living much like a camel, and laying up in fat times for the lean days ahead.

When he wakened, the mustang was neighing softly — an inquisitive whine, as it were, and tossing his head as he looked to the east through the trees.

Fantom got out of his blanket sleepily, and, looking down through the tree trunks in the same direction, he beheld a dozen riders coming out of the woods and riding by the edge of the lake, with their images, beside them in the still water, making another cavalcade. The leader stopped to give his mount a swallow of water. That was Bud Cross. Then, reining the head of his horse away from the water, he waved straight toward the trees where Fantom was hidden!

Fantom was madly at work, by this time. He dragged saddle and bridle onto the gelding, and kept chucking him under the jaw to irritate him. In that way he could keep the little fellow from whinnying to his kind. Yet they were *not* his kind. Would they had been! He was a stump-legged little rat, as much at home on rough trails as a mountain sheep, and he could jog or lope endlessly; but behind him were the blooded speedsters of Bud Cross. It seemed to him that he could now remember having heard, while he was in the penitentiary, that Bud Cross had induced the county to give him a selection of fast runners of proved endurance. The allowance had been made, and after that he ran down criminals as a good pack of wolf hounds will run down wolves. Here they were behind Fantom now. It seemed to him that he never had seen horses with necks and legs so long!

Now he was in the saddle and twisting the bay snake-like into the deeper recesses of the woods. He was off in a moment to a considerable distance. Behind him the voices of the pursuers died off faintly, like bells that are carried on the wind, dying and coming again.

There was a small open glade beneath the slope of the hill, and this he ventured to cross, confident that the woods from behind would screen him from any observation. He was almost across, and entering the farther side, when something rustled through the foliage before him, and immediately afterward the clanging report of a rifle smote sharply against his ears.

They had seen him, after all!

He gave one fleeting glance to the rear, and made out in three or four places the shadowy forms of the long-striding horses that worked behind him.

He must keep to the rough ground, if he hoped

for life! So, to the rough ground he kept, edging higher along the slope until like a handclap of a giant at his very ear, a Winchester spoke from a brake beside him.

He reined the bay headlong down the slope, through scattering brush and trees, and saw three men flying behind him. And to the right, and before him, other guns were popping. Yet he seemed to bear a charmed life. Perhaps it would have been better to point out that the shooting had been done by men on horseback, than which, there can be no more accurate marksmanship!

He sliced off to the left, but always it was downhill, and always they were gaining behind him. Thoroughbred though they might be, these man-hunting horses knew all about their business of running across country. They did not let up. They came on so freshly that Fantom desperately conjectured that the sheriff must have sent out from the town a relay of fresh horses to take up the work on the trail.

Never had the sheriff worked at any trail as he would work at this one, as the boy well knew. There was a broad white bandage around the head of Bud Cross, and that seemed to Fantom like a battle flag which the sheriff could not forget.

It was quirt and spur now, cruelly fed into the sides of the bay gelding to keep him going. He would not last long at this pace. His short legs, that could jog patiently all day long, had not the stroking power to match against the sleek, bounding forms behind. But Fantom dodged him through a dense tangle of brush; then down a sheer slope, sliding on his haunches and braced legs like a bear sliding down a snow bank.

He rattled down a twisting gully at the bottom of the draw and, looking back, saw the posse come out of the upper edge of the woods, and scoot down the slope one after another, enveloped in a cloud of dust, and kicking pebbles in noisy showers before them.

It meant death to Fantom, this fine riding, but an unwilling admiration rose in his heart. It seemed impossible that the whole number of the posse should have been able to follow that route across country. And, in fact, he numbered only eight who made the descent. Two more vainly urged their mounts forward on the edge of the slope, but could not make them take it.

In the meantime, there was nothing to do except to ride the bronco for all that it was worth, hoping for some branching gully from the main one down which he might dodge again. He could hear them shouting encouragement. They were whooping one another on, as if they were hunting a bear; and his lips began to curl with ferocity.

The draw swept around a bend, and, as the turn was made, there started out before him a rider on a bay horse, who drove at full speed down the cañon.

Fantom looked at him as at an illusion of the

eye. It was a man dressed in every respect as he was dressed, in a blue flannel shirt, with gauntlet gloves, with goatskin chaps, and wearing a red and white spotted bandana of silk, knotted around his throat and fluttering at the back of his neck in the wind of his galloping. The very sombrero which he wore was a white Stetson, like Fantom's, with a string of rawhide woven around the brim to give it stiffening! Even the look of his blanket roll behind the saddle was the same, with a yellow slicker strapped on top!

That was not all that the bewildered eyes of Fantom saw, for on the right, at the mouth of a small branching ravine, appeared Jonathan Quay, beckoning.

Fantom did not pause to think. He swung into the ravine at the side of Quay and in a moment had lost sight of the main ravine around a sharp angle of the smaller gully.

There Quay drew rein, holding up his hand to check his young companion, and as they sat their horses, and the sweat ran down the face of Fantom, he heard the roar of the pursuit, like the noise of turbulent waters, going down the big draw, the rocks flying under hammering hoofbeats. Like a withdrawing wave, the sound passed beyond their hearing, roared dimly around distant corners, then was gone completely.

After this, he was able to look at the older man.

"What —" began Jim Fantom.

Quay smiled at him. It was apparent that he

had been studying the face of Fantom ever since their horses were stopped.

"There'll be no more trouble," said Quay. "That young fellow who took your place knows how to ride a horse, and the horse he's on can travel. I think it could give the best of the sheriff's layout a close rub, in spite of its size, even if they were fresh for the race, which they're not!"

Fantom could only stare.

"They won't catch him," said Quay. "Even if they should, all he has to do is to turn about and hold up his hands. They'll see that they have the wrong man."

"And do what to him?"

"Nothing. He was simply riding down the draw, when he saw horsemen riding furiously and thought that they might mean harm to him. He took no chances and rode hard for it. That's all there is to the thing, as it seems to me!"

"You don't know Bud Cross," said Fantom grimly.

"There you're wrong. I know Bud Cross intimately, though I doubt if he's ever seen my face. I know him very well. He'll make no trouble for Chip Lander."

"Chip Lander!" cried Fantom.

"He said that he knew you," answered Quay. "He was glad to do something for you, on account of a little argument that you and he had a long time ago, when you were boys. Is that right?"

"My head's spinning a mite," said The

Phantom. "How did you manage to be here in the nick of time?"

"Does that seem like a miracle?" asked Quay gently. "I suppose it does, but if you were to take a bird's-eye view of Burned Hill and the lay of the land around it, you wouldn't be surprised. If you rode straight east, over the easy, rolling hills, they were sure to run you down in short order. If they caught you there, I couldn't help you until you were in jail. But if you turned in this direction, as I guessed that you would, either you'd get safely off into the upper country, above timberline, or else they would begin to hammer you in this region. With their faster horses, they would be apt to run you into this draw. At least, that was the way I guessed the game. And it happened to turn out that way. There was about one chance in four that Chip Lander and his horse would be useful at this spot at about this time. And as you see, the fourth chance was the one that turned up! No miracle, Jim Fantom — no miracle at all!"

He smiled again, but it seemed to Fantom that the eyes of the older man were not smiling — they were blazing with a strange triumph and excitement.

"I'm pretty paralyzed by all of this," said Fantom. "Which I sure aim to thank you for my skin, which would be dryin' on the rocks, by this time, otherwise."

"No, no!" answered Quay. "They never would have caught you!"

61

"Not catch me?" cried Fantom. "They was so close that the tail of my hoss fanned their faces every time we switched around a corner!"

"Before they got you," said Quay, "they would have had to eat fifteen shots out of your Winchester; and there weren't enough stomachs in the lot to digest that much lead, I believe!"

"Most of that lead would of been plastered on the faces of the stones, I suppose," said Fantom.

Quay shook his head. He seemed to speak with an amused omniscience, as though he were looking down from a height upon the soul of this boy.

"No, no," said he. "You'll never miss your mark now, Jim, until you've come to your last days!"

CHAPTER EIGHT

All mistiness of mind was highly objectionable to Jim Fantom. He waved a hand to exclude the present mystery from his ken.

"Look here, partner," said he, "I want to be on the level with you. You talk as if you'd read the book of my life right through to the last page, but I dunno that that's possible!"

"Ah, no," said Quay. "One never can quite tell! There's that squirrel, for instance."

He pointed above his head at a little tree squirrel which stood on its hind legs upon the branch of a pine tree and looked impudently down upon them, unafraid.

"Take it ordinarily," said Quay, "you wouldn't think that that squirrel would die until maybe some kind of a ferret caught it, or it misjudged a jump in some big wind and got killed by the fall, or a famine in the winter took it off. But just the same, Jim Fantom might feel squirrel hungry at this minute and blow its head off!"

"I wouldn't waste my lead," said Fantom. He added hastily: "Besides it'd be a hard mark to hit."

Quay smiled again.

"Of course," said he. "But it goes to show that prophecies are dangerous. Nevertheless, I dare say that I can tell you what you'll do today."

"What's that?" asked Fantom.

"You'll ride home with me."

Jim Fantom loosened the bandana around his neck, although already it seemed free enough.

"You're sort of takin' me in hand, ain't you?"

"My lad," said the older man, "you're not the first boy that I've tried to help out!"

He laid his hand on the arm of Fantom.

"Come along," said he. "I'm going to show you how to ride away from all of your troubles!"

At this, Fantom hesitated. He was, after all, a sufficiently romantic young man in the beginning, but when one has spent five years in a state penitentiary, it serves largely to rub away the gloss from the mind. It seemed to him that this was like a chapter out of a fairytale. But fairytales did not exist in this blinding light of the Twentieth Century.

If it was not a fairytale, then there lurked something behind the smiling benevolence of Quay. He would have given some of the blood nearest his heart to have penetrated the secret of the other, if a secret there were. At any rate, he balanced between the two feelings — that this was the most generous, kindly, and open-hearted man that ever rode into the wild West; or else he was the most cunning and deeply designing rascal that ever drew breath in any part of the world.

Looking again at the bright, thoughtful eyes of Quay, Fantom felt the same thing reinforced. Either this man was a saint, or a devil. And, perhaps because of the five years in prison, he was a little inclined to the second definition.

"It's a mighty kind thing of you to ask me home with you, Mr. Quay," said he. "But I reckon that you ain't thought of all sides of it. You dunno the sort of trouble that I might get you into, if the sheriff was to find out —"

"That I am sheltering a man wanted by the law?"

"Ay, that's it."

"Now, look here, my friend," said Quay. "The fact is that you're putting me in scales and weighing me. I don't blame you. It's not the first time that I've had it happen to me. You want to know why I have put myself out so much for your sake. Is that the fact?"

Fantom turned crimson, but he was sufficiently frank to answer:

"I guess that's right. It don't seem hardly nacheral for a man to do so much for a stranger!"

"It isn't natural," said Quay. "But if you see my home, you'll understand why I want you. In fact, I need all of the brave men I can get together! You'll soon see what I mean if you come with me to my ranch!"

"This sounds a mite better to me," said Fantom. "It ain't easy for me to go ahead until I can see around the corners of the thing that I'm doing. I'm sorry it's so, but that's the way of it!"

"I understand you perfectly," said Quay. "I don't want to force you. If you think that work for me would interest you, come along. There's another thing against it. I couldn't ask you to enter my employ unless I had your word that you would not think of leaving me before the next year is ended. We'd have to shake hands on that, in the beginning. What do you think of it, Fantom?"

The other scratched his chin.

"It would be sixty dollars a month."

"*And* found?"

"Yes."

"I never heard of no cowpuncher getting pay like that," said Fantom, frankly pessimistic.

"Of course you haven't. You've not often seen cowpunchers who have to ride herd one minute and fight rustlers the next, either."

"Ah, is that it!" cried Fantom, as light broke in upon his brain. "You're in some country where there's plenty of holes in the wall, and the boys drop down on you and use their runnin' irons to free hand your brands into something else. Is that it?"

Quay chuckled.

"There's a good deal of that going on," said he. "I can see that you appreciate the other side of the fence, Fantom."

"I've rustled a cow or two myself," said Jim Fantom frankly, "but for fun more than for the market. I ain't been a saint, Mr. Quay. But the way I look at it is, you've saved my life. You've picked me up there in that cañon and give me my life again — well, you pretty near got a right to ask me for anything you want out of me!"

Quay raised a protesting hand.

"Don't say that!" said he. "You may say that I've kept you from killing more than one man in that draw — enough men, my boy, to make you an outlaw for the rest of your days. But, otherwise, what I've done is not as important as you think. As I said before, you could have beaten them off! I could have laughed at an experienced man like Bud Cross charging straight down into the mouth of a fire, as it were! Great heavens, you could have riddled six men with bullets before that party was able to rein up its horses!"

Watching him closely, it appeared to Fantom that there was a glint in the eye of Quay as he said this, though what the glint could mean, he could not tell, unless it were that Quay half regretted that the fight had not taken place, with him to stand by as spectator of the fun.

"A year, then," said Quay, "but only if the idea appeals to you. A year, at sixty dollars a month, and found."

"A year," muttered Fantom. "In a year, a lot of things could happen, I suppose!"

"What is it that you're snubbed to on so short a line?" asked Quay. "What's in your mind, Jim? What's so pleasant in the world that you couldn't take a chance and leave it for a year?"

Jim Fantom rubbed his chin again and sighed.

"Why, nothin', I suppose," said he.

"Ah," said Quay instantly. "A girl, my boy?"

"A girl? I got nothin' to do with 'em," protested Fantom in haste.

"A girl," went on Quay, not heeding the protest. "Let me see. The one that you talked to that evening in Burned Hill. That pretty youngster, the Dolan girl! Is that the one?"

"I never seen her but once!" said Fantom gloomily.

"The more reason that you'll want to see her again. You couldn't make a better choice than that, Jim Fantom. Was she pleasant to you?"

Fantom considered.

"She acted like she wasn't considerin' it wasted time," he said finally. "But toward the end, I begun to crowd her a little and she passed me a frosty look or two. Nothin' much to matter, though!"

"You'd be willing to face her again, I suppose?"

"Why, Quay," said he, "don't you savvy that I never seen her but once, and that was the evenin' light, that tells a lot of lies?"

"Not about her," answered Quay serenely. "She's a little beauty, as certainly meant to queen it in the wilderness for some man's house as Mount Kinsell, yonder, is meant to lord it over this range. I congratulate you, Jim. But I could have known that you would take one like her — if there *is* another with her lines!" He added, while Fantom drew a long and sighing breath: "Clipper built, and finished like a yacht!"

Then the boy broke out, almost angrily: "Look here, Mr. Quay, are you askin' me to go to work for you, or to go and marry that girl, if she'll have me? Doggone me if I understand what you're drivin' at!"

"Well, well," answered the older man, soothingly. "It's not a bit strange to me that you're put out. As a matter of fact, I intend that you combine both things under one heading."

"Now, what in hell might you mean by that?" asked Fantom darkly.

"Simply this. You go to work for me, you shake hands on staying with me for a year — no matter what ups and downs we have — you promise to work for me like a soldier and take orders without talking back, Jim," and here he laughed, to make the words lighter in meaning, "and in return for that, I'll bring you that girl, and put you into a pleasant house with her, and marry her to you."

Jim Fantom was shocked back to an oath which he had not heard since the days of his childhood.

"Holy jumpin' Jupiter!" said Fantom. "What are you talkin' about?"

"I'm offering you a bargain."

Fantom pulled out a handkerchief and mopped his brow, his face, his wet throat.

"I dunno what you'd be gettin' back from me!" he said, doubtfully.

At this, Quay frowned a little.

"I expected a little more of the gambling spirit in you, Fantom," he admitted. "I think I've been useful to you, this morning. Very well, I won't dwell on that; I don't *want* to dwell on that. In addition I offer you good wages, good keep, a house, a wife — the wife of your choosing! Very well! What more? I ask you to give me a contract for one year. Not a signed contract, but your word of honor to obey orders for one year. Obviously, I need you. Just what for, I can't tell you. I hardly know myself. What's your alternative? To be hounded here and there indefinitely by the law, from which I can promise you a good deal of protection. Now, then, Fantom, what is your decision?"

"If she — if Jo Dolan — I mean, if she's the kind that would pick up and marry anybody —" he stammered.

"Young man," said the other sternly, "can't you read character better than this? I know nothing about that girl — except that I can make her your wife, if you want!"

Jim Fantom threw up both his hands.

"Then for God's sake get her!" said he, "and I'm your man!"

CHAPTER NINE

It was late in that day when they reached Quay Valley. It was named after Quay for the simple reason that he owned every inch of it, and when Fantom had his first view of it, it seemed to him a wonderful little kingdom. The valley was flat-bottomed, with a lake in the center and a small stream running down to the lake and out from it again. Little creeks and brooks streaked down from the upper lands and joined the larger bodies of water, and here and there a waterfall streamed in the air a transparent banner of white. All the rough upper slopes were covered with big timber, a virgin forest which now, as Quay pointed out, was being dealt with scientifically, so that not more would be cut than would healthily thin the woods. Below the forested ground came a wide belt of pasturage, and the bottom of the valley was checked and rechecked by the patches of farm land. Some of it was lying fallow, making red squares, for the soil was of that color when it showed naked; some of it was silver with oats; other squares were the darker green of wheat; but all of the level soil had been put to good use. Young Jim Fantom saw and admired.

"You're pretty rich!" he said.

Quay shook his head.

"It doesn't mean money to me," he asserted

solemnly. "This is my kingdom, Jim. But as for money — how could I handle those crops at a profit, considering that there are no proper roads across the mountains? I'd have to haul that wheat, for instance, sixty miles!"

"You don't waste it!" exclaimed the boy.

"No, we don't waste it. There's the granaries down yonder."

"Where the river cuts out of the lake?"

"Yes."

"It's a big enough set of buildings!"

With a pleasant thrill, the boy looked up and down the valley, which they were so high above that it seemed as if he could hold it in his outstretched arms.

"Ay, big enough," said Quay. "The two biggest are all stored with seasoned wheat and oat hay. Some ten sack wheat was cut to make that hay! But there it is, stored up and kept sweet! And there's enough hay there of the first quality to feed all the stock in the valley from October to June! That's in case of a very bad winter, but winters can't be that long and hard!"

"They can't," agreed the boy, "but I see that you make everything safe."

"That's my pleasure. I never take chances if I can avoid it!"

"And besides the hay warehouse?" asked Jim Fantom.

"That's the flour house, yonder. There are the mills, the low-looking buildings there where the river is white with the rapids. We grind out flour there, and cart it over to the warehouse. It's the flour itself that we haul out the sixty miles. That pays much better than the wheat, of course, because a ton of it is a good deal more valuable. Opposite is the warehouse where we keep the barley, crushed and uncrushed; the oats; and the corn. Do you see that corn patch there on the banks of the lake?"

"Yes, I can just make out the rows!"

"Well, that corn will stand eight feet high before the summer's over. We have a corn-roast when the green corn is ripe enough. Oh, we have some jolly times in the valley, as you'll find out, Jim!"

Jim Fantom looked with glistening eyes. In his heart of hearts there was nothing after which he more yearned than a life on the soil. To plant, to cherish, and to reap with his own hand what his own hand had sowed seemed to him the fundamental joy of life. So he laughed, with shining eyes, as he looked down on the valley as on a map.

"You're stocked up with everything, I suppose?" said he. "What are the smaller buildings down there in that circle?"

"Why, one is the store. You can get everything from a darning needle to a center-fire saddle, in that store. The smaller cabin is the blacksmith shop. I have a blacksmith down there who can make you anything between a Spanish bit and a wrought-iron grill, or a stiletto that would sink into a man's flesh by its own weight alone. He's a master, is old Josh Wilkes!"

"That's your headquarters, then?"

"Yes, that's what you might call town. The boys have named it Quayville! Well, from Quayville just west down the bank of the lake — there on the far side — is my house."

Jim Fantom could see a handsome park of gigantic trees, and the white-painted house settled among them, with a garden traced out around it.

"You see it's not pretentious," said Quay. "It's simply a log cabin, though it's a bit larger than the others. However, my men live as well as I do!"

"In those cottages?"

For, here and there in the valley, there were cottages dotted in pleasant locations.

"Yes," said Quay, "wherever you see a cottage, you can take it for granted that it's occupied by a happy family of my friends. Perhaps you've heard of —"

"I've heard of the Quay Reform Colony!" broke out Fantom, striking his knuckles against his forehead. "What a fool I was to forget about it!"

"I don't like to call it a reform colony," said Quay. "If now and then I am able to do a little — why, I thank God for it. But I don't believe in reform. I believe in letting men do what will make them happy. For instance, there's not a single man there who doesn't love the soil! You see the fields around their houses? Forty acres to each! If you look more closely, you'll see that each man has his own orchard patch. Pears, plums, prunes, apricots, peaches, and we grow apples as good as anything that ever came out of the state of Oregon, I assure you! Well, as I was saying, every man has his orchard patch, a few acres of pasture, a bit of vineyard, and some choice farm land — about twenty-five acres of good soil, to do what he pleases with."

"That's great!" said the boy through his teeth. "That's a way to live!"

"They have their tools furnished to 'em, a house to live in; enough chuck is furnished to 'em to make the first year easy; and they're given seed for their acreage. Besides that, they all get pay from me by the month."

"Hold on," said the boy. "How much does it cost you, then? Must pretty near cost you a fortune, don't it?"

"No, not a bit. I make a pretty good thing out of it. The houses and the equipment cost a good deal to start with, but those men board themselves, which saves me a lot! In addition, I have the pleasure of seeing them start their families, remake their lives. It doesn't cost a great part of their time to take care of their orchards. We do everything at a time — like fruit picking, pruning, etc. The work's soon ended, and every man has his crop harvested in one week! They have enough time to spend on my range, looking after my cattle."

"And working that farm land in the bottom?"

"Oh, no. I can't ask men like those fellows to

75

work behind a plow for me. I have some Chinese labor, for that. They're very steady, and they make no trouble."

"But look here," said Fantom, "do you mean to tell me that every doggone one of those cottages has a crook livin' in it?"

"No, no!" exclaimed the other. "I should say not! It's my hope that every man in the valley is as honest as the world needs to find him!"

He laughed a little as he said this, though Fantom felt that the remark probably had to do with some meaning which he did not quite understand.

"There are people down there who have completely altered and turned over a new leaf in life," said Quay, rubbing his hands together and laughing in the same odd manner. "That cottage by the creek, yonder, the one with the two trees just in front of it —"

"I see it."

"Joe Porson lives in that with his wife. As pretty a girl as you ever saw!"

"I never heard of Porson."

"He was in prison for eleven years for a gunfight in Texas. It was his tenth man, and the judge thought that Joe ought to take a rest."

Again Quay laughed, and again Fantom grew a little uneasy.

"Do you see the cottage with the green roof?"

"No."

"Yonder, where the river comes down into the

lake. You can just make it out through the trees."

"Yes, I see it now."

"That's where Mack Rhiner lives —"

"Rhiner the murderer?"

"Tut, tut!" said Quay. "I wouldn't call him that. He's as steady a man as you'd like to see, now! Married, too, and very happy, I take it! Just across the river from him is Steve Upton."

"He's the one who blew the First National safe in Crooked Horn?"

"That's the one. Married like the others. Married men in all of those cottages. That is to say — in all of the ones that are occupied. I have in mind the very one for you and your girl. You see near my house, where that creek makes a riffle of white water — the cottage with the orchard laid out all around it —"

"Look here, Mr. Quay," said the boy, delighted but rather overawed, "you were joking when you said that about Jo Dolan, of course!"

"Joking? Not a bit, not a bit! I've managed stranger things than that! Come down with me to my house. You'll stay there for a while, until your own house is put in order. Mind you, Jim. This is to be a one-year's experiment, and at the end of that time, if either of us doesn't like the bargain, the deal can be called off. How does it sound to you?"

"It sounds to me," said the boy slowly, "like a dream. A queer kind of a dream. I'm waiting to wake up!"

Quay chuckled.

"You'll be sure of one year of that dream, anyway," said he. "And perhaps for the rest of your life! That is, if you like the idea of this sort of a life?"

"Like it?" cried the boy.

He looked rather wildly around him.

"Why," he said at last, "it's the way I'd have laid out everything for myself, if I'd been able. Only it's more perfect than anything that I could have thought up. I'll shake hands with you again on that bargain, Mr. Quay!"

So, gravely, they shook hands, and then rode down into the valley.

CHAPTER TEN

They swung down into the valley on the hauling road. The surface was enough to convince Jim Fantom that no money could be made, or very little, by carting even a refined product like flour for sixty miles over such going. It was deeply rutted. Rocks and broken roots of trees made great humps in it, here and there, and the general appearance of the trail was like the roll of a ship in a quartering sea.

"What sort of wagons can haul over this sort of a surface?" asked Fantom.

"Listen," said his companion, "for here comes one now!"

As he spoke, Fantom heard behind him a faint, dull thunder. They reined up beside the road, and presently around the curve came a great wagon with wheels seven feet in diameter and fourteen mules stretched out before it. The brakes were slammed on at that moment by the teamster, and down the grade went the big vehicle with a continual scream of the pad of wet, green twigs which served as brake cushions against the great iron rims of the wheels.

The teamster turned the corner with his leaders trotting fast, the swing couples ambling, and the wheelers and pointers pulling against the brakes.

Through the dust, Fantom saw a lean, erect man on the seat beneath the canvas canopy of the "schooner." He gave a careless salute to Quay, and favored Fantom with a long stare; then the wagon went down the slope.

They waited for the dust to blow away, and as they waited, it gave Fantom a chance to ponder this accidental meeting. He was not thinking of the huge wheels, able to lumber over worse impediments than the surface of the way before him. He was thinking of the carelessness of the teamster in saluting his employer.

In two ways it was remarkable. In the first place, because even in the West a hired man had some respect for his employer; in the second place because Quay was the reputed benefactor of all of his employees. Fantom could remember hearing of the organization of this valley, and that Quay refused to take a single man who was not recruited from a jail or a penitentiary. The lives of these men he was said to build up from the beginning, treating them as children in a great family. There was not a great deal of talk about this ideal society, for the simple reason that it was buried so deep among the mountains. Range after range lifted its head between the hidden valley and the nearest town; apparently there was no trail except this same hideous road over which a horseman would stumble with difficulty, and which no wagon except these specially devised monsters could travel a hundred yards.

Men in such a situation were apt to look upon

Quay more as a god than as a man, and yet there had been utter carelessness and indifference in the salute of the teamster.

As the dust cleared away before them, powdering the brush at the roadside white, Quay was saying:

"That's Terry Samuels. He's a rare good man with a team. Nearly always on the road for us."

"Samuels? Samuels?" said the boy. "Wasn't there a Terry Samuels who held up the D. & S. express and robbed the Wells Fargo box?"

"Yes. That was eight years ago. You have a fine memory, Jim. We're hoping that the rest of the world will forget that unlucky little affair, so that Terry can go on with his happy life up here with us in the valley. The Happy Valley. Some of the boys call it that, you know!"

"Ay, it looks happy enough," said Fantom. "But do they all get on, so far from a town? Don't some of 'em get mighty lonesome?"

"Mostly they're married," said Quay. "I like to have married men up here, as you can imagine. I'm one who likes to see the families of little youngsters grow up around the knees of their parents. There's no way so sure as that of chaining a man — to a new life, my boy!"

He looked at Fantom and smiled as he said it, and Jim Fantom could not help feeling a real element of mockery in that smile, and it troubled and baffled him. Certainly there was much about this man and this valley which he did not, as yet, faintly realize. He rode on down the way with his companion, determined to keep his eyes very wide open, indeed, and for the first time he began to regret the solemn promise which he had made to Quay.

Because it included everything! For one year, he was totally under the direction of this man, and during that year whatever Quay willed, he must will, also! Sidewise he glanced at Quay, doubtful, and saw that the other was smiling again, straight before him, like a man who is well pleased with himself.

So they dropped slowly down toward the valley floor, descending with bends and windings until they issued out at the bottom.

From this point of view, the place was more extraordinary even than from the height; for the tall mountains seemed to lean in upon it from either side, and the trees, which were hardly more than smudges of shadow from above, now appeared as monster forests of silver spruce and of pine.

They put their horses into a canter, cut through the dust cloud of the wagon and its long string of laboring mules, and headed straight down the central road of the valley. They were following the river that wound down from the lake in the middle of the place, and as the road came to a bridge that arched the water of a little tributary, Quay drew rein again. He turned to Fantom and said:

"Whatever arrangement I've made with you, my boy, is to be kept silent. Do you understand?"

He said it crisply, sharply, like a man driving home an important point. Fantom frowned, but he nodded.

"That goes," said he.

"One other thing," said Quay in the same manner. "You'll find these men very open and free-spoken. No matter what they say to you, take it with a grain of salt. There are things they don't understand, about themselves, and about me. Is that agreed?"

Fantom was irritated.

"Look here," said he. "I've given you my word, and that holds."

"Ay," said Quay. "The first thing I heard of you was that your word was better than the other fellow's bond. I build on that, Jim!"

"I've given you my word," repeated Fantom, "and that means that you can handle me the way that you please, so far as talkin' and doin' things is concerned. But it don't mean that I ain't got a right to think what I please!"

"My dear boy," said Quay, and he laughed with the same intonation of mockery which had disturbed Fantom before, "you're as free as the wind to think what you please, be sure. Thoughts never have harmed me, and I don't think that they've been the death of many others. Words, however, are a different matter. Words and actions, Jim! Words and actions! They're what make the world spin around. Remember while you're here that every word you speak is by rights something that I should be able to control.

I have your promise. I trust to that!"

"What sort of a place is this?" asked Jim Fantom. "What sort of a place, if words are like dynamite?"

"Why, my boy, words always are like dynamite. Dynamite and poison, no matter where one may be, but especially in a place like this where you're surrounded by the thugs from a dozen prisons!"

"I thought," said the boy, "that they was chiefly made over?"

Quay did not appear to notice the sarcasm in this remark. He answered seriously:

"Do you think I imagine that I can change the innate nature of a man, my young friend? No, no! But a fire can't live unless it has fuel to feed on. And I've removed these men from temptation, as you may say, and also from the danger of the law. However, I cannot say that the fire is extinguished in every case. It simply smoulders and burns low. That's why I say that you must be careful of your words here in the valley. To mix the metaphor a little, suppose I suggest that many of these men are dry powder. Don't let sparks fall!"

There was sufficient common sense and clarity in this speech to remove any sense of mystery from the mind of Jim Fantom. He rode on in silence beside his companion, using his eyes eagerly, and finding enough to occupy his attention and his mind. They wound across a rich bottom land beside the river. It was checked into small fields of vegetables and berries, and a few dusky forms were moving out of them in the twilight with large-bladed hoes draped over their shoulders.

"Chinamen are great workers," said Quay. "Those poor fellows are very happy, however. They get a good share of everything that is made off the ground. No, white men wouldn't be contented with such earnings, but the Chinamen are different. Enough for life and just a little bit more is all that they require. They are content to go on adding one to one. They'll give three generations to making a fortune that a white man would want to heap up in three years. I admire those fellows. I can learn something from them!"

They went out over a narrow, highly arched bridge of wood that spanned the little river, and in the center of it, Quay drew rein.

Here, where the water issued from the foot of the lake, there was well-nigh no current; still as the lake itself, appeared the stream, except that the current whispered softly around the big wooden piers that supported the bridge. And it seemed a river a thousand fathoms deep, because on its still face appeared the colors of the sunset, now rusting away, and the white heads of a few of the loftiest mountains, looking as deep in the water as they really were high in the air.

A breeze stirred. It brought to Jim Fantom a sudden sense of the sweetness of newly cut hay, and suddenly he exclaimed:

"Ay, a man could live here. He wouldn't want

to bother with the rest of the world, I guess! He wouldn't want to bother with it!"

He lifted his head and breathed deep. There were scars in the soul of Fantom, but it seemed to him, now, as though five years of pain were being stolen away by the whisper of the water beneath the bridge; the peace of the Happy Valley passed into his spirit.

Then, with a rush of emotion, he turned toward the man beside him. He had been troubled by a feeling that there was too ancient a wisdom in Jonathan Quay, a cynicism of too great knowledge of men and life; but now it seemed to Fantom that all that was dignified, all that was kind and merciful, was gathered into the face of the older man. In this dim light his bearded face appeared patriarchal, and reverence, as for a father, came up out of the heart of Fantom. He stretched out his hand and laid it on the shoulder of his companion.

"I'm your man, Mr. Quay," said he. "You picked me up when I was a gone goose, and gave me another chance. No matter what happens, you can do my thinking for me. I'll go the way you point!"

He said it slowly. As he spoke, he felt that he was pouring out his life and placing it in the hands of Jonathan Quay.

CHAPTER ELEVEN

There was no answer from Quay to this emotional outburst, but Jim Fantom felt no shame for the violence with which he had expressed himself. The deep gratitude which had moved him still made his heart tremble.

They rode on across the bridge, the reflected color in the river faded behind them, the white peaks vanished from the water, and they entered a tall and gloomy forest. No timberman's ax had yet entered it. Six and eight foot trunks began on either side of the road and lifted a staggering distance into the sunset sky. They passed a lightning-blasted giant, holding out white arms, like a ghost; and so they came suddenly upon a small clearing, in the midst of which there was a log cabin, with a stout shed behind it, built of logs, also, and a streak of water, rosy in this dim light, beginning beside the cabin door and trickling across the open, lost presently under the shadow of the forest.

The horse of The Phantom stopped. Instinctively he had reined it in to stare at the place.

"Well?" asked Quay.

Jim Fantom made a little gesture. All the muscles of his arms and shoulders were stirring restlessly, flexing and unflexing. His fingers stiffened as though about the handle of an ax.

87

"It sort of hits me in the eye," said he.

"Do you like it, my son?" asked Quay.

"I mean," explained Jim Fantom, "to clear the ground — to be sinking an ax into those trees, and clearing the ground, to be making it your own — that would be something!"

"It would be a lot of work, for one thing," said Quay.

"You could sit in your door in the evening," said Fantom, dreaming, "and have a smoke, and see how far back you'd pushed the trees that day — or that month. Well, that would be a life!"

"I thought you were a horseman, a rider, a fellow who loved freedom, Jim?"

"Me? Sure I've always been. But all at once it got me. I mean, seeing the cabin, that looks like it needed company, and smelling the ground, sort of. Listen! D'you hear?"

"What?"

"The run of the water! Who lives here?"

"No one," said Quay. "The clearing is bigger than you think. There's a good-sized meadow to the back of it." He started his horse on, and added, as Fantom joined him, "I'm getting it ready now for a new man!"

The heart of Fantom fell for an instant, all his thoughts had leaped eagerly forward with hope that this might be his; he said nothing, but it seemed to him that the night had come over them with one step.

They left the dark of the woods a little later and came into the open, where the last of the afterglow still lived in the sky above them. Straight ahead appeared an avenue of trees, beyond it the front of a large cabin, of logs also.

"Your house?" said Fantom.

"I live there. But it's a sort of a clubhouse for the boys, too. They're free to go where they like in it, except that Kendal shuts down on them, now and then. He likes quiet, does Kendal!"

"Kendal?"

"Louis Kendal. He's in charge of everything for me. I have to be away a good deal — as on this trip, you see. So Kendal takes charge in the valley, and he gives orders."

"To everybody?" asked Fantom uneasily.

"Yes, to everybody. I might have mentioned him before, to you. Kendal's a good fellow, but a little grim, and sometimes silent. I think some of the boys don't like him, at first, but after a while, they never complain. You'll get on with him, Jim!"

A gate creaked open near by, and out of the field half a dozen cows lumbered and went waddling down the road, with a man walking behind them.

"You're late for the milking, Dutchy, aren't you?" asked Quay.

Dutchy fell back a little. He was as fat and waddling as one of the animals in his charge.

"I'll tell you how it is, Mr. Quay," said he. "That long-legged brindle heifer, yonder — bad luck to her! — she'd broke through the fence and got into Wallace's field of young wheat. I been an hour, about, chasin' her. All cows is fools, but they're two kinds of fools, plain fools and mean fools, and she's a mean one. I've lost five pounds sprintin' after her."

"Too bad," sympathized Quay. "That'll be bad for her milk, too, won't it?"

"Sure it will," said Dutchy. "She should a been a race hoss. Every time that I hollered soo-o-o, boss! she thought she was starting for a stake. She'd carry my money, on a track — damn her mean eyes!"

Quay laughed, and they jogged slowly by the cattle, up the road toward the house.

"Kendal's idea," said Quay. "When the ground was cleared, he left this double row of the big trees; he wanted me to build a real mansion at the other end of it, but I couldn't let him have his way as far as that! For my part, I'd be as happy in a tent. Where a man lives doesn't matter. It's the manner of housing heart and soul that counts, I suppose. Here we are, Jim."

It was a long, low building to which they had come, and, rounding this, they arrived at a barn, in front of which a man was watering a string of four horses at a trough. They threw up their heads and snorted at the sight of the two newcomers.

"Chip Lander!" cried Quay. "How did you manage to get here so soon?"

The young fellow waved a hand to them, and laughed.

"I'll tell you how," said he. "Mack Rhiner was

right on hand with a relay of fresh horses five mile from the start. I had that gang of the sheriff's pretty sick and dizzy by that time, anyway, and when I got into the saddle on a brand new hoss, why, Mack and me simply walked away from 'em. Bud Cross is back there somewhere in the hills damnin' his luck! I've been here an hour!"

"How did you come in? You didn't pass us on the road."

"Nope. There didn't seem any use of comin' all the way round. We used the short cut in from the south side. It was right under our noses. There was no use goin' all the way around."

"Use enough!" said Quay in rebuke. "Are you trying to lead the sheriff straight in on us, Chip?"

"Him?" said Lander uneasily. "Aw, he'll never guess!"

Quay said no more, but dismounted in obvious displeasure.

"I'll take your hoss, chief," suggested Lander, placatingly.

"I'll take care of him myself," said Quay. He added readily, "I'm not angry, Chip. After all, it's only for the sake of the rest of you that I want some of the passes kept secret."

He led his horse into the barn, but Jim Fantom remained behind. He said to Lander:

"You fished me out of boiling water, Chip. I was nearly cooked when you popped up in the way!"

Lander laughed as he shook hands with great

cordiality. Even in the half-light of the dusk, Fantom could see that the other had grown into as handsome a fellow as he had given promise of becoming when a lad.

"I was mighty glad of the chance," said Lander. "I was afraid that one of these days you'd come sashayin' along to get back at me for the last time I saw you!"

He laughed again, a cheerful, fearless laughter which suggested that his words were more modest than his thoughts.

"I'm glad to have you here," went on Chip. "You'll be stayin' here at the main house, I guess? You ain't a married man, Jim?"

"No."

"We might throw in together, then, unless his Nibs gives you a room by yourself."

"You mean Mr. Quay?"

"No. I mean that long slice of the devil, Kendal! He has the say around here about everything, as you'll soon find out."

"You don't like him?"

"Him? Like him? Well — I've talked too much already!" said Lander. "Come along and I'll show you the hang of things in the barn."

In the barn, which had stall-room for a dozen horses or more on a side, and a capacious mow in the center, Lander pointed out the situation of the feed box and the saddle room, where great masses of tackle of all sorts hung from the walls.

He tethered his four horses and then forked down some hay to Fantom's horse. After that, he came down from the mow by the ladder and joined Jim.

"How long have you been here?" asked the latter.

"Why, about five months," said Lander.

"And how come, if you're tellin' the story?"

"Sure I'm tellin' it."

They sauntered from the barn together as Lander chatted.

"I was in Montana in the town of New Lincoln. You know that place?"

"Yeah. In a blizzard I seen it once."

"I was in the most comfortable part of New Lincoln, which was the jail. The day before, twelve gents had stood up and said that I'd been guilty of manslaughter, which is a funny thing to call the killin' of a Swede that already had me down with a knife at my throat, eh?"

"Yeah. A funny thing, to call that manslaughter. They ought of given you a medal for that, Chip."

"The judge did. He gives me a ten-year medal, with a certificate attached, and something discounted for good behavior. I had one more night in jail before they shipped me to the pen, and that night my door clinked and opened. In comes somebody in the dark, but I thought I could see him by his own light, so to speak, like he'd been rubbed with phosphorus. You'll understand when you see him for yourself."

"Who do you mean?"

"Why, I mean Louis Kendal, of course. He

comes slippin' in, unlocks my irons, and whispers to me to foller him. It give me a chill, even then — I mean, the idea of bein' free, and the idea of bein' close to this here Kendal at the same minute. You'll understand when you see him, how snaky he is! But he walked me out of that jail by the back way, and unlocked about four doors as smooth as oil runnin' down hill! Aw, he's slick, that Kendal! He brought me up through the hills and never said a word to me. I didn't know whether he wanted to set me free or cut my throat, until we met up with old Mr. Quay on the road. God bless him! It was him that had sent Kendal, of course! There's as much gold in him as there is steel in Kendal!"

"He's the pure quill, all right," said Fantom, vastly relieved from the last of the doubts that had shot through his mind on the way to the valley.

Before they could speak again, a door screeched open, a gong was banged, and a cheerful cry pealed through the air:

"Come and get it! Come and get it!"

They started hungrily for the house.

CHAPTER TWELVE

All was rough comfort, inside the house. The logs were not even faced or their bark taken off, and plainly in view was the moss and mud which had been used to calk the interstices. The long table in the dining room was simply split logs, supported by two hurdles, and lashed together with rawhide.

However, the place was not unpleasant. A big fireplace yawned at the side of the dining room, and, since the night air was cold, a tangle of wood flamed in it. All was liberal and rude as a lumber camp, in this house of Jonathan Quay.

He was sunning himself before the fire when the two came in, but Fantom gave him hardly a glance, for the door had opened at the farther end of the room, at that moment, and, framed in the shadows, he saw Louis Kendal for the first time.

He recognized the man at once from what Chip Lander had said of him. Although only the faintest illumination reached to him from the lamp and the fire, yet, as Lander had said, it seemed that the fellow could be seen by his own light. The long, pale face, once glanced at, never could be forgotten. Moreover, Jim Fantom knew that he himself had been fixed by the first glance of those eyes, and that he was valued, summed up, and jotted down in the brain of the other.

Jonathan Quay introduced in a cheerful voice, and Kendal came forward slowly with his eyes still gleaming at Fantom as though he were striving to push aside a veil and get at the truth behind Fantom's face. Instantly, with all his heart, Jim Fantom loathed the man and feared him. A cold and bony hand gripped his, closing slowly, with a suggestion of great strength. Then they turned to the table and sat down.

It was a relief to be freed from the surveillance of Kendal; yet Fantom resented the judgment of the other, even before he knew the verdict which had been passed upon him. He was uneasy, nervous. Like a frightened boy, he found himself studying Kendal with side glances.

The man should have been an object of pity, he decided, on account of the pallor of his skin and, most of all, a suggestion of deformity in his body. What it was, in which he was wrong, Fantom could not tell, but the suggestion was there in the narrow shoulders, the long arms, the pale and bony hands. He ate awkwardly, as though his elbows were crowded against his sides by near neighbors. His eyes never lifted from his plate, though there was no doubt that he saw everything that happened in the room.

Fantom had the impression of being closed in a cage with an animal. He felt helpless, and dreaded the time when Kendal should speak to him. Hot resentment against his weakness followed.

Then he was aware that Quay had been talking

for some time, talking about the new recruit, telling pale Louis Kendal all about him, while Kendal never lifted his eyes or nodded his head, or in any way gave token that he heard.

"We are going to make it easy for James Fantom to start a new life, Louis," said Quay. "He has the material in him out of which law-abiding citizens are formed. That's the sort of fellow we want in the valley!"

Kendal stirred his food together on his plate.

"How many men have you killed?" he said in a twanging voice, startlingly loud.

Fantom started in his chair. He started so violently that the feet of the chair squeaked against the floor, and he saw Kendal smile with a secret satisfaction. At that, anger drove the fear from Fantom's mind.

"Not enough to interest you, I guess," said he.

He raised his head and stared fixedly. There was challenge in his voice, challenge in his manner, but Kendal paid no heed. He continued to share his secret thought with his plate alone, and to smile at it.

Quay seemed anxious.

"Don't misunderstand Kendal," he assured Fantom. "Louis has a dry way, but he's vitally interested in you and your problems — as vitally as I am, in fact! But I can answer for you, I think. I make it my business to follow the careers of the boys who had flown a little high. There was an affair in Tombstone. A pair of Mexicans looking for trouble who stumbled over Jim Fantom."

"There were four of them Mexicans," said Kendal, still smiling at his plate.

"Well, well — you know the details of that affair better than I do," murmured Quay. "Well, then, out of the four two were killed. Fantom was fighting for his life against four aggressors. Of course, everyone thought all the better of him for that. Then there were the affairs of Lynch and Harry Lord. I think that's about all. Four men, let us say, Jim?"

Fantom was about to answer, but Kendal drawled in the same disagreeably loud, nasal voice:

"And about three more to fill in, here and there!"

"Really?" sighed Quay. "And now young Phelan —"

"I didn't touch Phelan," broke in Fantom.

"Very well, very well!" said Quay hastily. "You didn't touch Phelan! We won't argue about that. But it's the viewpoint of the law, I suppose we may say? You wouldn't feel lucky if the sheriff had you for that death, would you?"

"No," said Fantom slowly. "They'd hang me, I suppose. But — why did you ask about killings, Kendal?"

"You was eighteen when you went to the pen. I was just thinkin'," said Kendal, "that seven was a tidy lot for a kid of eighteen. No harm in thinkin', is there?"

Suddenly his eyes flashed from his plate to the face of Fantom. They were eyes almost as pale as his face, but marked with a peculiar glow such as Fantom never had seen before. He shuddered, but he faced that stare, though he had to frown to do so.

"No harm, I guess," muttered Fantom.

Sweat was breaking out on his face. He wanted nothing in the world so much as to turn his eyes from the steady stare of Kendal. It was like a weight, turning his glance into corners of the room, but he fought away the temptation. It occurred to him that this was utterly childish, as when two boys in remote corners of a schoolroom resolutely strive to stare one another down, until the balls of their eyes ache with the strain and grow dry, yet fiercely they keep from winking.

So it was now that he stared at Kendal, until he felt his whole body leaning forward a little. Suddenly the eyes of Kendal narrowed and looked away; then he was aware that the strain had not lasted for more than a few seconds. But the sweat now ran freely down his face.

Quay noticed it.

"It's hot in here. You're too near the fire!" said he. "Why don't you move down the table, a little?"

"I guess I will," said Fantom.

The cook, at this moment, was refilling the coffee cups when the kitchen door opened with a jerk that caused the air to suck toward it and pulled the fragile columns of steam aslant. A panting man in scarred leather chaps, with a quirt dangling like a living snake at his wrist, stood in the doorway. He put his hand against the jamb to support himself, while he panted:

"Bud Cross! He's comin' down the valley! Whacha say, Kendal? Do we get him or let him come through?"

Louis Kendal made a peculiar gesture, with the palm of his hand turned up.

"You better ask the boss," said he.

"Bud Cross! The sheriff!" said Quay. "Coming here? Did he ride down the road?"

"He came over the south pass," said the other.

Quay turned reproachful eyes upon Chip Lander.

"I knew that there might be trouble from this day's riding," said he. "How far away is the sheriff now?"

"About a half mile."

"Tut, tut!" said Quay, only mildly dismayed. "Has he many men with him?"

"Only four," said the other. "We could blot them up as easy as nothing if you say the word to —"

"Blot them up?" echoed Quay. "Murder those men? Because they're riding to enforce the law? Great heavens, young man, how little you know me! No, no! Let them come on, freely."

He waved toward the table.

"Perhaps we'd better have everything taken away, except the dishes for two. Cook, will you manage that? Chip and Jim, I'm afraid that the sheriff would be too much interested if he should find you here with me. May I ask you to step into

100

the next room? Everything will be all right. Don't be alarmed in the least. This is unlucky. That's all! We'll manage everything for the best!"

His voice was very gentle. He talked as though to two children, reassuring them in a time of sickness or of alarm.

So Jim Fantom left the table with Lander and they crowded through the doorway into the next room.

They closed the heavy door behind them. A cold, damp air surrounded them, chilling after the warmth and brightness of the dining room's atmosphere. In that darkness they waited, standing close to the door. Fantom had his grip on the handles of a Colt; he could guess that his companion had done the same thing, and no matter what else the sheriff did in that house, it behoved him not to open the door to this room!

They could hear the voices of Quay and Kendal clearly, though those voices were lowered a little.

"There mustn't be any violence, Louis," Quay was saying. "Remember that the sheriff represents the law, and the law represents the good of the land. After all, you and I are working to the same end, are we not?"

"Oh, ay," said Kendal. "But a damned lot of belief Bud Cross would have in it if he was to find Lander or the new one in the house! You'll have to talk him out, Quay!"

"I'll do my best," said Quay.

101

"And if the pinch comes, Quay? What then?"

"Whatever happens," said Quay, "no violence! Remember! No violence whatever!"

There was no answer to this.

In the distance, Fantom heard the noise of hoofs, as if on a culvert or a bridge. The sound beat out for one moment, and then was muffled again. Doubtless those were the horses of the sheriff.

His heart began to beat fast. He had an almost irresistible impulse to flee, throw himself on a horse, and spur away, for the shadow of the law already was like ice fallen upon him.

But he remembered his word plighted to Jonathan Quay. For one year his body and his soul lay in the hand of that man! He could not stir without orders!

CHAPTER THIRTEEN

Now there was a silence in the next room, broken only by a gradual pulse of a footfall going up and down the floor. There was a slight drag of the heel, a slight jingle of spurs, and Fantom was sure that he recognized the slouching gait of tall Louis Kendal, pacing like a beast in the cage! He heard the whisper of Lander beside him, a whisper choked with a nervous tension.

"Sure as the devil, Cross will search the whole house!"

"I hope he don't come into this room. I hope for his own sake!" said Fantom.

"Don't I hope the same thing? Oh, I ain't fearin' for us. Kendal would blow them to bits, without our help. But if there's a slaughter like that, it's the end of the Happy Valley! It's the dead finish!"

He paused. He had murmured with such emotion that Fantom could see the youngster was speaking as of the end of the world.

"That devil — that Kendal!" whispered Lander again. "He's ready for a kill, now, since you've looked him down! That's never happened before. How did you manage it?"

"I didn't look him down!"

"I watched. I seen you sweat, sure, but I seen him look away first. Why, there ain't a man in the valley that wouldn't rather face a gun than to face Louis Kendal's eye. *I'd* rather to face a gun — any day!"

He fumbled for the arm of Fantom and gripped it.

"Right from now on, you watch yourself, because he ain't ever gunna forgive you!"

But Fantom could have gasped with relief. If there had been a moral victory for him, he never had guessed it. It was far from his thoughts, indeed! But it seemed that somehow the triumph had been his, and he was stunned and rejoiced, at the same instant.

However, there was something else to think of now. Close to the house the noise of the hoofs began again and drummed heavily, then paused.

"They're here!" he heard Kendal say.

Immediately afterward, a door slammed; he heard the clanking of heels on the floor coming into the dining room.

"Why," called out Quay cheerfully, "hello! Hello! Glad to see you, Sheriff Cross. And the rest of you boys. Sit down and have something to eat — or have you come here to eat *me!*"

He laughed good-naturedly as he talked, and Fantom was amazed by the theatrical skill of the man.

The voice of Bud Cross came in gloomily.

"I ain't after you, Mr. Quay, I guess. But I'm after one that I figger is somewhere in the valley, here. Have you seen hide or hair of young Jim Fantom?"

"Fantom? Ah, you mean the lad I saw in Burned Hill?"

"I don't mean nobody else," said the sheriff.

"Look here," broke in Kendal; "what's Fantom done? He's just out of the pen, ain't he?"

"He's killed Larry Phelan in Burned Hill," said the sheriff, "and he's gunna hang for it, and I'm gunna take him to the jail with my own hands or get bumped off tryin'! That's the story, stranger. I dunno that I have your name?"

"By name of Louis Kendal."

"Well, Kendal, what's your business?"

"Sort of straw boss for Mr. Quay, here."

The sheriff said, impatiently:

"The fact is, Mr. Quay, that everybody knows what you're doin' up here. You're tryin' to take the boys when they get loose from the pen and keep them from goin' wrong again. It's a fine job. Everybody admires you for doin' it. But they's another side of it that ain't so sweet. Some says that you sometimes don't wait for a gent to get loose from the law. You put out your hand and save him. Is that right?"

"Ah, I see," said Quay. "You mean that I deliberately take in men that the law is still hunting?"

The sheriff grunted.

"Here's this kid, this Fantom. We have him fallin' into our hands. We can almost reach out and tag him. His hoss is all in. Then suddenly he's scootin' away from us as though he had

105

wings — or a new hoss!"

"It was a new hoss," broke in one of the sheriff's men. "I never could of been fooled by that gait. I told you then and I knew it — that was a new hoss. He was stridin' two foot longer in the gallop than the nag that Fantom started out on. That's a fact! It run like a scared rabbit, that second hoss — like a rabbit makin' spy-hops!"

"It was a new hoss," said the sheriff. "Then, who put that hoss there, ready at hand for Fantom when he was in his pinch?"

"Do you point at me, Sheriff?" asked Quay, very quietly.

"Quay," said the other, "I don't like to throw fool talk around through the air, but the fact is that this gent rides away from us and fades out into the mountains. We follow on his line. We pick up his trail again, and it comes through broken ground right down into this here valley. There you are! It looks like he considered this place home. You can think it out for yourself!"

Louis Kendal muttered:

"You're goin' to search the house for him, are you, Cross?"

The sheriff answered crisply:

"I'm not goin' to be such a fool. If Fantom come here, he's already tucked himself off in the woods, the minute that I entered the house. Well, he's safe. I can't pick him up, this day. But I wanta tell you, Mr. Quay, that it's a mighty funny business. You're a mighty lot too intelligent for me to have to start in tellin' you that a man that gives help to a gent the law hunts is bein' a criminal himself!"

"Of course I know that," said Quay.

"One other thing," said the sheriff. "I'm gunna talk my heart right out to you, Mr. Quay, because I believe in you."

"That's a fine compliment, Sheriff, and I appreciate it, I do assure you!"

"Well, sir," said the sheriff, "the thing is this. We know that you have got a lot of ex-thugs up here — safe crackers an' thieves an' train robbers, an' out and out murderers. You've taken 'em up here and tried to rock 'em to sleep, as you might say. You've brought their wives up here. You've settled 'em down where they'll be a mighty long distance away from temptation. All right! But now they's another side of the picture!"

"I'll be glad to have you paint it for me," said the other gently.

"I'll do my best," went on Bud Cross. "Around here, in Leffingwell, an' in Trail's End, an' in Black Rock, an' in Chalmer's City, there have been bank robberies, stage holdups on the roads, all kinds of monkeyshines. They've busted into Thompson's store in Leffingwell, Thompson the jeweler. They've taken out forty-five thousand dollars' worth of stock, and they've left Thompson bleedin' to death on the floor and his head clerk lyin' dead in front of the safe. They've done a lot of other jobs like that one. There was the bank in Chalmer's City. A fine new safe; a good pair of watchmen on the job, but the watchmen are got, an' the safe blowed as easy as though it was made out of tissue paper!"

"These are very unpleasant things you tell me," said Quay. "Will you tell me what they point toward?"

"I'll tell you," said the sheriff. "I'll tell you, because I want you to know what I think you don't know! Now, then, you've got a flock of ex-crooks in this valley. Do they stay here all the time?"

"It's not a prison," said Quay. "Of course they go off hunting in the hills, now and then; fishing, too!"

"Ay, fishin' — an' they catch some fat suckers," said the sheriff fiercely. "Now, then, they's a special technique that every professional crook works up. I ain't gunna mention no names, but I'll say that all the jobs that have been done around here have been done in ways that look like the handwork of some of the men that you got up here in the valley!"

"Great heavens!" breathed Quay. "What are you saying, man?"

"I'm sayin' things that look like facts to us! I ain't the only one, Mr. Quay. Do you keep tab on the goin's and the comin's of these here — huntin' parties, as you call 'em?"

"Why, I follow in a general way the movements of the boys. I'm not a prison keeper, as I said before, Sheriff!"

"Sure you ain't," agreed the other. "Well,

then, you ain't a prison keeper, and you don't keep a close tab. But I'd like to know, was Josh Wilkes, your blacksmith, out on a fishin' trip along about the end of March?"

"That I can't say. Wilkes? He's an honest, cheerful fellow, Sheriff!"

"Why, Mr. Quay, it would make any gent cheerful to be able to get a safe place like this here valley, an' then ride out an' do his real work now and then, two or three times a year, eh? Wilkes served fourteen years, all together. And the blowin' of the safe in the Ranch and Farmer's Bank at Clivesdale, it sure looked like one of his neat old jobs!"

"One moment," said Quay sternly. "Are you suggesting that my men steal out of the valley and — and actually raid the surrounding country?"

The sheriff answered hotly:

"I don't accuse nothin'. All that I gotta say is that inside of the past five year, every good-sized town within two days' ride of your Happy Valley, here, has been raided, one way or another. The bigger ones more than once. Well, I don't accuse nobody, but thinkin' is free, Mr. Quay, an' I'd like to give you my thought on the subject!"

"Sheriff," said Quay, "this is a great shock to me, but I'm ready to hear what you have to say!"

"Then this here is the answer. You've taken in these gents an' tried to make them decent. Maybe you've succeeded with some of 'em. But with the others, they're makin' a fool and a false

109

front out of you. They're pretendin' to lie low and go straight, but, as a matter of fact, they're slidin' out an' 'huntin' and fishin' ', where they can sink their hooks on a fine fat safe or a jeweler's stock. Mr. Quay, I'm givin' you the idea. If you stop trustin' everybody so much and keep your eyes wide open, I'll bet my wad that you'll see some things that you'll want to tell me about in a hurry!"

"Good heavens!" muttered Quay. "Louis, is it possible?"

"Possible?" said the loud, twanging voice of Kendal. "Anything's possible with a gang of ex-thugs. You ain't able to change their spots for 'em. But we'll watch 'em like a cat watches mice, Sheriff!"

"The sneakin' hypocrite!" murmured Lander softly.

CHAPTER FOURTEEN

Whatever irritation was in the mind of the sheriff, it seemed to be thoroughly exhausted by his own speech. He and his men stayed to swallow a cup of steaming coffee, during the drinking of which he assured Jonathan Quay again that there was no personal malice in what he had stated.

"Sheriff," said Quay heartily, "I think you're wrong; I know you're wrong; but that won't prevent me from keeping a keener lookout!"

The sheriff left at once. He refused all invitations to spend the night, for he wished to get well started back toward civilization before the morning came. If not in the valley, he was sure that Jim Fantom would now be well on the way to Spenserville, and thence north and north toward the Canadian border.

He wanted to try that trail for the fugitive, perhaps to intercept him on it, if Fantom tried to linger over night in the valley.

"I've talked out freely," said the sheriff in leaving. "You're too good a man, Mr. Quay, an' too well known for me to accuse you of anything. But maybe I've opened your eyes to something. I don't know!"

He left at once with his men, though they groaned at the thought of the long ride which lay ahead of them. The noise of horses disappeared, and presently Quay opened the door, and admitted the two who were in hiding. He looked weary and sad.

"You've heard me tell lies," he said almost angrily to Fantom. "And those lies were spoken to an honest man. May God forgive me for them!"

However, as though he did not wish to hurt the feelings of Fantom, he added at once:

"I won't regret what I've done. If we are working outside the law, we're working in a good cause, Jim! I trust you! I trust that you have the making of a thoroughly honest citizen, and that you'll develop into one. If it turns out that way, then I'll bless the lies that I've told to the sheriff this day. If it turns out any other way, I'll send for him and take you with my own men!"

His teeth clicked. Those wonderfully steady eyes dwelt firmly upon the face of the boy, and Fantom straightened and raised his chin.

"If I make one crooked move!" he exclaimed. And he paused there, filled with a great emotion and a noble determination. Love for this strange man rose up in his heart, as it had risen when they paused their horses at the bridge.

"I believe you, my lad, I believe you!" said Quay.

He turned hurriedly to Lander.

"Chip," said he, "you're a quick-eyed boy, though you haven't been with us long. Have you noticed anything such as the sheriff suspects? Have you seen or heard anything?"

Chip Lander muttered — it was almost a growl:

"I've only just come, you might say. You ask Louis Kendal. He'd know everything that's happenin'!"

"Poor Louis Kendal!" said Quay, shaking his head. "He's been so sickened by this accusation that he's gone up to bed! I don't blame him. Such a thing is a shock. Murders, Chip — murders and wholesale robberies laid on the heads of my boys!"

He shook his head again and then turned away with a sigh. A moment later he had said good night.

"Such a thing as this makes me realize that I'm growing old!" said he. "Chip, you look after Jim and see that he has everything that he wants."

When they were left alone, the two youngsters faced each other, Fantom with an eye burning with questions, and Chip Lander biting his lip and staring at the floor.

"Let's get out of here and have a walk in the open," suggested Fantom.

They went out at once and walked up the slope past the barn. Inside it, they could hear the horses contentedly stamping, the grinding of one or two slow eaters against their grain boxes, and the rustle of the hay as it was nosed about.

Those sounds were a comfort to Fantom. They eased his soul. They gave a sense of permanence and well-being to this odd society in the Happy Valley, upon whose happiness this

113

shadow had fallen.

So they climbed the hill until they came to its bare shoulder. Other, more heavily forested heights, rose behind them. Below lay the house of Quay, with a few lighted windows, warmly yellow. Beyond that, the avenue of trees walked down to the lower woodland; and in the hollow of the valley was the lake, like tarnished silver, with the dim river leading into it, and out again.

"Why," muttered Fantom, "it's kind of like heaven, this here place, Chip."

"You like it, eh? Well, it ain't bad," said Lander.

"If you ever been like me, inside of walls and bars for five years," said Fantom; "if you ever had grabbed hold of steel bars and shook 'em; if you ever —"

He paused.

"I guess it's hell," said Lander with respect.

"I used to lie an' groan," said Fantom. "Maybe that sounds kind of funny. But it's true. I used to lie an' groan. Then I used to feel as though my breathin' had used up all of the good air in the cell. I'd lie there an' choke an' sweat with fear of stranglin'."

"It don't sound funny to me," said Lander.

"Once I said to a guard: 'For God's sake, wangle it so's I can get a cell where there's more air stirrin', will you?' He looked at me an' grinned. 'Them that you've done for, kid,' says he, 'they got less air than you, where they're packed away,' says he. That's what he says, an' grins at me. It made me kind of sick."

"It must of been hell," said Lander.

His voice was apprehensive, for the shadow of the long arm of the law fell upon him, also.

"Before they get me again," said Fantom fiercely, "they'll collect all that I got in my guns — except one bullet!"

Lander drew in a quick little breath.

"I guess you're right," said he.

"But this here," went on Fantom, "it's what I used to dream about. Open your lungs and take a whiff of this here air. It's sweet, ain't it? I'll tell a man! An' the trees, an' the open hills — why, I've dreamed about 'em, old son, and waked up, and seen the light of the mornin' streaked across by the bars!"

He paused.

"It's what they call it. It's the Happy Valley," said Lander. "Except for —"

He stopped short.

"You mean, except for Kendal? I wanted to ask you. Is there something in what the sheriff said?"

Lander made a wide gesture.

"I don't know nothing," he said. "I don't want to know. Don't ask me, Jimmy!"

"What's that?" asked Fantom.

They both listened. From the hollow to their left they distinctly heard the rubbing of leather, the clinking of bit-chains. In a moment they could see a shadowy procession of five horsemen passing through the dell, and climbing the farther slope. They went out of view over the next rise.

"The sheriff?" muttered Fantom. "Has he been layin' back here all of this time?"

Lander said nothing. He merely shrugged his shoulders.

"Not the sheriff," Fantom answered his own question. "That second horse from the tail of the procession, he was dancin' too much for a mustang that had covered the ground that the sheriff has rode over today. An' there was no slump in the backs of those gents in the saddle. They ain't been ridin' all day!"

Still Lander did not speak.

"What's up?" demanded Fantom, whirling upon him.

And then Lander said, as though cornered:

"Jimmy, I dunno. I don't wanta know. Maybe it's old Quay himself startin' out to fish in another poor devil like you and me. He'll work day and night, for that. Maybe it's some of the boys goin' to camp out in the high hills and start trailin' bear early in the mornin'. I dunno who it is. We better go back and get to bed!"

There seemed nothing else to do. Fantom had to walk slowly back toward the house, his mind whirling with doubts. At last, when they were close to the house, he paused and muttered:

"The one thing seems to be to stick to Quay, an' trust everything to him, Chip."

Lander gripped his arm impulsively.

"That's my own scheme," said he, "no matter

116

what Kendal is or what Kendal does. If he's wrong, some day the chief will find out about him and put everything right. What more can you ask?"

"Nothing!" agreed Jim Fantom.

They entered the house and went up to Lander's room. There were two beds and Fantom took one. He undressed in silence, a dozen times looking inquisitively toward his companion, and each time feeling something in the face of the other which discouraged further question.

Undoubtedly there was a mystery connected with the Happy Valley. What it was, he would find out all in good time. At last he said:

"Well, Quay himself don't advise many questions."

"Sure he don't," assented Lander. "What's the use of askin' questions in a place where everybody's got a lot that he don't want to talk about? If he didn't have, he wouldn't be in here with the rest of us, I guess?"

"I guess not!" said Fantom.

Presently he had stretched himself out between the blankets. The lamp burned beside the bed of Lander, who was reading a battered magazine and smoking a cigarette. Through the open window blew the mountain wind. It caught at the wreaths of smoke and jerked them away into nothingness. It seemed to catch the thoughts and the doubts of Jim Fantom and scatter them, also, as though declaring to his soul that nothing mattered except the purity and the strength of the great outdoors.

The whole picture of the valley crowded upon his mind, the reaching mountains, the shadowy forests, the gleam of water in the hollow, the fat fields beside the river.

Far off, in some corral, he heard a calf bawl incessantly, mourning for its mother, but even that sound was dignified and softened by distance.

This was the world that he wanted. There was only one thing lacking, pricking at his heart of hearts; but even this Quay had promised to supply, by some miracle.

All doubts left him. He heard the voice of Lander asking some question, but he was too numbed with sleep to answer. Then sleep came gently over his brain.

CHAPTER FIFTEEN

It seemed that one of Lander's conjectures about the five night-riders had been correct. In the morning, Quay was gone. There was left only Louis Kendal to start Fantom in his new life. Kendal was crisp and curt.

"What can you do?" he asked at the breakfast table. "Can you use a rope?"

"I used to daub a rope on now and then," said Fantom. "That was a long time ago, though. I never did much of it."

"You know how to work cows? Can you tell what flies are after a cow by the way she kicks up in the distance, ag'in the skyline?"

"I guess I can't. I'd be mighty glad to learn."

"Got no time for schoolwork here," said the other briefly. "Lemme see. What *can* you do?"

"I'll do anything," said Fantom. "I don't care where I start. You can gimme an ax and feed trees to me. I'll cut firewood. I'll run a cross-cut. Or I'll be a blacksmith apprentice, if you like!"

At this, Louis Kendal looked almost dreamily past the boy.

"That's what you're willin' to do. Or say, handle a plow?"

"Glad to — like to! I wanta get close down to the ground."

Kendal laughed. And his laughter had a harsh,

penetrating clangor like the beating together of hammer and metal.

"You'll ride a hoss and use a gun!" he said tersely. "That's what you'll do!" He laughed again, amused by his thought. "Why give a violinist a piano to pound, or a harp player a maul to swing? You get your hoss and oil up your rifle. We got a lot of sheep lost every year from the coyotes. Go up there and fetch me six coyote scalps, and I'll call that a day's work!"

He took Fantom to the open door and indicated the northern hills.

There was enough in his manner that was disagreeable in the extreme, but Jim Fantom would not have dreamed of disagreeing. At any rate, the open country was before him, and, after the meal ended, he hurried out to his horse, loaded his rifle, and started away.

Six coyotes were no small order for any man to bag with a rifle in a day's hunting, but he vowed to himself that he would not return until he had performed the work.

He held on into the upper hills until he came to the sheep grounds, where big herds were closely grazing over rich grass. In the distance, he saw three herders, men who wore cloaks, and he would have sworn that they were Basques such as wander lonely through all parts of the West keeping their flocks.

He went on, wondering what crimes these men might have committed. They were knife users, and doubtless they had been sent up for knife fights. His blood thickened a little at the thought!

Among the rocks beyond the flocks he dismounted and began to cut for sign. Luck came to him. He had reached a veritable army of coyotes in their own network of holes in the ground. And there he worked, probed, and sweated, and took snap shots at fleeting, tawny shadows.

He was a good shot, though a little out of practice, but with twenty chances in the course of the day, he could collect only seven scalps.

He had not come away with a lunch; he had disdained going back to the house for the noon meal. Out of a muddy little runlet hc had half quenched his thirst; and therefore the end of his first day in the Happy Valley left him with a singing head, a blistered neck, and little black spots dancing before his eyes.

However, he was happy. For him the valley was not misnamed; and, as he came down, one of the Basque shepherds walked close to him and stared with a grin of interest at the seven scalps, as though well he knew what they meant to his flock!

When he got back to the house, both Chip Lander and Kendal were gone; the cook prepared supper for him alone.

"Did you buy some of these?" he asked, when he saw the trophies.

"Look at 'em," suggested Fantom.

The cook, with hairy, tattooed hands, turned them over.

"All fresh as eggs," he declared. "Whatcha do, son? Whistle 'em out and make 'em stand for their pictures, or how?"

"I know their lingo," said Fantom. "I was raised among the rocks when I was a kid, an' I learned a lot of little things like that."

"You go an' murder 'em now, eh?" chuckled the cook. "You persuade 'em out into the light an' then soak 'em?"

"Never touch nothin' but the bad characters," Fantom assured him. "Coyote police, as you might say. Shove that stew a little closer, will you?"

The cook grinned again.

"You're gunna be at home up here," he declared, "if you get by with that Kendal. But it looks like he means trouble for you, maybe!"

"How come?"

"Why, that's his old gag for them he don't like. He sends 'em up to go after the coyotes, and mostly they get a headache and nothin' but a smell of gunpowder to bring back with 'em. Fact is, those coyotes move too fast for most of the boys. But I guess that you got a quick eye, old son. Try some more of this corn bread. How'd you happen to come up here, anyway?"

"A friend of mine was shot in Burned Hill. I got the glory," said Fantom briefly. "And you?"

"Well, sir, that's a story," said the cook. "I used to foller the sea. I picked up this on the China Coast —"

Here he paused to indicate the tattooing on his

hands and the beginning of a great design at the base of his hairy neck.

"— but afterward, I figgered that it would be an easier life to sit still and wait for suckers to come up an' ask to be caught. I sold some green goods; I pushed some queer; and everything would of been all right if the dirty dog that was my partner hadn't crooked me out of a lot of my share. I sapped him with a chunk of lead pipe, and they put me away for nine year on account of it. The boss brought me up here afterward, and I've been workin' in his galley ever since. So there you are!"

"Like it?" asked Fantom.

"I like it fine! Except Kendal, damn his heart. Nobody likes him, I guess!"

"What's wrong with him?"

The cook's face clouded.

"You don't know, eh?"

"Not everything, I guess."

"You gotta learn him for yourself," said the cook. "I don't sell no extras about that bird! He flies too fast for the news to keep up with him, anyway."

He went off sourly to the kitchen, and Fantom went out into the crimson heart of the sunset.

He wandered aimlessly across the fields, then followed a twisting lane into the woods. It joined the main road, and he went on, enjoying the cool sense of dew in the air, and looking ever up past the dark heads of the trees to the color in the sky above him. So he came, unawares, on the cabin which had charmed him the night before.

It resounded with the noise of hammers. Lights shone; the door was open; and Fantom wandered to the threshold.

Three men were putting together a rough-hewn table in the center of the room. It was a big room, with a capacious fireplace at the farther side. Chairs of the same fashioning as the table stood here and there. A fresh smell of new wood greeted him.

"Hello," said Fantom, "you boys are workin' late."

The chief of the three looked askance at him.

"Rush order," said he.

"Somebody movin' in?" asked Fantom.

"One of Quay's pets," said the other.

They paid no attention to him, but went on seriously with their work, so he drifted on through the house.

It had a bedroom, a kitchen, and the larger apartment which he already had seen. All the furniture was of the same rough pattern which he already had noticed, but it looked comfortable and strong. Rows of pots and pans hung on the kitchen walls. In a closet he saw blankets, linen. Behind the cabin was a small outhouse arranged as a combination of creamery and pantry, with a fine array of smoked hams and bacons in the latter, and shining new milk tins in the former.

The woodshed adjoining was unstocked, but there was a set of axes leaning in a corner, and who could ask for more, when the whole forest surrounded the place?

He went slowly back through the place, taking note of the comforts about him. The workmen were preparing to leave, putting out their lanterns and gathering up their tools. The head man stepped up to him.

"You're The Phantom?"

"I'm Jim Fantom."

"I'm Josh Wilkes. Glad to know you. When your pony needs new shoes, I'll be seein' you again. This house ain't for you, Fantom?"

"No. Not for me."

"The chief has fixed it up fine. He gets new ideas every year. They's enough pots and pans in yonder to run a hotel kitchen. So long, Fantom. When you got nothin' to do, drop down to the village and see me. My wife cooks the only good coffee in the valley. Come on, boys."

They left, piled their tools into a buckboard which was standing in front of the cabin, and drove away.

Jim Fantom remained behind, and hungrily circled the cabin, as a wolf circles a moose caught in the snow but still formidable with horns and deadly cutting hoofs. He never had seen a thing in his life that he wanted as much as he wanted this place. It filled his mind. It enchanted him with the possibilities of the future. But some other man would step in here, grasp those axes in the woodshed, and begin to push back the forest frontier!

Bitterly he envied that man!

He remained there until the darkness was complete and he could no longer see the runlet of water from the spring, only hear its whisper at his feet.

Then he turned away again with a sense of emptiness that made his heart ache. There might be another cabin built for him, twice the size of this one, but none that would fit so exactly into his mind!

He passed up the road, out from the shadow of the trees, and then slowly on, with the clear field of the stars blossoming over his head.

CHAPTER SIXTEEN

When he reached the house, he gave a last look at the stars, and went in by the kitchen door, in hope of getting a cup of coffee from the cook, whose deep bass voice could be heard singing as he rattled the supper pans in the sink.

The broad back of the cook was bent over the kitchen sink, as Fantom went in, but the eyes of the latter were jerked as by compulsion to a corner of the room. There he saw the lank form of Kendal, with the seven coyote scalps in his hands. He appeared to be studying them with an intense interest, thoughtfully, squinting as though at small type.

"Who sold you these?" he asked, without looking up.

"The same gent that sold the Winchester I was usin'," answered Fantom. "It had those scalps attached, as you might say."

Kendal put his finger through a bullet hole.

"You only got five of 'em through the head," said he.

"They were all runnin'," answered Fantom.

He frowned, wondering what this questioning led toward.

The cook guffawed.

"He was havin' an off day," said he, turning around. "He missed two heads out of seven!"

"I missed thirteen of 'em clean and altogether," confessed Fantom, who began to guess that this bantering was really praise of his marksmanship.

"You missed thirteen an' you got seven, an' five through the head," said Kendal dryly, as though stating a problem for solution. "Are you tired?"

"No. Not much."

"Do you know the Creston Road?"

"No. Never heard of it."

"The doctor, here," said Kendal, "he'll show you the way to it. I'll tell you what you'll do when you get there. Doc, go out and saddle a couple of hosses. You might take that bay gelding with the four white stockin's for the kid, here. Get something good for yourself, and two led hosses. Hop to it!"

The cook grunted and instantly left the kitchen.

Kendal went on, still thumbing over the coyote scalps:

"You'll come to the Creston Road in about thirty mile. You can make that in two hours and a half, if you stir up your hosses a little. Maybe less. Better make it in less."

He fondly smoothed a scalp which had a white streak running down between the eyes.

"Now when you get there," went on Kendal, still squinting at the scalp and never glancing at the boy, "you send back the cook. You won't need him. You change your saddle onto the best

128

of the led hosses an' send the cook away. After you've done that, you ride down the Creston Road for a couple of miles until the woods break away an' you come into the open. There'll only be a few scatterings of brush and saplings. Find a place that'll give cover to you and your hoss. When you get in there, you wait. It won't be long before the Creston stage comes along. In that stage there won't be more'n one man outside of the driver. Take a look at that man as the stage goes by. If he's small, and has got a lump on his back, you sashay out from your cover, after the stage is past, and ride up alongside. You stop that stage and take the hunchback out of it. You savvy?"

"I hear what you're sayin'," said Fantom slowly.

"Take him out, cut a hoss out of the harness, and put the runt on his back. Then you break off through the woods, headin' east. Afterward, circle around, and come back onto the road that leads back into the valley. Bring that gent in here with you. You foller me?"

"Will he want to come?"

"He'd rather come to hell!" said the other fiercely. "But you get him an' bring him!"

"If he fights back?"

"He'll be bigger than a coyote and not movin' so fast," said Kendal.

For the first time he looked up, straight into the face of Fantom, and his eyes burned coldly at the boy.

"You want a little job of murder done. Is that all?" asked Fantom.

"I want the crook-back, that's all. That's all you gotta know. You ain't up here to do any thinkin' when I tell you what to do!"

He spoke with a deliberate malice, and Fantom could see plainly that Kendal wanted nothing so much as a direct refusal of the command.

He went over the matter in his mind.

He was to stop a stage; having held it up, he was to abstract one of the passengers from it, and carry the man back to the valley. The odds, he was promised, were at least two to one.

Furthermore, here he had in a nutshell the proof of all that the sheriff had said the night before in this house. The Happy Valley housed a den of thieves who rode forth at the bidding of Louis Kendal!

He shrugged his shoulders.

"Is that the regular game here?" he asked.

"You've got your marchin' orders," said Kendal tersely. "Start on your way!"

Abruptly he got up and slouched from the room with his peculiar gait, the heels of his boots dragging on the floor, the spurs jingling softly.

Fantom remained at a stand. It was not of Kendal that he was thinking at this moment. It was Quay who filled his mind. He had given his solemn word to be Quay's man for a year, and almost the first of Quay's commands had been that he should yield an implicit obedience to

130

Louis Kendal. There had been further commands — no talk, no questions, no desire on the part of Quay that his new protégé should try to peer behind the face of things and see the facts concerning them. All of this could be explained by the character of the men who had been gathered to populate the Happy Valley. But he wondered what an expression of bewilderment would come over the face of Jonathan Quay, if he should learn of this present errand!

But his hands and his tongue were tied.

He jerked his Stetson lower over his eyes, pulled up his belt a notch, and took the rifle from the place where it rested against the wall. Then he went out to the barn.

The "doctor" already was leading out the horses; in a moment they were mounted and off down the valley. They crossed the bridge. The river flashed beneath them; the loud thunder of the hoofs beat sullenly against the ear of Fantom, and then they were swinging at a steady lope along the trail.

They walked or jogged the steep up-grade; then again it was gallop, gallop, gallop through the night, with the woods whirling back on either hand.

Presently a pale fire rose among the eastern trees, and the moon swayed with the rhythm of the gallop into the upper branches, then floated clear like a great golden bubble and sailed up into the steel-dark sky, putting out a crowd of stars around its course.

A strange content arose in Fantom. It was as though all need for moral judgments on his own part had disappeared. He was in the hands of others, who must do his thinking for him! He even laughed aloud, and saw the head of the cook jerk around and felt the eyes of the man staring at him rather wildly.

Suddenly the trail emerged upon a roadway, a rough mountain road, dipping up and down, rutted, deep with dust. Here the cook drew rein, and dismounted. Fantom imitated him.

"Now what's the next step, Chief?" asked the cook.

His voice was hushed; he looked around him in awe, and winced a little when the long hoot of an owl sounded mysteriously from the forest darkness near by.

White moonlight fell upon them, a patch that slid down through the great trees, and the cook seemed troubled by the light. The horses stood with heads down, their sides heaving, and the steam of their bodies rising faintly. From their bellies the sweat dripped down into the dust.

"You don't know this job?" asked Fantom

"I dunno nothin'," said the cook.

He moistened his lips, which looked black in the moonshine.

"I ain't been on the road for a long time," he muttered.

"Are you sick?" asked Fantom coldly.

The cook made a sudden gesture with both hands, as though surrendering.

"I guess I'm no good!" he said hurriedly. "I been through hell, and some of it stuck to the skin — I guess!"

No doubt that was why he was merely a cook in the Happy Valley, doing a Chinaman's work; no doubt, also, that was why Kendal had sent along such a companion, who could not be used for battle, even if Fantom wished to try him!

He looked at the big, burly fellow with compassion and some scorn.

"It's all right, Doctor," said he. "This job is for a lone hand, Kendal said. You're to take the hosses and go back. I go on alone."

He could hear the man sigh with relief, while Fantom went about the work of changing saddles.

There was a darkly dappled gray, one of the led horses, which seemed fresh as the morning, even after the long journey over the dusty roads. Upon him, Fantom cinched up the saddle, after looking into his eye and assuring himself that the horse was not merely a picture without real heart.

He saw, then, that his rifle was in the holster, loose, that his revolvers were working with a free action, and the girths were holding well. Then he turned to the cook.

The latter had finished changing his own saddle, and now had backed the trio of horses into the shadow, as though he disliked even this pale and lonely illumination from the moon.

"You're dead sure," said the cook rather

133

faintly, "that I couldn't help you none?"

"Why, maybe you could," said Fantom gently, "but I got my orders from Kendal. What happened to you, partner?"

The cook hesitated, and then blurted out:

"I done a fiver. I thought that I was stronger than the chains and the bars. They showed me that I wasn't. They showed me that I was a fool —"

He broke off with a shudder that was audible in his voice.

"Go on back to the valley," said Fantom, more kindly than before. "I know what happens in the pen. I been there. It almost got me, too!"

"You ever got solitary?"

"Ay," said Fantom dreamily. "Once! Once I got it!"

And he found himself moistening his own lips, as the cook had done before. Then, in haste to rouse himself, he leaped into the saddle, waved his hand, and dashed off down the road.

CHAPTER SEVENTEEN

A swing of the way instantly put him out of sight of the led horses and the cook. Finding himself alone, he drew rein. The gray danced and leaned against the bit strongly. His blood was up. His quarters trembled with eagerness and with strength anxious to be unleashed. His ears pricked stiffly forward. It was as though he knew what game was before them and yearned to enter upon it.

Fantom soothed him to a jog. A nervous horse might undo him with a whinny, a snort, or a leap at the wrong moment. So he stroked the neck of the big gelding and talked to him until the ears of the animal inclined back a little, twitching in understanding of the mood of his rider.

They went on until the great woods suddenly gave way to second-growth forest. A fire had cloven its path down the mountainside, here, and plowed the huge virgin trees under. Afterward, the quick-growing and stubborn lodgepole pines had sprung up, and tangles of brush; only now and again, like a frozen giant of stone, the naked trunk of one of the earlier trees arose, minus head, minus limbs, but with the tallest of the second-growth wood barely brushing the base of its enormous torso.

The Phantom, looking at these solitary monsters, thought of the tales he had heard in his boyhood of the great heroes of the early frontier — Carson, Wild Bill. They had been to him like legendary giants, and his boy's heart had swelled with a desire to emulate their deeds; but now it seemed to him that he could see his folly illustrated. He was of the second growth; he reached not even to the knees of the great of old!

Into a close cluster of the lodge-poles he rode, dismounted, and peered out from this covert. The horse snorted hot breath down the back of his neck, then nosed his shoulder as though for companionship. But he did not stamp, he did not swing his head about; apparently the gray was not a nervous fool.

The road, marble-white with dust, swept down from among the higher trees, on the farther side of this excavation which the fire had made in the forest, and looped its way as swift as a running snake across the level, disappearing again into the shadows from which Fantom had ridden. And as he watched the road, its moving curves, its unknown destination, he felt his heart grow light and his nerves grow steady.

All that the flight of soaring birds could mean to a poet, all that a ship with the full burden of the wind loading its hollow sails could mean to a seaman, this open and empty road meant to Jim Fantom. It was not really empty to him, but it seemed to him that he saw stages lumber down it soundlessly, and horsemen lope, with rifles balanced at their saddle-bows; he saw half-naked

Indians trooping, with the moon glistening on their stalwart shoulders; he saw prospectors steering their burros, with testing hammer in hand and prophetic eyes turned forward; he saw masked men sweeping at full gallop, looking back with poised guns; he saw the grim posse following, spurring hard.

His lips parted in a silent laugh. What was the life inside the shelter of the law? This, this was that for which he was meant! His blood sang; he could have blessed Kendal for the mission on which he had been dispatched.

The silence grew around him. Only once, far away, an owl hooted, the note dying as though it were sailing on raid wing away. Then nothing stirred. The wind was frozen under the eye of the moon. Not a tree top bent; not a bough rustled its leaves. Where the peaked shadows fell on the white road, there did they stay as though painted.

Jim Fantom smiled in his concealment. Again he handled his weapons, softly and surely. There was no tremor of his hands. A slow heat of savagery entered his blood, mounted slowly to his brain. He had become a beast of prey, couched here, waiting.

Then, far up among the trees, he heard a rumbling. It died, began again like thunder on the horizon, swelled, fell off, swelled louder and nearer. He heard a distinct rattling of chains, then the groan of a hub on an axle of steel.

Nearer came these sounds. A horse snorted

loudly, seeming almost at the edge of the woods. Instantly Fantom grasped the nostrils of the gray, but it made no effort to whinny a reply.

The next instant the leaders of the stagecoach trotted into the open. The two remaining spans followed, then the stage itself, heeling on the rough road like a ship in a wallowing sea. It was an old-fashioned conveyance, whose tough hickory had survived twenty years of usage, and on the lofty seat was a driver without a guard beside him, an old driver, reeling drunkenly back and forth with the movement of the vehicle — Fantom well-wished him to be a younger man, for these veterans were as apt to fight as a cornered wildcat!

The stage drew closer. He heard a woman's laughter peal suddenly; then the open seats of the stage were in view, containing two women and one man. His nerves jumped at the prescience of Kendal, who had known these facts from afar.

But the man? He turned, at that instant, and spoke with a gesture to the woman beside him. It seemed as though a pillow had been stuffed under his coat and fastened between the shoulder blades. Fantom knew that this was the goal of his errand, and he was glad with all his heart that he would have an excuse for action!

Rapidly, as the stage lumbered past, he knotted his bandana over his nose and mouth. Only his eyes could be seen, of all his face, and the eyes were nearly lost in the broad shadow cast by the brim of his sombrero.

As he finished these preparations, the stage swung into the dark of the woods beyond, and Fantom went into the saddle like a jumping cat.

The gelding gained the road in a jump and veered, without a touch of the reins, in pursuit, as though he knew perfectly well what was to come. Rapidly they gained. The dust turned up by the spinning wheels was like a fog before them, and, cutting through this, Fantom was suddenly beside the stage.

He dropped the reins over the pommel of the saddle; both his hands were occupied with Colts.

"Halt, and hands up!" sang out the voice of Jim Fantom.

It rang joyously through the gloom beneath the old trees. The driver yelled out, "Whoa!" with a groan, and slammed on the brake. His left hand had reached for the gun that lay in the broad seat beside him, but he did not actually pick it up. He was brave enough, but not for such a danger as this, coming from behind.

In the seats, the women raised shrill cries, like the screaming of terrified birds in a gale; they clasped their faces, as though they wished to shut out the sight of the robber, but could not quite decide to cover their eyes.

It was the hunchback who occupied the attention of Jim Fantom. He had twisted sidewise in his seat and reached back for a gun with a lightning movement. But with his hand at his hip, there it froze in place, for he saw the leveled, steady gun in the right hand of Fantom looking him in the eye. Death was too certain here to be played with!

The tired stage horses slowed instantly to a halt; the brakes groaned; the coach was still.

In that stillness, the babble of the women filled the ears of Fantom. One of them was standing up, wringing her hands.

"Oh my God!" she shrieked. "That this should happen to *me!* That this should happen to *me!*" As though fate had tricked her, and basely gone back upon some guarantee.

The other was weeping and blubbering out words at the same time. It angered Fantom. He felt no pity or remorse for them.

"You fools!" he exclaimed. "Be quiet! You there — driver! — get those hands over your head. Here, you in the back seat, get out of this!"

The women were silent as though hands had been clapped over their mouths. The arms of the driver rose stiffly above his head. The hunchback climbed carefully down to the ground — not an easy thing to do while his arms were stiffly erected above his head.

But there was no satisfaction for Fantom in this mute surrender. His blood craved something more. It seemed an unfair trick that this whole conveyance of many horses, of four human beings, of the great lumbering stage itself should have paused and meekly given up without a shot fired.

That, as he knew in the instant, was what he

140

had wanted. That was what he had waited for so eagerly in front of his horse, in the nest of lodgepole pines! His lips sneered stiffly back from his teeth.

"Get up there and cut out the near leader from the traces," he commanded the hunchback. "You, Grandpa, make another pass at that gun of yours, and I'll break your back for you!"

He sidestepped the gray horse a little forward until he could sit at ease, facing all the people of the stage, and watching the hunchback obediently working to free the near leader.

The driver spoke:

"Say, kid —"

"Well?"

"I'd like to have my left hand free for a minute."

"What's your dodge, Grandpa?"

"I'd mighty like a chaw of tobacco, now that we're standin' here. Throat's plumb parched with the dust these fool hosses have been kickin' up!"

Fantom laughed, but only a fool would throw away chances.

"Keep hangin' onto the stars with those hands, Grandpa," said he. "You can eat a ton of tobacco, as soon as I'm gone!"

The hunchback had freed the lead horse; he turned and faced his captor. It was a long, white, bloodless face. Great dark pouches hung beneath the eyes, and the eyes, even in the moonlight, appeared covered with a film, like the eyes of a dead fish.

He reminded Fantom of someone he had seen; yet he swore that no man in the world could have been ugly enough to resemble this fellow.

"Climb on that hoss!" he commanded.

The hunchback tried, and failed. He had to lead the animal up to the step of the stage, and from this he managed to scramble awkwardly up to the back of the horse.

"Ride ahead — straight into the woods — there — go east!"

And the hunchback obeyed.

CHAPTER EIGHTEEN

As the shadows of the woods closed behind him, Fantom could hear the women break out in a shrill whimpering again, to which the old stage driver responded:

"Don't you go bustin' your hearts about him. He ain't gunna be ate, I guess, and if he is, he'll sure kill the young gent with indigestion. Why, just the look of him kind of brung on my liver complaint ag'in!"

Then the noise of weeping and the gruff voice of the driver died behind them. Fantom came with his captive into a clearing.

"Halt and hoist your arms ag'in!" said Fantom.

"You might as well finish the business now," said the hunchback calmly. "I don't care how you shoot me. Front or back. But what's the tomfoolery about having my hands up?"

Fantom nudged the muzzle of a revolver into the man's back.

"That persuade you?" he asked.

The body of the hunchback quaked — with laughter! Utter amazement flowed through the mind of Fantom, and chilled his blood, also. This was madness, surely. Said the hunchback:

"I amuse myself. Here I walk on the rim of my last second of life. Off of it I shall fall, in an in-

143

stant, and be dashed to pieces. But still I obey blindly, stupidly, as a dog obeys, when its master calls and stands ready to shoot its brains out as it comes nearer! However, there you are, with my hands in the air!"

Dexterously, Fantom "fanned" him.

He located a revolver in a hip pocket and drew it forth — a dainty, nickeled thing, fit more for a woman than for a man's grasp.

"Ah, it's the gun, the gun!" said the hunchback. "I should have thought of that. I should have drawn it in the first moment, in fact. But then, I saw death in the hollow end of your Colt, my young friend, and that dissuaded me. Besides, I don't regret the delay. Why should I care to die like a hero, fighting? Not at all! I prefer the treasure of a little added knowledge."

"What more d'you know than you knew before?" asked Fantom.

"I know infinitely more about myself. If I had drawn the gun, I should have died in a quick flurry of bullets that would have torn out my brains or smashed through my heart —"

"You'd of got a slug through the right shoulder. That's all!" said Fantom calmly.

"Ah, ah," said the hunchback. "You're an expert, and I took you to be only a butcher! Only a butcher — a slaughterer!"

"Look here," said Fantom, "you ain't gunna be murdered, if that's what's gallin' you so much!"

"There, there!" said the other. "I might have

known that such a young and gallant boy wouldn't consent to kill the poor ox. He'd go out and drive the creature into the slaughter pen, but he wouldn't strike him, himself. He would as soon kick a dog, no doubt! A dog that was near and dear to him, I mean!"

Fantom growled:

"We got no time to stand here an' chatter. You're talkin' crazy, besides. You can turn your hoss, now, and drift west, ag'in. I can hear the rumble of the stage. Old tobacco face, yonder, is drivin' on with his four hosses! Good luck to him!"

"It's to be on the road to the Happy Valley, then?" said the prisoner, as he obediently turned his horse in the bidden direction. "I'm to die as I come so close to the Happy Valley? Well, there's a moral and an allegory in that. I can't complain of my fate, at least, since it's that of the greater part of mankind. I'm to ride on, and the final bullet will come at the moment when hope is restored to me in part. Is that the plan? Well, it's worthy of Louis. He always was a master of such situations!"

At this, Fantom exclaimed sharply:

"I dunno where you got the ideas, partner. Wherever I'm takin' you, you're gunna be taken safe. You can put your money on that!"

The hunchback rode on for a moment, his body shaken with laughter as before.

"You don't believe it?" asked Fantom sharply.

"Tush, tush," said the other impatiently. "I'm a grown man — and I know Louis rather well!"

It sent a second chill through the blood of

145

Fantom to hear the man speak in this casual manner of his coming death. He could not help breaking out:

"I've told you that you're ridin' safe when you're ridin' with me! That's final!"

The hunchback twisted suddenly around in the saddle, so suddenly that the revolver jerked instinctively into the hand of Fantom. He put it away again, hurriedly, ashamed of the start which he had received.

The prisoner was staring at him fixedly. His horse sidled and then stopped.

"Young man," said the hunchback, "I think that you mean what you say!"

"Mean it?" cried Fantom. "Have I been talkin' through my hat, all this time?" He added tersely, "Ride on."

The prisoner clucked to his horse and they went on at a walk, the big, thick shadows of the tree trunks brushing softly over them. But the hunchback seemed buried in profoundest thought. Sometimes he shook his head, as though arguing with himself against the facts of the case. And several times he turned his head with a quick, startled motion that was peculiar to him, and stared at Fantom, bewildered.

At length, they came out onto the road and jogged their horses along it. But the back of the lead horse was sharp, and the hunchback was a poor horseman, so that Fantom in pity made the pace a walk.

"Young man," said the prisoner at last, "by

the eternal heavens, I think that you're a truth-teller! I don't think that you're lying to me!"

"Thanks," said Fantom ironically.

"He's sent you down here to get me, and never told you a word about what he intends to do with me!"

"That's true," said Fantom, and then bit his lip. It was unnecessary for him to discuss the future with his captive.

"It's plain to me," went on the other, "that you have faith in your ability to escort me safely into the Happy Valley?"

"I've talked enough an' too much," said Fantom. "Now I'm through an' I'll talk no more, if you don't mind! There's the road. I'll be mighty obliged if you'll keep your hoss movin' along it as fast as you can!"

The hunchback nodded, his long chin seeming to tap his chest as he did so. He rode on for some time, in perfect silence, his eyes narrowed, as though he were making out the way through a dense mist.

"Louis, Louis, Louis!" he sighed at last. "More manifold than the ways of the snake, more manifold, deeper, more dangerous. Poison in the tooth — but what's that compared with poison in the eye? How long have you known my dear Louis?" he asked Fantom at last.

"Two days," said Fantom. Then he broke in sternly, "We'll have no more questionin', stranger. I don't know you, an' you don't know me. An' that's the end of it, I figger."

"I don't know you?" said the other. "Let me see! Let me see! If I could turn back to the right page — somewhere before this I've seen the same face — very stern for the years that it owns! A young face and a bitter look — penitentiary stuff, I'd say!"

The captor started in his saddle.

"I touched you there," commented the hunchback. "I touched you on the raw, I'd say. Let me see, let me see!"

The shadow of a hunting owl slid silently across the road. Fantom, lifting his eye, was barely in time to see the hint of a form drift away among the upper branches of the trees.

"Well — young — prison — hold on, then. I think I've found the right page, after all! Ghost — phantom — James Fantom, as I live!"

He clapped his hands together, and the noise seemed to Fantom's ears like the report of a gun in the stillness of the forest. The hunchback went on:

"James Fantom, stage robber, gunman extraordinary — three men down — betrayed by a pair of rascally companions — penitentiary — Why, of course! It all runs back on my mind, now. I never should have hesitated a moment, if I'd had the good, honest sunlight to see your face by!"

Fantom bit his lip.

"You know me, stranger," he said. "I don't know you. I dunno that I want to know you. But I figger that no good comes out of the talk —"

148

The hunchback turned sideways upon his horse and considered the boy, his long face jutting out, his filmed eyes considering Fantom and, as it were, the vast distance beyond him.

"Young, hard, tempered like steel, out of the fire of the law, with the whip-marks on your soul — why, yes, there's the very material that Louis would be hungry to put his hands on. And this same night to send you down here alone, to stop a stagecoach with two armed men in it — there's the test. No, I don't doubt that Louis had known you only two days. But by the end of this second day he will know that you're the man for him. Oh, he'll know that after you've delivered me up to the knife! I tell you, James Fantom, that there's little that's human about that fellow, but there's enough humanity to permit him to be really grateful to you after this service that you've done to him. A thing that he'll never forget. Unless —"

He stopped, and, laughing suddenly with a strange malevolence, he rubbed his hands together.

"Unless," he said, "Louis should take it into his head that perhaps I had talked to you too much!"

He laughed again, and again he rubbed his hands together.

It began to occur to Fantom that this man was indubitably mad. And yet there was something more than madness in his air and in his words. The boy said nothing.

"But if Louis should think that perhaps I had talked freely, and that your ear had been open to me — then, perhaps, he would think it as well to brush out all possibilities of danger. He would kill me, and then kill the last shadow that I cast upon the ground. In fact, young man, perhaps you ride at this moment in a danger almost as great as mine!"

As he spoke, he thrust out one of his long, skinny arms, and with a bony forefinger, he pointed at the boy.

Young Jim Fantom regarded the gesture with a scowl. He would almost rather have had a gun aimed at him than that half fierce and half mocking face.

"But we'll soon see," said the hunchback, "for there are guns waiting for us in that clump of brush just ahead!"

CHAPTER NINETEEN

Fantom looked straight before him up the road.

Upon the right, the primeval forest rose up like the side of a black cliff a hundred and fifty feet into the air. To the left, the same monstrous wood had been shattered and broken by some landslide which had battered the trunks to pieces for a distance of a hundred yards or so, and in this broken space there was the usual growth of brush and of small pines.

It was toward the center of this open patch that a dense growth of high brush glimmered in the moon as the wind touched it lightly, the same wind that stirred the dust upon the surface of the road and hurried it like a fleeing ghost before them.

Keen as the eye of a bird, the glance of Fantom worked among the quivering branches of this shrubbery, and saw, distinctly, that, while the tops wavered rhythmically back and forth in the hand of the wind, one small bough was pressed to the side. And that was enough. Either man or beast was in that covert, and man he took it to be. He said aside to his companion:

"Stranger, I figger that you're right. Somebody's layin' for you, or for us both, up there in the brush. They won't shoot, yet. They'll wait till we come closer. Now, then, just drift your hoss over to the side of the road."

"That side, then," said the hunchback, his mouth working suddenly, as though a strange taste disturbed him, and had to be relished in haste.

"No, the side closest to the bush," said Fantom. "They'll suspect less, that way."

"And have an easier shot!" said the hunchback.

"Do as I tell you!" snapped Fantom. "Edge to the left, the left, do you hear? Mind you! My hand's for you in this. No matter who's behind the game, if there's murder in the air, my hand's for you against 'em all!"

The hunchback was tense with expectation, and yet he had time to allow his eyes to wander with wonder and with awe toward the face of his companion.

"If I live — if I live," he said through his teeth, "you'll have a reason one day to thank God that you've done this for me. If I live!" he repeated, and the voice was a hushed groan of desire.

It was strange to see the manner in which the philosopher, who so readily had surrendered all hope, was now lost in the human being, craving life as bitterly as any frightened child, now that a ghost of hope had returned to him! This Jim Fantom noted.

In the meantime, they were slanting their horses gradually toward the left hand side of the road. In the meantime, from beneath the shadowy brim of his hat, he studied the threatening bush ahead, and suddenly he saw distinctly through a gap among the boughs a straightened finger of steel, pointing at him, with the moonlight glistening like silver upon it.

"Spurs!" he said to the hunchback, and leaped the gray horse for cover.

At the same instant a wasp sound stung the air beside his head. Another, and a jerk at his hat. Then a double report cracked in his ear.

That instant the shadows of the tall trees swept over him and he looked about for the hunchback. But the latter was not with him!

The fusillade of rifles continued. Anxiously he looked back, in fear to see the little man sprawled upon the road, riddled with bullets that now flew from the guns of the murderers, but the road was empty. Only, in the distance, he thought that he heard the crackling of brush, as though a rider were plunging furiously away on the downward slope!

His captive had escaped, and he was almost tempted to plunge in pursuit, but between him and the other wall of the forest lay the blank and gleaming stretch of the road. Already he had had two bullets sent his way!

It might be that these were men from the Happy Valley. It might be that the shots which had missed him so narrowly had been intended for the hunchback. But it seemed strange indeed that shots should have been missed so widely at such a narrow distance.

No, decidedly he would not venture out upon

the naked road! Let the hunchback go. It might also be that the captive had been right when he said that Louis Kendal would strive to wipe out prisoner and captor at one moment! Certainly the waspish singing of the bullets had seemed to sing that sort of a song.

In the meantime, he was filled with admiration for the cunning of the hunchback, who had dared to take the longer way to safety, and, so doing, had placed such a barrier between himself and pursuit! And with all his heart he was now glad that the man was free.

These thoughts, requiring space for their telling, had not occupied his mind for two seconds. Then he started working up through the woods, aiming to get behind the place from which the rifle practice had begun.

There was a hot vengeance in his heart. The grip of his fingers on his gun handles worked feverishly, and his jaw was set hard. Little mercy would there have been, then, for any living creature that crossed the path of Jim Fantom!

Yet he worked his way cautiously. The noise of the rifles had ceased after the first rapid burst. The wood was still, so that when his horse stepped on a twig the report seemed to the tense nerves of Fantom almost like the report of another gun.

He dismounted, and ran forward swiftly, noiselessly, on foot. He knew woodcraft, and he knew how to go as an Indian goes, making no sound, letting the toe of the foot fall first, gingerly, and so making sure of the footing before the weight of the body followed and rested upon it.

So he wove forward among the trees, until he made sure that he had covered a distance, sufficient to put him behind the ambushers. Then he turned in to hunt them from their covert. They had not retreated back into the wood. He could be reasonably sure that they would not take to the road, for fear lest he should be waiting at the margin of it, ready to open an avenging fire.

He came to the edge of the big trees; the ruin of the tumbled rocks of the landslide was before him, spotted with its growth of brush and lodgepoles. Vengeance, if it was to be his, was close before. But as he hung there, hesitant, uncertain how he should go forward, he heard a burst of galloping up the roadway.

He sprang out into the open with a curse. There was no doubt about it. It was the ringing of the hoofs of horses, pounding already far up the road!

He could see what had happened, now. They had left their covert the instant their volleys from ambush had been fired, and slipping away under the shelter of the woods near the road, at a sufficient distance to round the first turn, they had ridden out and given their horses the spur.

More than two. Three at least, he was sure of; perhaps four were in that fleeing group.

He turned and sprinted back with all his might. He found the gray gelding, flung himself upon the back of the horse, and rushed him out upon the road.

There, as the gray reached the soft, muffling dust of the road, he heard, far, far away, the ring of the hoofs of the fugitives as they fled over some rocky spot that gave the noise of the shod hoofs loud as rifle shots into the air.

At once, Fantom reined up his horse. Already it had traveled far, and, against such desperate riders as these, it was doubtful if the gray could gain. Or, even so, the noise of his coming might warn the fugitives to prepare another ambush.

There seemed nothing for it but miserable submission for the moment, and Fantom jogged the good gray slowly forward, grinding his teeth with fury.

In all things this day he had been blocked and foiled. He had performed his mission, and then his captive had escaped from him. He had been fired upon from cowardly ambush, and the assassins had escaped from his hands. Wrath enlarged him. Bullets alone no longer seemed sufficient for his vengeance, but a slow fire, and Indian torments for these subtle scoundrels.

But the words of the hunchback still sounded in his ears. He had known! Not his death alone would suffice Louis Kendal, but the death of the man to whom he might have talked.

That raised other questions. What was it that the captive might have said? What was the information he had to give, so deadly that he who heard it must also die, to satisfy the rage or the fear of Louis Kendal?

But, doubtless, Kendal had expected that this would be no simple affair — this capture of the hunchback. He had expected the little man to fight for his life, and to die beneath bullets crashing into his brain, as the rifle shots had crashed into the skulls of the coyotes that same day. Failing that, there was the trap set, which would swallow both captive and captor!

But the trap had failed, and how would Kendal face him on his return to the valley? He thought of that with a savage satisfaction. He would have something to say to the man when they encountered one another; and God give Kendal a swift hand upon his gun, and a sure aim, or he would die in that encounter. With such thoughts his blood boiled all the weary way back to the valley.

The night ended while he was still upon the way. The gray of the dawn began, and the birds sang in the upper branches cheerfully. Their fresh voices made him feel more keenly the ache of fatigue in his own bones.

Then the day began to glitter from above. Rosy fire flooded dangerously close behind the forest at every hilltop in the east, and finally he came out upon the brow of the Happy Valley just before the sun arose.

The spaciousness beneath his eye was a wonderful stimulant after the closed dimness of the forest ways; the lake in the valley's heart was one entire ruby, small enough, with distance, to be fitted into the palm of his hand; and the window panes of the cabin blinked golden bright, here and there.

All was peace. He heard cattle bawling faintly, far down the hillsides of the valley wall; a bell tinkled not far away; sheep spotted the upper heights; and a wind of sweetness blew gently in his face.

The heart of the boy relaxed, like the unflexed hand of a fighter. After all, there must be no haste. There must be no rash step, imperiling his existence in this fallen bit of heaven!

CHAPTER TWENTY

His passion against Louis Kendal increased again, as soon as the gray gelding dipped over the edge of the valley wall and started the descent. For every stumble in the road, for every puff of dust that the hoofs of the horse kicked up, an increased ugliness formed in the mind of Fantom.

It seemed to him the most complete and dastardly treason that he ever had known or dreamed of; and ever and anon before his eye came again the vision of the big shrub, glimmering in the moonshine, and then the steady finger of steel that had pointed out at him.

It was no headlong fury in Fantom, however. He realized that, of all the men he ever had crossed, none compared with Louis Kendal. He was more formidable in brain; perhaps in that strange, lank body of his there was more physical strength and skill, likewise. So rage rose higher within him, and fear mingled with it.

He thought the miles were long that separated him from his vengeance, and yet the last rose was hardly out of the sky before he was across the bridge and the gray streaming up the drive to the house of Jonathan Quay.

In the stable he jerked off the saddle and bridle from the gray and tethered him in a stall. From the corner of his eyes, as he did so, he took note

159

of a powerful chestnut mare which, perhaps, would be carrying him out of the valley at high speed before another five minutes had passed. So he gripped his guns, inside the stable door, breathed deep, and then marched straight for the big log house.

To either side, he was aware of the valley, more sparkingly beautiful, as it seemed to him at this moment, than it ever had been before. But this he was now preparing to shut himself out from.

He reached the very door of the house before he remembered Quay again. The thought struck him like a bullet to the heart, and he leaned his forehead against the side of the house, sick and dizzy. He had promised to Quay absolute obedience to this lieutenant of his; and for one mortal year that promise would have to be kept.

At any rate, he could confront Kendal and make him admit his guilt, or curse him to his face! This fierce thought comforted him. He entered through the kitchen door, and the cook turned toward him, a sleepy yawn altering suddenly to surprise and keenest inquiry.

"How was everything, kid?" he demanded. "Nothin' happened wrong?"

Fantom went to the stove and sniffed the steaming coffee. His fury was turning into cold deliberation in his heart.

"What you think, Doctor?" he asked. "Lemme have a cup of this stuff."

The cook obediently poured out the inky liquid.

"What do I think?" he repeated. "I dunno what to think, Fantom. But I know that Kendal's in the front room lookin' whiter and sicker than ever!"

Fantom swallowed the coffee at a gulp. All of his suspicions were instantly confirmed, as he strode off through the house and came to the room where Kendal sat by the window.

The man was hunched like a watcher at a death bed, his head fallen forward, his gaze intent upon a corner of the room. Yet the rosy brightness of the morning was outside the window pane where he sat and all the world was tempting his attention.

"Kendal!" called the boy.

Kendal did not stir.

His head remained bowed, and his lank, pale hands did not stir in his lap. One would have thought that he had fallen asleep with open eyes, so great was his concentration in his thoughts.

So Fantom strode up before him.

"Kendal!" he called again.

There was no answer.

To be treated thus, like a child unworthy of attention, enraged Fantom still more, when he needed no extra fire in his indignation.

"Kendal," he said, "you've double crossed me. You've tried to trap me. You've sent me out to hunt game and tried to bag me when I was bringin' it in!"

Not an eyelid of Kendal stirred. He remained

fixed in contemplation of the farther corner of the room.

Fantom stepped still closer. He was so furious that he trembled from head to foot and his teeth gritted.

"Kendal," he said, "are you gunna try to bluff me out like this — like a fool, or a baby?"

He touched the shoulder of the man as he spoke.

There was no flesh in that shoulder; it was all bone and sinew, hard as iron. But now the tendons twitched beneath the hand of Fantom and the hand of Kendal flashed up as the head of a snake curls back, swifter than belief.

The long hand closed upon the wrist of Fantom; the finger tips thrust into the flesh and found the bone. It was such a grip as he would not have credited, except from a giant, or a madman. It froze the nerves of his arm to numbness; his right hand was taken from him, as it were, and now the pale, strange eyes of the man glowed at him, the long face jerked up to stare at him.

"When I'm thinking, Fantom, let me be!" said he.

He loosed the hand of the boy, and it fell back limp against Fantom's side. A cold weight of awe descended upon him, and fear such as he never had felt since, as a little boy, he had dreaded the dark.

"You've had your job cut out for you; you failed at it!" said Louis Kendal.

"You were there. You saw!" exclaimed Fantom. "By God, Kendal, I think you were the one that sent the bullets at my head!"

"At you? At you?" said Kendal. Suddenly he laughed.

It was an appalling thing to see, this laughter. His jaws sagged, and his lips twitched back, but only a panting sound came forth.

"You?" he said. "Shoot at a thing like you, when *he* was there?"

He gasped. Then, slowly, his face resumed its former frozen expression; his head fell forward; his gaze fixed upon the corner of the room as though he were studying an infinite problem.

Jim Fantom strove to speak again. He felt that his manhood demanded that he should challenge the fellow again, and yet he did not find a word to say. His legs of their own volition carried him toward the door. His hand opened it. He passed from the house like one issuing from an ugly dream, and stood again in the open with the bright sun staring into his face.

Still it was a world of illusion, because it could hold such a creature as Louis Kendal.

He walked, he did not care where, but away from the house. He did not see where he went. He stumbled over rocks. He headed across the fields, still with a shudder in the small of his back. The great dark forest arose before him, but it seemed a cheerful thing to him, compared with the soul of Louis Kendal. He was not even oppressed with a sense of shame for the manner in which he had been subdued and overawed by this man. His wrist yet tingled with the grasp of the monster; but all that mattered was the strange coldness in his heart.

He hurried on, breathing deeply, shaking his head from time to time, like a dog newly out of icy water. And so he found himself suddenly on the horizon of a song!

It came to him delicately small with distance, the singing of a child or a woman, which fell upon the gloomy soul of Fantom as the sun falls through the forest heart and drops golden warmth upon the ground.

He stopped in mid-step, as one who rouses suddenly to the knowledge that he is invading sacred precincts. Instinctively he smiled, then went on slowly, led by the music, winding among the great trunks of the trees. The voice ended, but, ending, it left the thrill of its beauty in his blood.

Louis Kendal, his long pale face, his unhuman eyes, his maniac grip, vanished from the mind of Fantom, and he became a boy, unhappy and alone in the world. The whole passionate longing arose in him as never before, except on one day. The walls and the bars of the prison had not separated him from his freedom so completely as he now felt shut off from all that his heart desired.

He could not name the thing, except to call it happiness, which all other men seemed to possess, but from which he was barred. It seemed to

Jim Fantom that all others moved in company with their kind, laughing, rejoicing; whereas he stood alone in the dark of the forest and no man cared.

He remained there with his hand gripping the rough rind of a tree, his head fallen, his eyes upon the pine needles at his feet; and every breath he drew was labored with sorrow. He tried to reason with himself, saying that this was nothing but some random child, singing in the woods. But no matter how he argued with his reason, he knew in his heart of hearts that he felt as though a sentence of eternal outlawry had been passed upon him.

The song recommenced, seeming nearer, richer; and he went forward, guided by the sound as by a light. He only paused when a question passed through his mind — was it a child? was it a woman? Such a piping sweetness could issue only from the throat of a child, such beauty must come from the lips of a woman!

The song still seemed far away, when he came to the edge of a clearing in the wood, and saw there a small log cabin with sheds behind it, and a silver streak of water across it, bubbling up with an audible murmur from beside the door of the house.

That door was open. Through it the singing poured, welled up into the air, floated off sweetly among the trees. It seemed to him like a palpable presence, which should be harvested and saved, a joy that must be laid up against the sour and sad future. Now it was scattered headlong, seeds all wasted, falling upon unprofitable ground, except that he, like a poor winter exile, could hear from a distance and gain from it nothing but an empty and an aching heart.

Then, suddenly, a veil was snatched from his eyes, and he realized that this was the cabin of his choice, that the woodhouse, that the horse and cowshed, that the spring which bobbed its bright head beside the door! He simply had come blindly upon the place from a different direction.

CHAPTER TWENTY ONE

This realization brought him a few hasty steps beyond the verge of the trees, but there he paused, for song and singer issued suddenly from the doorway, and he saw before him the girl of Burned Hill, Josephine Dolan, as far more beautiful now to him as the fresh morning is more lovely than the twilight.

She wore a blue gingham dress, with the sleeves turned up to the elbows, and a pail was in her hand; but all was so transformed to the excited eyes of Jim Fantom that she could not have stirred him more if she had been a bright spirit, wrapped in the blue of heaven.

On the threshold she paused, ended a song, and began another, like a bird whose throat is continually crowded with music on a spring morning. Then she went to the spring, the silver of the dew-wet grass turning dark beneath her feet, and dipped the bucket into the cup of the water.

She was straightening again when she saw him. The song stopped with a jar; the bucket dropped to the ground, and the water sloshed out from side to side under the impact.

"Hello!" she called to him. "How did you come here, Jim Fantom?"

He went stumbling across the clearing toward

her. He could not see his way, but only the girl, her brightness, her laughter, and the streaking of morning mist across the trees behind her.

"But you," said Fantom. "How are you here? I'd like to know. Unless — ay, your father has moved up here! I should have thought of that!"

He half choked, and gasped with relief at the thought, for the first thought had been that she had come here for another man, he for whom Quay had built the house.

"My dad!" chuckled the girl. "That's likely, ain't it? My dad up here in the Happy Valley? Nope! He's never done a thing that would get him — this high!"

She laughed again. She was all full of laughter or of song. And with one hand dropped on her hip, she eyed Jim Fantom now and passed from her laughter into the hum of a tune.

He could not speak at once, in answer, but his glance drifted over her and his thought embraced her beauty. It was her radiant mirthfulness that thrust him away at arm's length and made him ill at ease. She ran on:

"What's Dad done that Mr. Quay should have to save him, or want to save him? It's the lucky ones like you that he's interested in! You fellows who are long riders and take the long chances — and here you wind up in the Happy Valley!"

She laughed again. He could not tell how much mockery there was in her, but partly he knew that this laughter was the bubbling over of the mere joy of living.

A sterner thread of thought and of fear made him say:

"If it's not your father, then who is it? You can't be up here alone, I s'pose?"

"Here? With these woods all around? I should say not!" answered she. "I'm up here to be married, Jim!"

"Married?" said he. "Married?"

"Well, it's not as bad as all that, I hope," said the girl. "Has to be some time."

"Ay," said the boy huskily. "Of course you'd have to marry, some time."

His eyes opened with despair as he looked at her.

"And up here in the Happy Valley," said she, "there's no rent. That puts us a jump ahead of the game!"

"Who's the man?" he asked suddenly.

Then he looked down at the ground, nerving himself, desperately determined to withstand the shock.

She waited a moment.

"Why, you know him," she said.

Suddenly the handsome face of Chip Lander jumped into his mind. He, too, was from Burned Hill.

"Maybe I do! Maybe I do!" he muttered.

"He's been pretty bad," said the girl, "but I suppose that Mr. Quay will make him tame enough."

"He ain't been settled long, then?"

"Oh, no, not long."

It was Chip Lander, then, a newcomer in the

valley! He recalled with a sudden bitterness how Quay had promised him, so easily, that this girl should be his. It cast a fierce light upon the entire character of the man. It cheapened and reduced him. He was one of those glib and oily talkers, it appeared, always ready with promises — anything to give a cheerful moment!

"I'll take the bucket in for you," said he.

He picked it up and carried it into the house, through the door into the kitchen. That room was transformed. Not in actual form or contents, but a spirit had entered it. A fire hummed in the stove, a sweet scent of cinnamon was in the air. On the surface of a white-scrubbed mixing board on the table was a thin layer of biscuit dough, rolled out ready for the cutting.

He looked down to her hands. For the first time he saw that they were whitened by the flour, and this little touch drew her down from the region of the bright spirits and made her a woman. But not for him. Some other man had claimed and won her!

"You've — you've started things going," said he.

He looked vaguely around him. Already he knew all that he would see, but he was inhaling the new atmosphere of the house with a sad interest.

"Well, I have to pitch in and see how things'll go," said she.

"Ay," he answered. "Before the wedding, I guess."

"Yes, before the wedding."

"When will that be?"

"Well, I dunno, exactly. But pretty quick, I suppose."

He sighed.

"I've been busy as a beaver. I only got in here late last night. I couldn't sleep. I've been up all night getting things ready. D'you want to see?"

"Well, I'd sort of like to."

She led him into the dining-living room, the one big room of the cabin.

"Look at that!" she said. "I picked 'em at sunup."

These were armfuls of yellow and white blossomed branches which she had cut from some shrub in the woods. Their fragrance was ethereally thin in the air, mingled with the heavier sweet of the kitchen cookery.

On the hearth a fire had been kindled, and the flames weltered low.

"I wanted to try the flue. It works fine, you see. It's going to be a warm house when the winter snows come. It'll be snug, don't you think?"

"Why, I guess it will," said he.

"I'll hope you'll be here a lot," said she.

He started.

"Me?"

"Yes. We could talk about Burned Hill, and folks down there."

"I won't be here," said he.

"You won't?"

She looked at him, puzzled.

"I'm gonna make a trip," he said. "I've gotta make a long trip. I won't be here."

She was smiling at him, half quizzically, and half doubtfully.

"Well, that would be too bad," said she. "I sort of counted on you. Here's the other room."

They went into the bedroom. There were other flowering branches here; and big enlarged photographs on the wall, of a gentleman with sadly drooping moustaches and a tight-waisted woman.

"Dad and mother to keep an eye on me," said the girl. "They make it sort of more homelike. That coverlet came all the way from Boston. It was hand made at home. In grandma's house. It's sort of cheerful."

"Ay, it's sort of cheerful," he said dismally.

The whole house was filled with perfume, and with bright beauty, as it seemed to his hungry soul. The very pattern of the rag rug upon the floor was to him a marvel, and a sad marvel. Other feet would tread upon it, other eyes would dwell upon its rioting colors. And it seemed to the boy that the care, the infinite patience, the loving hands which had worked to make this rug — all of this was a type and a symbol of the past out of which this girl had come. His own forebears were rough, rude people, savage as himself. But she came from a gentler stock, a stock of home lovers and of home makers. So it was that she had given to this house, in an instant, a touch beyond his imagining.

He turned gloomily away.

"I'm pretty much afraid you don't like it," she said.

She followed him anxiously, and touched his arm.

"You don't like it!" she repeated.

And she looked up to him with fear and doubt dwelling in her eyes.

"Like it? Like it?" muttered Fantom thickly.

"You don't think it'll please — him?" said she.

There was infinite appeal in her voice, in her eyes.

And then Jim Fantom went mad in a sudden stroke, for he caught her close to him and held her there, soft beneath his hands, until the warmth of her body came to him, and the fragrance from her hair was in his face.

He, with a hand of iron, found her chin, and forced her head back.

She had not struggled against him. Her eyes were closed. It seemed to Jim Fantom that he had been walled out and excluded from her life by this fact more than by lofty walls of stone. Holding her in his arms, she still was a thousand leagues from him.

"Look!" said he. "I'm a swine. I never should of touched you, even with my eyes. But I love you. God, God, how I'm lovin' you! I'm gunna go. I won't see you again. Him — if he wants satisfaction — he can come and kick me in the face. He's got the right —"

He whirled away from her. His shoulder

crashed against the side of the door, spinning him over the threshold, and so he ran blundering across the clearing, wishing in his heart that he never had seen this place, the valley, the girl's face, yet knowing there was nothing in life remaining so precious to him as the thought of this.

The cool shadows beneath the trees washed like water over his face. His hat was knocked off by a low branch. He ran on, unheeding, like one striving to escape from himself.

CHAPTER TWENTY TWO

That outburst of physical action saved him from himself, as it were. When he came to the house, again, his brain had cleared a little. As he neared it, he walked slowly, and found himself repeating aloud, over and over, rhythmically, "I've gotta be calm! I've gotta be calm. She's gone!"

Coming fully back to consciousness, he stopped short, and with cold sweat standing on his face, he told himself that he was going mad. The shock of that suggestion sobered him still more, and the next moment he saw the tall form of Louis Kendal striding up and down behind the house.

He paused as the boy drew nearer, and said brusquely:

"Get into the buckboard — you'll find it in that shed. Harness the pair of buckskin broncs at the end of the east side of the barn. You see that pile of rusty plowshares? Take 'em down to the village and give 'em to Wilkes to be sharpened. Tell him I want 'em back by tonight. While you're down there, get three boxes of half-inch copper rivets. Here's the order for them."

He extended a slip of paper to Fantom, and the latter took it in silence. He was almost glad of the terseness of the tall man's language. As he turned away, Kendal snapped at him:

"One minute!"

He turned back.

"You're here maybe to stay," said Kendal. "All right. Now keep a head on your shoulders. What's happened between us, I'll put out of my head. You do the same, and we'll get on. If you don't, I'll make you think the Happy Valley is a happy hell. That's all!"

He did not wait to hear the reaction of the boy, but continued his striding back and forth, deep in the solution of his problem.

That problem, as Fantom could guess clearly enough, doubtless had something to do with the mysterious hunchback; and as he went into the barn, his thoughts turned a little from the cabin in the clearing and the loveliness of Jo Dolan to the hunchback, the filmed eyes, the pale, long face, as pale and as long as that of Louis Kendal, and infinitely more ugly.

Were they related?

The shock of that thought stopped him again; he grew so absent-minded that, when he came to the buckskin mustangs, his head was nearly clipped from his shoulders by the flying heels of the off horse.

That wakened him to reality. He paid heed to himself as he tossed the harness upon them and led them out into the open, as tough and cunning a pair as ever he had handled.

The buckboard was soon drawn out from the wagon shed, but it took ten or fifteen minutes of backing and filling to get the broncos into their positions. But at last they were hitched, the plowshares piled in, and away went Fantom down the drive.

The mustangs, their tails switching with vicious energy, leaned on the bits, shouldering out as the mighty pull of Fantom dragged their heads together, and so they flew down the road, sometimes breaking from a trot into a hump-backed gallop.

He could not help wondering, as the wheels crunched and whirred upon the stones of the road, whether Mr. Louis Kendal had had some hidden purpose in assigning him to such a team as this. The white flank of a bird tree was enough to make them bound like deer into the ditch, almost overturning the wagon, and the clangor of the spilled heap of plowshares in the body of the vehicle frightened them back into the middle of the road.

For a moment they were uncontrollable, leaping ahead in a panic. But the strong hands and the cunning craft of Fantom sufficed to reduce their gait again. The bridge crashed beneath them, as though thunder were dropping upon their heads from above. Then they whirled on down the road, with the trees blended almost into a solid wall on either side, a solid heaven of green above them.

Into the village he came at last, standing up, with his feet almost jammed through the foot-boards, and his arm and leg muscles aching from the strain. Yet he managed to bring the team to a prancing halt in front of the blacksmith shop.

Josh Wilkes came out, grinning widely. He was a fat man, with hanging cheeks and little eyes like the eyes of a pig, quick with greed and with cunning inspired by hunger.

"You've got the Dynamiters, have you?" said he.

"Is that what they're called?" asked Fantom.

"Sure. The last time that they were hitched up they exploded poor Bill Watkins into a black-berry patch and blew the wagon into the lake. When we fished poor Bill out, he hollered like a kid. Them berry thorns, they'd scratched him like twenty wildcats. Pretty near put out his eyes. The Dynamiters ain't been used since then. How come you picked 'em out?"

"They was give to me," said Fantom, his teeth clicking on the end of the words.

The little eyes of the blacksmith gleamed.

"Well," said he, "you needn't say 'thank you, ma'am' for 'em. Was it Kendal that throwed 'em at you?"

"Ay."

"Well, maybe he's got a lot of confidence in you; maybe he thinks that you can bounce, like a rubber ball! That near hoss is a pack of hell-fire! He's showin' me the red of his eye, the devil! Well, good luck to you, son, and give this pair plenty for air and don't let 'em turn you inside out like an old coat. They got a scientific spirit, these here. They wanta get right under the skin, like a doctor!"

He carried the shares into the shop, and

Fantom drove across to the general merchandise store which stood on the farther side of the square which composed the village. It was something like a New England common; three or four cows, a mare and its colt, were staked out, browsing contentedly. And the buildings were spaced about it, solidly built and capacious structures, as though Quay expected that this might be the nucleus of quite a town.

Two women had just climbed down from a pair of buggies in front of the store. And they came willingly to hold the heads of the buckskins while Fantom jumped out with the tie ropes to secure them to the hitching post.

"It's the new man," said one. "It's Jim Fantom!"

"Of course it is," said the other. "You better introduce us. Go ahead, Mary!"

"I'm Mack Rhiner's wife," said the other. "You've heard of Mack, I guess, Mr. Fantom?"

"He did me a round good turn the other day," said Fantom. "You bet I've heard of him. I'm mighty glad to know you, Mrs. Rhiner."

"Thanks," said she. "This here is Harriet Samuels. Maybe you have heard of Terry Samuels, too?"

"Of course he has," said Mrs. Samuels. "Sometimes I wish that I hadn't though!"

She was a handsome woman of close to middle age, with a shrewd face and a shrewder look, but her manner was very open.

They walked on into the store, together.

"That's a fine thing to say about poor Terry!" commented Mrs. Rhiner, who was pretty, and blonde, with a dappling of freckles over her nose.

"Poor Terry!" exclaimed Mrs. Samuels. "He sat up till two, last night, working over a new kind of lock."

"Inventing?"

"Inventing nothing! Inventing new ways of taking the thing to bits. He's gotta read the mind of every new-fangled lock that comes out, or else he ain't happy. You never seen such a man. 'You better get to bed,' says I. 'I can't sleep,' says he. 'They got a droppin' bolt inside of this here. Who would of thought of that? Jumps down, and then slides up when the key turns, and sets the rest of the lock free to work. What good would a skeleton key be, I'm askin' you, on a lock like this? They's been too much brains spent on locks. Kind of makes a profession like mine get poor and skinny!' "

"Does he talk like that?"

"Yeah. You'd never think that Terry was an honest teamster, now. If it wasn't for Mr. Quay, he'd be gone like a shot. But he's sure interested in his old business. The other night, I heard a scratchin' for ten minutes at the front door. It was Terry. He was tryin' to work back the bolt with just a common pin! Drat the man! How's things, Mr. Fantom?"

"Fine," said Fantom without conviction. "Everything is fine."

"You'll like it up here," said Mrs. Samuels.

"Won't he, Mary?"

"Yep. If he don't get sleepy and bored with it all," said Mrs. Rhiner. "Mack cuts up a little, now and then. If only there was a greaser or an Indian or something that he could work off his steam on! But there ain't!"

"Listen to her," said the pacific Mrs. Samuels. "She'd like to see her husband eatin' up Mexicans and Injuns. Ain't you ashamed of yourself, Mary?"

Mary Rhiner shrugged her young shoulders.

"Well, he was born with teeth," said she, "and he's gotta use 'em. God made him that way. I didn't. And all I want is Mack to be happy. Yesterday he was settin' on the front porch and a squirrel jumped down from the trunk of one tree and scooted for another. Out comes Mack's gun and he blazes away. He knocked that squirrel over, but it was only the dirt that the bullet kicked into the side of the poor thing. It rolled over and scrambled up the bark of another tree and switched its puff of a tail out of sight. It got away. Mack was near wild. He walked around and around that tree, lookin' for a second shot.

" 'I'm gettin' old!' says he, and he spends the rest of the day throwin' pebbles into the air and shootin' at them.

" 'Pebbles ain't men,' says I to Mack.

" 'Neither is squirrels,' says he, 'but men eat 'em! I'm gettin' old and shaky, I tell you!'

"That's the way with him. But he's been a real artist. You can't expect him to settle down easy,

181

like some other men."

"Sure he's an artist," admitted Mrs. Samuels. "I heard Terry once say that Mack could make a Colt talk English and three other languages, none of which was understood outside of himself and the gun. But it's better to have him up here where there's more trees than men."

"Oh, but ain't it!" sighed Mary Rhiner. "I God bless Jonathan Quay every day of my life, I'm tellin' you!"

So talking, they wandered into the General Merchandise store, and Fantom ran his eyes over a wide display of stocks that ran from overalls to Winchester rifles in racks.

One thing of importance had happened, at least. He had liked both of these women, for their frankness, their direct speaking. Beyond that, their faith in Quay moved him, and made him feel that his feet were based upon the bedrock!

CHAPTER TWENTY THREE

"Hey, Mrs. Rhiner," said the clerk, coming from behind the counter. "Look at here what we got in that your kid will be crazy about!"

He wound up a spring and placed a gay little toy bird, painted yellow and red, upon the floor. At once it began a jig, pecking busily at invisible grains of wheat.

"Whacha think?" demanded the clerk, stepping back and eyeing the toy with as much pride as though he had himself devised it.

"Why, it's a beaut," said Mrs. Rhiner heartily. "Jimmy'll love it to pieces in about five shakes. You better gimme half a dozen of 'em, if you got that many."

"Hold on!" broke in Mrs. Samuels. "Little Terry will be eatin' his heart out if he sees Jimmy with one and none for himself."

"We got four," said the clerk. "We'll split 'em two ways!"

He disappeared behind the counter.

"You know him?" whispered Mrs. Rhiner, aside to Fantom. "That's Don Pilson, the slickest second-story man you ever seen. He done the Marlborough robbery in Chicago. That's him! You wouldn't think it, would you? Say, Don, meet Jim Fantom, will you?"

They shook hands, Don Pilson grinning his welcome.

"Glad to have you here, son," said the ex-robber. "What can I do for you?"

"Half-inch copper rivets," said Fantom. "Here's Kendal's ticket."

It seemed to him that he could see the other scowl as his eye fell upon the writing of Quay's lieutenant and manager.

Then he stood by while Pilson looked over some shelves at the rear of the store. The two women were busily engaged, with much laughter, in working the dancing bird, when the door slammed, and Chip Lander came into the store.

"Here's the handsome bachelor," said Mary Rhiner. "Hullo, Chip. How's things?"

"Dizzy," said Chip, grinning.

"Dizzy with what?"

"Girl," said Chip.

The heart of Fantom grew small and hard within him.

"Listen to him!" said Harriet Samuels. "He's talkin' right out loud. You must be runnin' a temperature, Chip!"

"What girl, where?" demanded Mrs. Rhiner, more to the point.

"In the new cabin," said Chip Lander.

"Is there a girl there?" asked Mrs. Samuels. "The poor thing will have rheumatism, sure, livin' among the shadows of all of them trees!"

"Who is she, Chip?"

"She's a beauty," said he.

"Sure. I could guess that. How beautiful, child?"

"She wins before she starts," said Chip.

He thrust his thumbs inside his belt and teetered exultantly from heel to toe, and back again.

Fantom, watching him, hungered to shout an insult, and then snatch at a gun. Never had he detested anything in the world so much as he now loathed the handsome, flushed face of Chip Lander.

"Look at him!" chuckled pretty Mary Rhiner. "The poor thing's in a trance!"

Mrs. Samuels laughed gaily.

"The fast fish," said she, "is the one that gets hooked the deepest. Is she a black-eyed darlin', Chip?"

"She's all gold," said Chip. "Gold an' blue an' pink."

"Sugar an' cream an' butter," scoffed Mary Rhiner good-naturedly.

"If you was to see her," said Chip Lander, "you'd forget to be jealous."

"Of you?" asked Mrs. Samuels.

"Of her. If you was to see her, Harriet, you'd thank God that she was livin' in a cabin fenced around with tall trees."

"How come, Handsome?" asked the older woman.

"Because when the gents in this here valley see her, they're gunna lose their sense of direction like a carrier pigeon that's been tapped on the

185

bean! They're gunna run wild! I'm tellin' you that!"

"All right," said Mrs. Samuels. "My Terry has rode some long rides, but he always comes back as sure as a boomerang, and has to be dodged ag'in!"

"They're all gunna run wild," went on Chip Lander complacently. "And they're all gunna head in one direction."

"Because you're dizzy, child," said Mrs. Samuels, "that ain't a sign that they's only one pair of eyes to serve all the men in this here valley! She's probably a peroxide and paints her eyelashes."

Chip Lander laughed loudly.

"Sure," he said, "you better start knockin'. You better practice. Because you're all gunna need to do some talkin'. You married women will all be hobblin' your husbands or takin' them out on the lead."

"There never was a girl in the world," said Mrs. Rhiner philosophically, "that could please every man. Some see faces and some see deeper."

She touched the end of her rather upturned nose and frowned with gravity.

"Men see the time of the year!" declared Mrs. Samuels. "When May comes around, you would think that the girls was in flower, like the earth. Along about May, when my Terry goes past a girl, he steps as light as a burglar and looks guilty."

"With my girl," declared young Chip Lander, "it's always spring, I tell you. The blossom is always on the doggone bough, as somebody wrote in a poem, I think."

"When did she come in?"

"Last night, for a surprise. I found her this morning."

"Have you known her long, Chip?" asked Mrs. Samuels.

"A coupla thousand years," said Chip, almost gravely.

"Is that all?"

"Yeah. I used to dream about her back in the days of old Pharaoh."

"You was likely a close bosom friend of Moses, you," suggested Mary Rhiner, half smiling and half in disdain.

"Him and me used to eat at the same lunch counter," said Chip Lander. "And we daubed our ropes on the lean kine and the fat ones, elbow to elbow. But then we fell out!"

"How come?" asked the clerk, returning with the boxes of rivets.

Fantom took them, but remained where he was, tormented into movelessness, tortured, but fascinated by pain, as it were.

"We fell out," said Chip Lander happily, "because he seen Beautiful and forgot to go home to supper. I had to show him the gate. An' for a long time, he forgot all the street numbers in that town except where I lived."

"Kind of was a bother to you and the girl, eh?"

said Mrs. Samuels, sarcastically.

"Sure," said Chip. "He was always hangin' around and leanin' on the front gate, combin' his beard and lookin' at the dog."

"How long did he keep that up?" asked Mrs. Rhiner.

"Well, he got tired. He kind of lost heart, and decided to leave the country," said Chip Lander. "That was why he marched off with all his friends, and wandered around a long time, and wrote a lot of Commandments, and started no end of trouble for the rest of the world. He never could forget her, d'you see?"

"Sure I see," said Mrs. Rhiner. "You been chummy with her ever since?"

"Dreamed of her every night since I was a kid," said Chip Lander. "We been mighty thick."

"Maybe you been the thickest of the two. Is she fond of you, Chip?"

"I'll tell you how it is," said Chip, "she's so doggone good-natured that she sees something even in me."

"She needs good advice," said Mrs. Rhiner.

"The poor simple thing," said Mrs. Samuels, chuckling. "Handsome, when are you gonna get married to her, and what's her name?"

"Her name is Beautiful," said Chip Lander, "and we're gonna get married as soon as I've put a lining of gold inside of that house and mounted the doors and windows with diamonds."

"That'll just take you a coupla days," said Mrs. Rhiner.

"Sure," said he. "After seein' her this mornin', I could take old Mount Baldy, yonder, and break him in two, and pick out the nuggets out of his insides."

"She ain't swelled you up any, Chip?"

"Her? Nope, she's just made me feel nacheral, and strong."

"How old is she, Handsome?"

"She's the right age for singin' and dancin'," said Chip. "She's about as old as the spring of the year, ma'am."

"I bet," said Mrs. Rhiner, "that she wears glasses and has a lantern jaw."

"Speakin' of glasses," said Chip, "you'll need smoked lenses when you look at her, she's that bright!"

"Chip, where did you get it?" asked Mrs. Samuels. "I didn't know that the moonshine they peddle out in this here Happy Valley was that good!"

"Aw, he ain't particular," suggested Mrs. Rhiner delicately. "God gave him one good gift, and that's a strong stomach. Don, have you got any canned salmon? We gotta eat, in our house, even if they's a peroxide sweetheart just come to town!"

"You'll eat, ma'am," said Chip Lander, "but Terry won't eat after he's seen her. They's gonna be a terrible loss of appetite among the gents in this here part of the world. They's gonna be a tunin' up of banjos and fiddles. They's gonna be a clearin' of throats and a mighty lot of caterwaulin' around in the night, over there by the new cabin. They's gonna be a lot of footmarks leadin' toward that cabin door, but they's all gonna stop at the threshold except one pair of shop-made boots. How d'you like 'em, ladies?"

He looked down admiringly at the narrowly pointed tips of his toes.

Fantom could endure no more. The gloating of young Chip Lander carried home to his very heart the remembered beauty of the girl, and now he started hastily out from the store.

"Hey," called Chip after him. "I wanta tell *you* some things about her, Jimmy!"

"I'm busy," croaked Fantom, and passed out the front door of the store, letting it slam heavily behind him.

There on the front veranda he waited for the mist to clear from his eyes — a red-stained mist of fury, and jealous hatred.

Behind him, in the store, he heard a sudden burst of loud laughter. That was the way, he said to himself, that Chip Lander had carelessly laughed his way into the heart of the girl.

CHAPTER TWENTY FOUR

It was that, he thought, which chiefly maddened him — the casual air of this man, the excessive buoyancy with which he floated through his talk about the girl.

To Fantom it seemed a sacred thing, to be closely housed in the secrecy of the soul. But the flamboyant Lander could not help rippling out his nonsense!

He breathed deeply, squared his shoulders, and was about to go down to the buckboard, when the door clanged again behind him, and he heard a cheerful whistle coming out. It was Lander, he knew, and his mind darkened with the thought, as though a shadow had fallen across his soul.

A hand clapped him heartily upon the shoulder.

"How are you, old boy?" asked Chip.

Fantom whirled, with a backward gliding step. It was that swift, light motion of his which had gained for him his sobriquet in an earlier day of The Phantom.

"He can walk on dry leaves and they'll never whisper a word of him!" someone had said.

So whirling, he scowled at Lander.

"Tell a man when you're comin'!" he exclaimed bitterly.

Lander stepped back in turn, amazed.

"Why, what's bitten you?" he asked.

Reason and natural gratitude to the man whose riding had saved him from the law surged up in the heart of Fantom, but instantly they were dismissed again, and beaten down. Only red anger, fiercely flaming jealousy remained to control him. He wanted nothing in the world, it seemed to him, except the death of this man.

So he remained a moment, his lips stiffening into a straight line.

"Don't sneak up behind and whang a man," he said. "They's parts of the country where it ain't safe!"

Lander turned crimson.

"Are you talkin' down to me, young feller?" said he, as hot as Fantom.

The latter smiled and drew in a quick breath. And there was that in his smile and in that thirsty intake of breath that banished most of the color from the face of Chip.

"Why not talk down?" asked Fantom.

"Why?" said the other, shrugging back his shoulders, as though he needed to harden his courage by some physical act. "Because they ain't enough inches in you to see over my head."

"I see over you, and I see through you!" said Fantom slowly. "I see over the top of you, and I see through you, like thin water. And all there is at the bottom, is scum!"

Lander started violently.

"Man," he exclaimed, "are you crazy? What's

started you after me?"

"I been raised," said Fantom, "in a part of the country where they's only one way of talkin' about a lady."

Lander parted his lips to speak, then closed them firmly together. He had seen the two women come out through the door of the store, and whatever explanation he might have offered, he would not be seen to take water in the presence of such witnesses.

"My way of talk is my own," said he.

"A damn poor way I call it!" answered Fantom.

"They's nothin' about me that you can damn and get away with it," replied Lander, quivering from head to foot with excitement.

"Great heavens," exclaimed Mrs. Rhiner. "They're goin' to fight! What's the matter with the pair of you two young idiots?"

She pushed in between them, boldly.

"Get back!" snapped Fantom.

She threw one glance at him, and that was enough. He had swayed a little forward upon his toes, his body crouched slightly, so that he gave the appearance of one about to leap. But they who watched knew well enough that all this energy, all this collected nerve power ready to explode, would be flashed into action in the movement of a hand and a gun.

The lean fingers were working slowly; the eyes of the boy gleamed as they clung to the target.

"He's goin' to shoot! He's goin' to shoot!

Mary, get back!" cried Harriet Samuels. And Mary Rhiner ran hastily back.

She was gone from the field of The Phantom's vision. All that remained in his eye was the form of his enemy, and a horseman coming down the street at a canter, a cloud of dust puffing up behind the heels of his horse.

"Scream — do something to stop 'em!" exclaimed Mrs. Rhiner.

But the older woman broke in. "Don't so much as stir, or it'll start 'em at each other. Chip, Chip, back out. Don't be ashamed. He's got a murder in him, and you won't have a chance. Chip, back out of it! Don't be a fool!"

"I'll see him damned, first," said Chip, white, but coldly resolute as one prepared to die.

"There can't be anything really wrong," said Mrs. Rhiner. "Jim Fantom, Chip never harmed any man."

"No," said The Phantom. "He never harmed no man. He never had the nerve to do it. It ain't men that he hunts down. That ain't his way! He's a sneak. He's a lyin' sneak, and I'm here to prove it on him."

Said Chip, his voice coming rather hoarsely, and far away:

"I've licked you before. I'll do it ag'in, today!"

"Good!" said Fantom through his teeth. "I wanted to hear you say that, and you've said it. Now, fill your hand, you skunk, and fill it with aces, because you're standin' around the corner from the finish of one of us!"

"Make your own move. I'll take care of myself," said Chip Lander.

"You fool!" snarled Fantom. "I'm givin' you the last chance. Make your move and fill your hand — or I'll start this game."

The fingers of Chip twitched. Plainly, he was sorely tempted, as one who knew that the odds were heavily against him. Yet his pride and his sense of honor controlled him to the end. He resisted that impulse and fought back the shameful temptation.

He was no better than a dead man, he knew; the coldness of that fear was numbing his wrists, tingling in his finger tips, and yet he faced Fantom without a stir.

"Make your own time," said Chip Lander firmly.

Then a shrilling voice clove the air. It was Mrs. Samuels, calling: "Mr. Quay!"

The hand of Fantom stopped mid-leap, and he saw the form of the nearing horseman turned into that of Jonathan Quay!

Savagely he resented the coming of his master, but master he admitted Quay to be. Into his hands he had given himself for a year!

There was no stir of Chip Lander, he had seen a change in the face of Fantom, and the first hope came to him, followed by the call of Quay himself: "Hello, what's the matter?"

"It's Jim Fantom and Lander — they're about to fight —"

"Nonsense," said Quay, coming close. "Fight?

Here in the valley? It's forbidden, and they both know it!"

Fantom turned on his heel toward Quay, his face as hard as iron.

"You've come in time," he admitted grimly. "I was about to bust loose."

Quay looked calmly upon them, his keen eyes searching each face in turn.

"What's happened to you two?" he asked. "What in the world is the matter? This is the man who helped you only the other day, Jim!"

"I know it," said Fantom, remorse swelling in him. "I know it. I — I turned into a mad dog. That's all!"

He started hastily down the steps of the veranda of the store and toward the waiting buckskins.

"One moment," said Quay, after him. "If you ladies will step on, a bit — we must talk alone —"

They drifted away, hungry eyes of gossip turned over their shoulders as they went.

"Now, Fantom, what's it all about?"

"I've talked enough. I've said that I was wrong," said Fantom sullenly, without meeting the eye of the older man.

"Chip, speak up," commanded Quay.

"If Jim wants to drop it, it's dropped," said Lander, "as far as I'm concerned."

"I drop it," answered Fantom.

Then his repentance grew strong in him.

"I'll apologize — with the women to listen to me, if you want," said he.

"My God no," answered Lander. "I never had a mean thought for you, Jim, from the day when we had our fight in Burned Hill. Has it been workin' in you all of this time? Man, man, I don't pretend to be what you are with the guns!"

"Guns?" said Quay.

"Ay," said Fantom slowly, making himself face the truth. "I would have killed him, quick enough!"

"Here in my valley?" demanded Quay angrily. He checked himself and controlled his voice at once. "I still don't know what's at the bottom of this."

"I slapped him on the shoulder as I came out of the store and found him waitin' here," said Lander. "He turned around, pretty black in the face, and give me a mean word and a bad look. Seems that he didn't like the way that I'd been talkin' about the new girl over yonder in the new cabin — I don't know her name."

Fantom reeled.

"You don't know her name?" he repeated.

"Me? Why, man, I was only blowin' off a little wind. I seen her. There ain't any harm in seein' a pretty girl — the finest I ever laid eyes on — and then talkin' a little large and foolish, is there?"

Fantom took him by the shoulders.

"D'ye mean it, Chip, d'ye mean it?" he asked.

There was such a groan of anguish and of hope in his voice, that the other gasped.

"Mean it? Why, man, I only was there long enough to ask her for a drink of water. I hardly

197

had a chance to see the color of her eyes; and she was off ag'in, singin' in the kitchen. But what's she to you, Jim? Will you tell me that?"

CHAPTER TWENTY FIVE

With trembling hands, Fantom drew forth a bandana and with it wiped his streaming face. He felt weak; he felt as though his blood had turned to water, so great was the reaction of his relief.

"What's she to me?" he said. "Why, I dunno — Mr. Quay — maybe he's got an idea!"

Jonathan Quay looked sharply from one of them to the other.

"She's to be his wife, Chip," he said at last.

Lander winced.

"Ah, man," said he. "I see it, now. I was drivin' you mad. Why'd you leave the store before I explained my joke to the two of the ladies? I called to you, but you wouldn't wait! I wouldn't of let you go out with a wrong idea!"

But Fantom had turned his back upon his friend. He stood beside Quay's horse and looked into his face with eyes of fire.

"There ain't any doubt, Mr. Quay? She's — she's —"

"She's doing her housework, I suppose," said Quay, rather tersely. "And probably a bit lonely, as well!"

It was to Fantom like the sight of blue water after the long desert march.

Somehow the lead ropes were taken from the horses, he was in the driver's seat, with Chip

Lander hanging to the heads of the rearing mustangs.

"Steady, Jim," he warned. "They're crampin' the wheel, there. They'll have you turned over, in another minute!"

"Let 'em go!" shouted Fantom.

He stood up and whirled the whip.

"Let 'em go, Chip!"

Lander released them. They flung themselves forward and high in the air, as though leaping together at a given signal. The buckboard flew after them, landed with a crash, and heeled far to one side. But Fantom kept himself erect. He seemed upheld by some extraneous force in that heaving, pitching vehicle; then, with a broad whirl of the lash, he cut both the mustangs at once.

One of them squealed with fury and with surprise. They were accustomed to having the reins held hard, their mettle feared, their paces regarded with awe. But now they were scourged forward.

They gathered speed. They burst into a full run, and with reins only tight enough to assure his balance, Jim Fantom, stood erect behind them and plied the whip again, and again, until their rumps were scored with welts.

From rut to rut they skidded in the dust, which arose in a lofty cloud behind them. At every bump the wagon vaulted into the air, and the frightened, infuriated ponies squealed again and again and bawled with excitement as they bucked and pitched and raced through the town.

Those who saw declared that, in front of the upward-curling rush of dust, Jim Fantom stood erect all this way, plying the whip, and laughing like a maniac.

So they tore out of the village, and turned into the out road with a skid that almost put them in the opposite ditch. Then they straightened out and fairly flew forward, with the whip still working. They struck the bridge, and the wheels sprang at one bound from the first rise to the high-curved center, then shot down the farther side.

They swept and skidded along the curves of the forest road, next, until Fantom drew rein and shouted. And at once that gallant pair of broncos, the Dynamiters, came back into his hand!

Their danger had been extracted from them, their explosiveness removed. With apprehensive eyes that glanced aside and backward at the strange madman who had so stroked them with fire, as though he rejoiced in their deviltry. They danced a little in their trot, but the bits were light in their mouths, and Fantom laughed again, softly and fiercely, as he regarded them.

At last, they stopped gently beside the road, and quietly they stood while he dismounted and tethered them, only wincing a little now and again as the pain of their recent whipstrokes burned them.

He left the span and went forward through the

trees. But when he saw the cabin beyond them, all of his courage disappeared. Perhaps it was apprehensive joy that stole the strength from his knees, and from his brain as well, and joy that made his body feel light as a bubble, ready to float in the air.

He stopped beside a tree at the edge of the clearing and there paused with his hand against the trunk, resting. He tried to think. He wanted to plan what he would say to her, how he would act. But his heart rose and choked him, as though he were about to face an audience of thousands.

But what were thousands to him? No, there was no other place in the world where he would be but this. And yet he could hardly force himself forward.

And then the voice rose sweetly from the house again. There seemed to him now more woman than child in the song; and yet the child was in it, also. That thought filled him with pity and gentleness, so that he had a sudden courage to go forward across the clearing until he came to the spring.

There he paused. It was this very grass that he had seen darkened beneath her footfall that morning. And this memory unnerved him again. He would have prayed for strength, but his numbed brain could not find words.

He went slowly on. Sometimes joyous confidence made him take a long stride forward. Then, abashed, he would halt.

But he came to the door.

It was shut, and this troubled him. The singing, as well, had stopped. Twice he raised his hand. The first time, he heard a poker rattled in the stove, and let the hand fall. Again, a pan clanged loudly. But the third time he was able to rap.

"Come!" called the clear voice of the girl.

It was so briskly matter-of-fact that he held his breath. He could not push that door open.

"Come, come!" she called impatiently.

Then rapid steps crossed the floor, and the door was jerked open. She stood frowning above him.

"Who wants —" she began. "Oh," she ended. "D'you leave something behind you, Mr. Fantom?"

"Matter of fact," began Jim Fantom, "matter of fact —"

He paused. He had stumbled on the word "mister" which she had prefixed to his name.

So he stood, uneasy, uncertain, looking wistfully up to her.

"It looks," she said severely, "as though you want to say something."

"I wanted to say," said he, "I wanted to say — that — that — I'd come back here —"

"So I see," said she.

She looked past him, above his head, absent-mindedly watching the woods.

He was glad that her eyes were off him, for that allowed him to think more easily.

"I wanted to sort of apologize," said he.

She looked at him with a puzzled air, as though trying to guess at some meaning hidden behind his words.

"What are you apologizing for?" she asked.

At this, a bit of color flicked into his face.

"Are you makin' a joke of me, Jo?" said he.

"Not a bit," said she. "Come in and sit down. You look all tired out."

"I don't wanta sit," said he.

"Why not?"

"Why — somehow I could talk better standing. What I gotta say to you is this —"

"Wait a minute," said she. "The biscuits will be burned to a crisp!"

She fled to the stove and dropped to her knees to open the oven door, while he climbed higher on the steps, pausing at the threshold to see her the better.

She had drawn out the baking pan; a mist of steam and smoke flew up into her face, and a good savor came to him. It made him hungry. That bread had been brooded over by her, touched by her hands. His hunger grew; his heart ached more bitterly.

"I wish that you'd stay out or come in," said the girl, sharply. "You're blocking all the light for me."

"She doesn't care," said he to himself, in sorrow. "What does she care a rap for a stupid fool like me that just stands around and can't talk? Look at Chip, the way that he always smiles and is bright. He's funny, too. My God how I wish that I could say something that would make her laugh!"

He communed with himself, in this manner.

"Please!" exclaimed the girl, impatient as he did not move.

The Phantom sighed.

"Well," he said, "I guess I'm in the way."

"In the way of the light, you are," said she.

He felt that pride demanded that he should leave at once, after this insult; yet, though his heart swelled with sullen anger, he could not take himself away.

Then, as he despaired, he remembered that Quay had said that she would come to the valley, and that she would be his wife. Quay was all powerful. He was omniscient, also. But though he could perhaps force the girl to marry Jim Fantom, even the great Quay could not make her love except where she chose to love.

Standing against the wall, miserable and uncertain, he regarded her as she dexterously wiped the tops of the biscuits with butter and then replaced the pan in the oven. What had brought her here, he wondered profoundly. What mighty lever of temptation had the great Jonathan Quay used upon her to lead her to his Happy Valley and place her in this house? She had been placed there for him! Out of Quay's own mouth he had heard the thing. The joy of that thought made his heart as light as a floating leaf; yet he dared not let his affection touch her with the weight of a word or of a finger's tip.

CHAPTER TWENTY SIX

"You'll excuse me, Mr. Fantom," she said over her shoulder, as she slid the pan of biscuits back into the oven. "You'll excuse me if I ain't got the time to listen to your apology, won't you? But I'd sure like to know what it's all about!"

She smiled at him in bright inquiry and then rose and went to the sink, where she washed some green salad. He watched the water flying from the crisp sprays of green and dissolving as diamond powder in the strong shaft of the sunlight; until it almost seemed that not water but mists of fire flew upward from her hands.

He, with enchanted eyes, watched, and had faith in miracles.

"You were goin' to say something, a minute ago," said she. "I hope I ain't been interruptin' you, too much."

"Ah," said The Phantom, "the fact is, I ain't a very slick talker, you see!"

"Well," said she, "you're too big to talk fast. It's allays the little dogs that start yappin' and waggin' their tails because they like their own music so much."

He chuckled a little. It was forced and rather shaky mirth that he managed to produce, and the girl turned fully about and looked him over.

"You laugh like you were sick," said she.

"Sick?" he murmured.

"Yeah. Sick in the stomach, or something."

"I'm not. I'm all right," said he.

He went on desperately:

"About apologizing, I meant, for having, er — laid hands on you the way that I did, and —"

"What hands?" said she. "Oh, I see what you mean. Why, that was nothing. My brother, Billy, has hugged me a lot harder than that. All you did was put a smudge on my sleeve, but you didn't break no bones. You'd oughta wash your hands before the next time you hug a girl. That's all, Mr. Fantom."

He looked earnestly at her and moistened his lips with the tip of his tongue, but she kept her facial expression entirely grave.

"Look here —" he broke out.

She said idly:

"Look at what? Heavens, the roast!"

She fled to the oven and jerking the door of it open, presently she had the lid off a roasting pan. Steam gushed out past her and the rich aroma of the cooking, browning meat dwelt about the room.

Her head tipped critically aside, she studied the roast for a moment, and then basted it thoroughly.

"That's a roast," said Jim Fantom intelligently.

"You bet you guessed right," she answered, without smiling. "That ain't no chicken stew! It never crowed when it was wearin' feet and hair."

She recovered the roast.

207

"I dunno that it browns as much under one of these lids, but it's tenderer."

"Ay," said he. "I'll bet it's tenderer."

"But sometimes these basters make a roast soggy."

"Yeah," said he. "I bet they do, all right."

She looked critically at him.

"Did you ever see a bastin' lid like that in all your born days?"

"No," said he.

She laughed, a real peal of merriment.

"All right," said Fantom. "I knew that was the only way that I ever could make you laugh. *At* me, I mean, instead of with me. But I don't care if you make a fool of me, Jo."

"I couldn't make a fool of you, Mr. Fantom," said she. "A great big important man, like you!"

Fantom flushed.

"All right," said he. "Go ahead and plaster me. I guess I got it comin'."

"I'm not tryin' to be mean," said she.

"Sure you ain't," he agreed. "It jus' comes nacheral to you, eh?"

His face was very red, but he laughed a little.

"There I go again," said he. "Sayin' the wrong thing, every time. I dunno what's the matter with me."

"The kitchen's pretty hot," said she.

"Is that a way of suggestin' that I go out into the fresh air?" he asked her.

"Not a bit," she answered. "Sit down and make yourself at home."

She carried a table cloth into the next room and he heard the clink of knives and forks as she laid them out. Through the doorway he saw that two places were arranged. Who would sit at the second one?

His bewilderment grew greater and greater while he watched the flash of her hands as she laid out the dishes with rapid dexterity. She looked up, and her eyes met his, with a smile.

"Jo," he said, inspired by the smile, "will you tell me what it's all about?"

"What, Mr. Fantom?"

"And why d'you have to be misterin' me so much?"

"I won't, then, Mr. Fantom," said she.

"All right," said he. "You're gunna keep it up?"

"Well," she answered, as she came toward the kitchen door, "who's little Jo Dolan to be talkin' familiar to a famous man like you, Mr. Fantom?"

"Famous?" he said, suddenly frowning.

She slipped past him.

"Famous, sure," said she.

"Famous for robbin' a stage, you mean! Well, I'll be goin' along. Only —"

He paused.

There was something to be done, or said. There was some word which, like a key, would open the door of his understanding.

"Look at what it meant to me," she suggested. "I mean, somebody that had done so much —"

"And been so long in jail. Is that it?"

"Well, a jail's a good, quiet place. Folks say that's where you got such a thoughtful look, Mr. Fantom."

"I'll be goin' along," he repeated, and got as far as the outer door.

Then he turned once more. Her back was toward him, as she laid out the salad on two plates, taking the bits of it daintily in her pink finger tips.

"Would you mind tellin' me," he burst out, "how you come to be here? Would you mind sayin' it again?"

"Why, Mr. Quay brought me up here," said she.

"And what made you want to come?"

She turned sufficiently far for him to see the curve of her cheek; and she rested a thoughtful finger against her chin.

"Well, a girl has to get married some time, Mr. Fantom. I guess you'd admit that."

He felt that he was going mad, with love of her, with incredible desire to touch her, if it were only to shake hands and say farewell.

"Jo," he almost shouted at her, "will you tell me who that man is? Will you name him, Jo?"

"How can I name him?" she said. "It's all in Mr. Quay's hands! He's old enough to pick and choose, I guess."

He gasped.

"Maybe he would wanta marry me himself, d'you think?"

"That old — my God, I'm gunna go crazy!" he panted. "Will you turn around and look at me?"

"As soon as I get this salad fixed."

She actually turned her back on him again.

"What did he say to make you come up here?"

"Well, he pointed out that I wouldn't be gettin' any younger from now on."

"You bein' pretty near out of your teens already, I guess," said Fantom with a fierce irony.

"I'm pretty near twenty-one," said she, "if you wanta know, young man!"

"Ha!" said he. "You was afraid of gettin' to be an old maid, maybe?"

"Well," said she, "you never can tell. I'm more'n two thirds of the way to thirty. Maybe I'll get fat."

She looked down at her arm, holding it out for judicial consideration, and moving her hand with a graceful flexure. A dimple appeared at the elbow, flickering out and in.

"Jo!" he cried.

"Well?"

"Will you stop it?"

"Stop what?" she asked him, and, opening the oven door, took out a pan of biscuits, marvelously browned.

"Stop drivin' me crazy!"

"Well, I wouldn't want to bother you that much," said she. "I'm afraid that oven heats a little uneven."

"Oh, damn the oven," said Jim Fantom. "I mean, I wanta ask you —"

"You see how much browner they are at that end of the pan?"

"Jo, will you for God's sake tell me who's gunna be here for lunch with you?"

"Why," she said, "I don't know. Have you invited anybody else?"

"Me?" said Jim Fantom. "Invited? Me invited somebody else?"

He drew toward her. The look of a sleepwalker was in his eyes.

She turned past him toward the sink, saying in a matter-of-fact voice:

"You better wash your hands, unless they're a lot cleaner than they were early this morning! Before you come to the table, I mean. There's some hot water in the steam-kettle at the back of the stove, there. You better take the yellow soap, here. It's good for gettin' the grease off the skin."

He made an impatient gesture. But still, obediently, he took the soap, got the wash basin, and poured some steaming water into it. He worked up a tremendous suds, and scoured his fingers furiously.

"Jo," he thundered at her suddenly, turning with soapy water and bubbles streaming from his wet hands.

"Yes!" she cried, starting violently.

She shrank against the wall as though she, who had been so carelessly gay and so insolently self-possessed all this time, had now been broken down with sudden alarm.

212

"Jo," he announced, as loudly and fiercely as before, "the fact is that Quay sent you up here because you'd promised to marry *me!*"

CHAPTER TWENTY SEVEN

She appeared as though she would shrink through the wall; she turned pale; he dreaded and wondered at the change in her, and yet he loved her for it.

"Answer me!" called Fantom, approaching her with a slow stride. "He sent you up here because you'd promised to marry me!"

"I couldn't remember little details," said the girl. "I wouldn't think that it was you, Mr. Fantom —"

"Ha," said he, "you may 'mister' me and mock me as much as you like, but I'm guessin' at something, right now!" He stretched out his arms to her. He was close, now, and she was shrinking away, straining back her head as a frightened horse strains it back in fear of punishment. Yet she managed to laugh.

"Look at yourself, Jim Fantom," said she. "In another minute you'll be spoilin' this dress with those wet hands of yours! Go be a man, will you now? And dry your hands, Jim, like a good boy!"

He hung over her. She was tense with fear, yet there was a smile somewhere in her eyes.

"Please, Jim," said she.

He turned on his heel and crossed the room to where a towel hung on a roller. It was glazed with newness, that towel, and the water came off slowly. But he was in no haste, now. His eyes followed her, adored her, rushed upon her, then shrank away in awe. His heart beat so thunderously, now, that he felt the pulse, like a finger, tapping at his lips.

She was busy taking out the roast, uncovering it, heating a platter with hot water, drying it, then putting the roast upon it. All about the edge she put garnishings of green things, then stood back to criticize as Fantom came upon her, again.

"Jo!" said he. She turned with a jerk, as pale as before, her lips parted, her breath panting.

"Oh, will you stop these charges, Mr. Fantom?" said she.

"Go on with your misterin'," said he. "Much good may it do you! Because I'm gunna have you. D'you see? Have you and hold you and keep you here in the Happy Valley forever!"

"You're all talk," said she. "An' the roast is gettin' cold."

"Aw, Jo," said he. "Be kind, will you? And be honest! Are you afraid of me?"

"Why should I be afraid?" she asked him. "I wouldn't be. And I wouldn't run a step from before you, Mr. Fantom."

She looked at a dainty finger and deliberately licked from it a drop of gravy, then with a forced insolence, stared straight at Fantom's face. But her glance wavered; she shrank as he came closer.

"You said that you wouldn't be runnin' away

from me," he taunted her. "Look at you now, though!"

"I'm gettin' the roast," said she.

"Look at me!" said he. "I'm gunna have you look at me, Jo."

She raised her eyes, but they flickered away again.

"You're not so pretty that a girl would have to be lookin' at you all the time," she explained.

"Jo," said he, "my heart is ragin' and achin' to have you close to me and to tell you that I love you!"

He could see the word strike her, with a physical impact. But she said:

"It's a likely thing, after seein' me once in the evening."

"As true," said he, "as God made me. I want to tell you —"

"You can stand off and tell me, then," said she. "Do you have to have your hands full before you can talk?"

"You can speak plenty of sharp words," said he, "but can you look me in the eye when you say them? Tell me that, now!"

Once more she tried to lift her glance, and once more it was overburdened and shrank from him.

Yet she did not retreat; she merely raised a hand and let it rest lightly against his breast. This was her one defense. He trembled from head to foot at her touch.

"I'm mighty busy — an' everything is gettin'

cold. Will you go sit down to have your lunch, Jim?"

"I've gotta talk a minute."

"Well, finish up your talk, then. Wouldn't you of made a lawyer though, the way that you carry on!"

He moved an inch closer. There was no greater pressure from the hand to keep him away, but he saw a tremor in her, as though a wind had touched her lightly.

"You never would of come here, if it hadn't been that you cared a little about me, Jo!"

"Wouldn't I?" said she. "I'm a practical-minded girl, you'd better know. The nice little cabin is what I came for."

"And the husband you got didn't make any difference?"

"Of course not. You take men, they're all about alike, I'd guess. There's nothing to choose, much."

"So long as you choose me, what do I care for your talk?" said Fantom joyously.

His arms hovered about her, and at that, she caught her breath and shrank smaller, though she would not give back.

"Don't be maulin' me, now," said she.

"Ah, Jo, will you care so much if I touch you?"

"I'm not a puppy or a calf that needs to be patted," she told him. "I can listen to what you have to say, Mr. Fantom."

"I want only to kiss you, Jo. Is there a great harm in that?"

"Why would you be philanderin' around?" she asked him. "We're not married yet, you know!"

"Is a girl to be married before she's ever kissed?" said he.

And he watched the rapid rise and fall of her breast, and felt the quivering of the hand that touched him.

"Ah, Jim," she murmured at last, "it's a mighty long way from my home and my folks to here! I'm all alone, d'you see?"

"Say no to me, then," said he, "an' I won't touch your bright hair, darling" — he touched it as he spoke, with a shaking hand — "or so much as the hem of your dress."

"Well, there would be no harm, perhaps, if you kissed me —"

She raised her face to him and it was warm and bright with tenderness; she held aside the hand that had kept him away.

"Once every day if you kissed me — until we're married, Jim."

"Only once, d'you mean?"

She tried to laugh, but the sound fluttered musically and faded.

"I've got housework to do, you idle man," said she.

"But the whole long day, from the mornin' to the middle mornin', and from that to noon, an' from that to the middle of the afternoon, where the sun sticks for whole hours and doesn't move in the sky, an' from that to the evenin', and from the evenin' to the night. Then all the long night until the dawn begins to come up — why, only to touch you once in all of that time?"

"It's best," said she.

"Do you fear me, Jo?"

"I wouldn't have you think lightly of me, even if I've come up here like something bought. But I won't be standin' here for hours and hours, holdin' out my hands to you. My shoulders are achin' now!"

He sighed, with sorrow, with impatience, with burning joy.

"You can put down your hands, then. If there's only one time in the day, I'll wait for it."

"And have me livin' in fear of your Injun charges, all the day long?"

She turned from him and picked up the platter of the roast but instantly put it down again.

"I guess," she said faintly, "that you'd better carry the things in to the table. I seem a little shaky."

"Because of me botherin'!" he cried in a passion of remorse.

"We had to talk," she said. "But I sort of dreaded it. And after I let you go away this mornin', I wondered when you'd come back. Well, it's over, now!"

She went to the door and leaned against the side of it, while Jim Fantom obediently carried in the dishes to the table. Then he went to her at the door and stood there a moment beside her, frightened by her pallor and the distance in her eyes.

"Are you no better?" he asked her.

"Oh. I'm better," she said.

"Would you come on in, then, and have lunch, Jo?"

"I'll be comin' in a minute."

"Are you grievin' about something?"

"No, I guess not."

"You look as though you were seein' things over the hills and far away."

"Well, it don't matter."

He took her hand. It was soft and small, and strangely cool.

"You'd best come in," said he. "You sort of scare me, standin' here lookin' at the other end of the world."

"Ah, but I've been terrible scared myself!" she whispered. "I've been so scared that I had to sing, to keep my heart up." She laughed, shakily. "I'll be all right. I'll go in with you now, Jim."

They went in. But at the door of the dining room her hand pulled back in his.

"Jo, Jo," said he, "you look like cryin'!"

"I won't, though," said she.

"Ah, but you're not happy. There's something that's forced you into this. It's Quay. He's got some hold on you, or on your family — you —"

"D'you think he's a wizard, Jim?"

"Ay, he's done something to you!"

"He has," said the girl. "By sayin' your name over and over to me. That's how he put the spell on me!"

"Ah, dear," said he, "will you tell me, then,

why you're so sad just now?"

"Well, I've been lookin' at everything and sayin' good-by to it. All the faces I've been seein'; all the voices I've been hearin'. They'll never seem or sound the same to me again. I belong to you. But it's only now and then that I'll look over my shoulder. The rest of the time, my life'll be yours. But will you think that I'm a light thing or a cheap thing, because I loved you all at once?"

"Do I think light and cheap of myself, for lovin' you the same way?"

She turned to him suddenly and drew down his face between both her hands, and kissed him; but he remained half stern, half sad, for he was enlarging his strength and bracing himself against the future. He had a sense of guilt, as though he had stolen this unbelievable treasure, but he swore that he would give it good care all the days of his life.

CHAPTER TWENTY EIGHT

The sun had marched well west before Fantom left the house and started for the team. He was half grave and half laughing, like a child. He even was partly blinded, on this day of days, and stumbled and almost fell over a root that twisted up from the ground before him.

Therefore, he was only aware as in a dream of a figure that appeared on his right hand, and actually rubbed his eyes as he turned and stared again.

It was the ugly white face of the hunchback, who leaned one hand against the trunk of a tree and regarded Fantom with a perfect nonchalance. The latter, utterly amazed, bewildered, instinctively reached for a gun. His mind cleared as it glided brightly into his hand.

"Well, well," said the hunchback, "do I frighten you into pulling a gun on me?"

And he smiled at Fantom. Even at that distance, the boy was aware of the glazed, fish-eyes of the little man. His face was the color of a fungus or one of those pale plants that grow in the dark heart of a forest, or in the damp of a cave.

"I missed you in the woods, stranger," said Fantom. "I'm glad that I've come up with you again here in the valley. You won't mind comin' along with me."

He approached aggressively as he said this.

However, the hunchback shook his head without the slightest perturbation.

"You won't do it," said he. "You're not the kind that does a good turn and then takes it back."

"You think," said Fantom, "that I won't bring you on to the house?"

"For Louis Kendal? No, you won't do that. You wouldn't care to stand by and see him swallow me alive."

Fantom frowned at him.

"You're sure of yourself, and me, too!" said he. "But the fact is that I was sent to get you, and you'll have to come with me."

Said the cripple:

"I don't think that I'm wrong in you. There's more manhood and honesty in you than you think. Why, my boy, it would have been easy enough for me to stay behind the trees while you went by."

Fantom paused, close to the other.

"It's true," he said. "I never would have seen you. Then why did you show yourself? Do you think, man, that I won't keep my promise to the people that I work for?"

"That's what they count on," said the hunchback. "Honor, honor, honor! They work on that. They turn it into hard cash by the hundreds of thousands of dollars. Your honor! They can be sure of that. They *are* sure of it. They plan on it, and scheme for it. *Your* honor, and *their* crookedness, makes a safe team! They'll cover a long mile with you in the harness and their crooked whips in the air above you!"

Fantom stared at him.

"You talk," said he, "as though you knew everything about everyone here in the valley."

"Isn't that possible? However, I don't know about them all. I don't know much about the poor dupes who are trying to work out their lives in a new way, here. But I know the brains at the top. I know the brains at the top!"

He laughed, without making a sound, and the ugliness of his face during this silent laughter was a thing to wonder at!

"Stranger," said Fantom, "I dunno that I'm right to stand here and let you talk!"

"You will, though," answered the other with perfect calm. "Not maybe for yourself, but because of the girl in the cabin, yonder."

Fantom stiffened a little.

The hunchback nodded, and went on:

"I've been watching her for some time. I watched the two of you, in fact."

"Hello! You mean that you came up to the house and looked in?"

The hunchback studied the face of the boy and nodded. Then he broke into his usual hideous and soundless laughter.

"I looked in," he said.

He wrung his hands together almost as though in pain, yet Fantom could tell that the little man was enjoying himself immensely.

"Love!" said the hunchback. "Love! Ha, ha, ha!"

This time his laughter was aloud, and it sounded like the cawing of a crow, harsh and ominous.

"She loves him, and he loves her. They live in each other. They cannot look at one another without blushing. They smile and simper and stare at the floor. Their flesh shakes; they are in pain. Oh, love, I know all about you, I know all about you! Baby food, baby food. Food for babies — and angels, not for men with broken backs, and dangling long arms like the arms of a monkey, and a hideous face. Not for me, but I know about it. However, you will run around the world ten times, and never find another like her. You agree with that, I suppose?"

Fantom was silent, not knowing how much mockery was mixed with this praise.

"And she," said the hunchback, "will travel ten times around the world before she finds another Jim Fantom — brave, simple, full of trust, worthy of trust. Some people get to heaven by the work of the left hand. This may save even Quay and send him there — this little work of his in bringing the girl to you."

He struck his lank, pale hands together and nodded, his eyes closed, obviously filled with satisfaction because of his thought.

"But think of her courage, her great heart, her beautiful spirit! One glance in the twilight. She who has had men around her like the bees around honey. One glance. A moment of talk. And she knows the man who is meant for her! Well, this thing makes hard hearts turn soft, opens the minds of cynics, seats God a little firmer on his throne. Yes, makes him an actuality. Tush! She is beautiful, and she is good. I wish you joy out of the bottom of my heart."

"Thanks," said Fantom doubtfully. "*Even* Quay, did you say?"

"Even the good Quay, the generous, gentle, thoughtful, wise, benevolent philosopher, Quay. Yes, even Quay, I said. Beside him, Louis Kendal is an angel of grace! Do you hear me? An angel of grace!"

He said it angrily, and scowled at the boy.

"I've heard enough from you," said Fantom firmly. "It's true that I can't take advantage of you when you gave yourself up to me. But I'll have no slander. Quay's been a father to me!"

"Ay, a father," said the other. "That's what he is. A father, and starts his children for hell! Ah, well, my lad, I won't feed you with slander, then. Keep your faith. Keep your faith, and your love, until your eyes are opened, and everything is lost — everything lost to you! The girl, the hope, everything gone!"

He waved his lank hands. Then he peered at the startled face of Fantom.

"You know for yourself," said the boy, "that your life ain't worth a penny, if you're found here in the valley?"

"I know it," said the hunchback. "I know it,

and I take my chance. Kendal the devil, Quay the emperor, and their myrmidons. I take my chance against them all. Courage, you see, can be locked up even in a little twisted body like mine. Courage, and hope, as well. Hope to find them, to talk to them. Only to talk."

"Without a gun?" asked the boy.

"Only a gun to keep their hands in the air and their ears open. That's all. No danger to them, my lad. Otherwise, I know that at least you'd take me out of the valley. Ay, but talk! What harm can I do them with a little conversation, spoken softly?"

He leered at Fantom.

"God knows what I should do," said the boy, doubtfully.

"God's not in the valley, except over that cabin, yonder," said the hunchback. "Ay, maybe there are shadowings of him in other houses around here. But little of God in the Happy Valley, Jim Fantom. There's Quay, instead. Quay, and his minister of evil. His Kendal!"

He waved toward the road.

"Go on with your team. Keep your eyes wide and your head clear. There'll be need of thinking, before you're done with your life here."

Fantom paused.

Never had he been more at a halt than he was at this moment, for he could not see where his duty lay.

To take this man by force and to bring him to

Louis Kendal according to order was now, he was sure, impossible. His soul revolted at the thought of taking advantage of a man who voluntarily had put himself in his hands. Moreover, it seemed impossible that the cripple could actually be dangerous to such a man as Louis Kendal, though he knew that that human monster dreaded the little man. He went back a pace and hesitated again.

"Go on," said the hunchback. "Hurry, hurry! Get through with your day's work. Come back to see her again in the evening. And ask Quay to bring the minister."

He tipped back his ugly face and laughed again.

"Ask Quay to bring the minister. Listen to his answer."

He began to laugh once more.

But this spectacle was so horrible to the boy that he suddenly turned his back, and without a word went on to where the team was tethered.

They were still tame. They tossed their heads up and danced a little, to be sure, but the instant that his hands were on the reins and the shadow of the whip dangled above them, they went off down the road at an easy trot, the bits light in their mouths.

And Jim Fantom could let his puzzled thoughts fly back to the girl, and to the hunchback. It seemed to him that she was like brightest sunlight, after which there comes the darkest shadow. The cripple was the shadow!

On Quay and on Kendal he had thrown his accusations, with such a surety that, in spite of all his loyalty, in spite of the gratitude which was bubbling up from his heart like water from a well, Fantom felt that there must be something in the words of the little man.

Yet he was happy. It was as though his mind were a slate, covered with joyous poetry. There was no room for more than scrawlings on the margin; and, no matter how ominous these might be, he would not heed them.

He saw the shadows of the trees jerked past him down the road. A blue jay darted through the air, a dazzling flash of color on some errand of mischief, and then he came out on the avenue to Quay's house. He knew that there was joy behind him; he guessed that there was danger before; but he could not keep the smile from his lips.

CHAPTER TWENTY NINE

He drove the span of buckskins with a certain pride up the driveway toward the big house of Quay, and as he came closer, saw something to the left, among the trees, that made him rein in his span and send them on at a soft walk.

It was Rhiner, the ex-murderer, the peaceful cottager of the Happy Valley, now, who was talking with Kendal among the woods. Rhiner was arguing closely. His horse was behind him, the reins over the crook of his right arm, and so violent were his gestures that the reins jumped and flung about in the air and the horse stood back with flattened ears, plainly in terror.

Kendal listened, half turned away, his head bowed with thought. Now and then he nodded. Now and again he raised a hand as though to protest against needless violence in the speech of the other. Finally he struck one hand through the air and shook his head in flat denial.

Rhiner recoiled as one amazed and incredulous. He started forward as if to repeat his argument, but was met with a similar gesture of definite refusal. At this, there was an appearance for a moment as though the ex-criminal would snatch out a weapon; but he changed his mind, threw himself onto his horse, and rode furiously away. Once or twice he reappeared through gaps in the trees, going at reckless speed. Then he was lost in the distance of the woods.

It sent Fantom on in gloomy thought; it was another conclusive proof that strange things went on in the Happy Valley. All its happiness might be of no more substantial stuff than the bright colors that are reflected in a bubble. The very face of lovely Jo Dolan might be to him no more than what dreams are made of!

This made his fingers slow and stiff upon the harness; his head and glance were so downward that he did not notice the approaching of Kendal until the strange voice of that man spoke at his back.

"Fantom!"

He whirled about and saw the long, pale face of the other sneering at him.

"I sent you out on an errand, Fantom," said he. "I didn't send you out to spend half the day!"

Fantom turned back to his unharnessing.

"D'you hear me?" barked Kendal.

"You needn't bawl at me like a calf," said Fantom. "The fact is that I hear you, but what you say don't mean anything to me, Kendal!"

He shuddered slightly as he said this. It was far from true!

"Means nothing, eh?" echoed Kendal.

"Nothin' at all! You can give me orders. Quay's handed you the right to do that. But as for houndin' me, they ain't a man in the world that I'd take that from, Kendal!"

He felt the other come up to him, though there

was no sound. The breathing of Kendal was almost on his neck as the other answered:

"We tried to give you your chance, young feller, and you wouldn't take it. I'll give you one more day to find out for yourself that the other dogs in this valley stops howling when I begin to bark! After that —"

He was gone, silently, at first; and only in the near distance did Fantom hear the trailing footfall and the jingling of the spurs begin.

The instant the danger was gone, he was sick at heart, for he realized that he had done a useless thing, which would only imperil his happiness, and the happiness of the girl he loved. Her very existence, perhaps, was involved, and more and more insistently the first image returned to him — the Happy Valley was a beautiful bubble, and when it dissolved, at some touch of tragic reality, the girl would disappear and all the rest, and leave him more lonely than death itself in the midst of the mountains.

A snarling order from Kendal, in the distance, told him to report to the straw boss, Hendricks, for work, and he willingly did so, after the team had been put up. From Hendricks, he received orders to ride fence in the river bottom, and there all the afternoon he worked up and down the line, tightening the loosened barbed wire, replacing fallen staples, and wondering, like all line-riders, at the slowness with which the time passed.

He was drawn in two ways. From the hillsides

along which he rode, he could see the bending of the lower river between its wooded banks; he could see the western windows of the cottages flash golden bright as the sun drew toward the horizon; he could see the lake take on color and deep in its arms the white clouds turn to fire. On the other hand were the uplands, with their spotting of cattle, and white mists of sheep far away.

Never had the valley seemed to him so beautiful; yet the sense of dread increased in him momently, and as the lower cañon and gorges which split the sides of the mountains filled with blue, the heart of the boy fell lower still. It was as though the coming of the night were bringing a danger with its shadows, welling up out of the ground.

Before sundown, he had used his last staple, and hurried back across the fields to the house of Quay; and Quay himself he found walking up and down before the stable, smoking a pipe and looking contentedly down across the darkening crimsons, blues, and greens of his valley.

Quay looked like the commonest laborer. He wore riding breeches of a cheap, heavy corduroy, gathered into the tops of high boots which laced up the front almost to the knees. He had on a canvas shooting coat that was badly stained with oil in several places and was ragged at the elbows. A flannel shirt, open at the throat, and a storm-battered and stained felt hat completed his outfit. Yet the eye of the boy dwelt upon this uncouth attire in kindly fashion. It brought the rich man closer to him. It made the heart of Quay seem more open to inspection, revealing kindness, deep sympathy with less rich and lucky men.

Indeed, it would have been an instinctive thing for the boy to snatch off his hat as he went into the presence of the older man. As it was, he approached him slowly and waited for Quay to speak, which he did with the kindest of smiles.

"You're reconciled with Chip Lander and your own fate, I hope," said he.

Said Fantom:

"You see how it is, Mr. Quay. I remembered your promise to bring her up here. But somehow it didn't seem that even you could do a thing like that. And the idea of losin' her was pretty hard to bear."

"I didn't bring her up," said Quay gently. "She came, herself. She used her own arts of persuasion. I was merely the agent who opened the door and showed her a way to travel. You yourself brought her here, my lad. Thank yourself for it. Yourself, and youth, youth, youth! That is the gold which buys women. Good luck to the pair of you!"

"Whatever luck we'll have is your giving!" said the boy. "Her — an' a house — an' everything fixed so fine in it — Mr. Quay, I'd ride to hell and back for you!"

Jonathan Quay lifted his big, bearded head, at this, and stared at the boy with a keen appreciation.

"I think you mean that," he said at last.

"I mean it. Aw, I know that it sounds loud and useless, but the time may come when something happens, and you can use me!"

Quay did not answer at once, merely remaining at a stand, while he looked across his valley, but at last he replied quietly:

"You see that I've taken dynamite and mixed in a little more clay with it. But if it should ever take fire, the Happy Valley might burn with a very bright flame, Jim!"

Fantom did not answer. He stared earnestly into the face of the other, yearning for a fuller answer, but Quay merely said:

"I trust that the time never will come, but if it should, I don't know of another man in the place that I could be so sure of — not one, so much as Jim Fantom!"

"You've saved and made 'em all," insisted Jim. "They'd all die for you, Mr. Quay!"

"Honest people and loyal people see honesty and loyalty in others," said Quay. "It warms my heart to hear you, Jim. Hello, there's the supper gong — if you're dining at home?"

The boy laughed, and instantly he was gone across the fields for the cottage in the woods. But as he went, the hope of seeing the girl could not altogether illumine his heart. There was more than that, a strongly possessing shadow which had been gathered about him all the afternoon, since the appearance of the hunchback. The talk with Kendal, the overlooking of the interview between Rhiner and Kendal, the interview with Quay himself had not reassured him.

Moreover, when a man has any strong cause for happiness, he cannot help but feel that Fate may easily be tempted.

It seemed to the boy that whatever power there is that watches men's lives must now be watching and envying him. As a boy watches a line of hurrying ants, and deliberately crushes the one that bears the heaviest seed, so it seemed to him that the Divine Watcher might now be looking down and ready to destroy him.

Or the girl! It might be she that would be taken away from him!

Suddenly he threw back his shoulders and laughed at himself for a foolishly impressionable lack-wit.

This was no fairy place, no valley taken from a book of myth or legend, but a real and living thing. The rocks and the trees were real, the people in the Happy Valley no different from others!

So he spoke to himself, but suddenly found himself sprinting ahead at full speed; and, as he labored, he found that fear had leaped up in his throat and was driving him on faster and faster. A shadow leaped behind him, a shadow fled before; madness whirled through his brain; his face ran wet with cold perspiration. And so he came suddenly upon the sight of the cabin!

It was all at peace. The rosy evening made color in the sky, but already a lamp had been lighted and glimmered like a bright yellow eye through the kitchen window; from the chimney, a column of wood smoke was rising, crystal white as it streaked across the trees, and then dyed with rose as it lifted higher. There was no wind. Up to heaven arose that smoke, like the smoke from a sacrificial fire. And Fantom laughed softly to himself.

He slipped to the living-room window, and, peering through, he saw the table laid for two, the fire fluttering on the hearth beyond, and a big white rug made of the skin of a mountain sheep, looking, on the fire-lit floor, like a cloud in the sky. He went back to the kitchen. She was not there!

"Jo!" he called.

She was hiding from him, no doubt, and would jump out, to laugh at him.

"Jo!" he shouted.

He got no answer, and the smile became a fixed grimace upon his lips.

Suddenly he was running from place to place, opening closets, growing cold at heart and desperate.

He made sure. She was not in the house, so he dashed outdoors and cried furiously:

"Jo! Jo!"

He cupped his hands, and cried again. Then he started to run toward the trees, but the black sight of the shadows beneath them told him that it was useless to search for her by this light.

He turned toward the house again, and now

the sight of the rising smoke, already dwindling as the wood burned out in the stove, and the increasing glimmer of the lamp from the kitchen, were to Fantom like the sight of a ghost.

He stood for a long time, wavering, and then a light voice called from the side of the clearing. Called his name! He ran toward her stumbling, with his arms outflung.

She was alight with a triumph, and held toward him a dripping, shimmering mass of pale green.

"Look what I've found! Water cress!" said she.

He took her into his arms.

"I thought you were gone!" he groaned.

"You're spoiling the cress," she complained, "and the fire's dyin'. We'll have to hurry in. Why, Jim, where would I go? Silly dear!"

She slipped from him and hurried away.

CHAPTER THIRTY

When they reached the house, he followed her aimlessly from place to place as she finished the preparations for supper.

"To go out at this time of night!" said he, "out alone — into the woods, when they're darkenin'! What a way to do, Jo!"

She turned at him, knocking the thrusting steam that spouted from the kettle into a silver mist that surrounded her.

"What could hurt me? The woods are just the same, night and day."

"Things go out huntin' in the end of the day and the start of it," he warned her soberly. "It sure scared me, Jo, not findin' you anywhere. It sure scared me. It was pretty bad. And you gladder of water cress you'd find, than findin' me."

She laughed as she turned back to the stove.

"You talk like a baby," said she.

"Maybe I'm kind of that way," he admitted. "I don't feel so big and strong. You ain't mad at me, Jo?"

"You've broken the cress. Look at the stems of it, and look at the way it's bruised! But that's the way that men are. Heavy-handed."

He dwelt upon her fondly, and yet half sadly. For still the figure that had entered his mind that day remained, and all her beauty and her laughter and her busy ways were as illusions seen through the bright film of a bubble, perishable with it.

"I don't like the idea of you stayin' here all alone," he burst out suddenly. "Especially at night."

"I've got the owls for company," she assured him. "There's packs of owls tootin' out of the trees pretty near all night. They're pretty wise company!"

"I'll talk to Mr. Quay. He'll probably send me off after a minister right away. First thing in the mornin'."

She stepped back from the steam of the stove for a minute and looked thoughtfully at the ceiling.

"I dunno," she said.

"You dunno what?"

"There was a man here this afternoon that looked around."

"What's that got to do with anything? He wasn't — I mean, he didn't get fresh nor nothing, Jo?"

"Him? Oh, no. He just looked around a little."

"What looking sort of a man was it?"

"Oh, just a man."

"Jo, what on earth has that got to do with what we were talkin' about — fetchin' the minister, I mean?"

"He looked around a good deal," she said uneasily. "Well, I guess it was nothing."

"No, that's not what you guess."

"I shouldn't of mentioned it."

"Why not? You can mention anything to me, I guess. Now, you tell me!"

"No. It wasn't anything."

He rose and stalked to her. He stood behind her, threateningly.

"You better tell me, Jo." He took her by the shoulders and at that, she tipped back her head and smiled suddenly, close to his face.

"All right," said she. "I'll tell you, only there's nothing to tell. He was a longish sort of a man, with a longish sort of a pale face."

"Ugly?"

"Nothing you'd put your finger on. Not very pleasant, though."

"Kendal!"

"I dunno his name."

"Why was *he* around?" he asked fiercely. "Why — what did he mean by coming around?"

"He came from Mr. Quay, to see if everything was all right for me, here!"

She stirred a pot busily.

"You got another meanin' behind that," he accused. "He looked at *you* mostly."

"He looked at me once. I think that he may make trouble, Jim."

Fantom drew a breath. He was half choked with emotion. "You think that he'd stop Quay from bringin' the minister for us, Jo?"

"I don't know. But while I was startin' supper, tonight, all at once I was afraid to stay in the cabin. I ran out into the woods. It was gettin' dark when I came to a run of water with the cress floatin' at the edges of it, an' the sight of it ripplin' with the current gave me better nerves, somehow. So I came back. I'm sorry to tell you all of this. But it had to come out, somehow!"

"It's Kendal! It's always Kendal!" he burst out. "Everything would be heaven up here, except for him! But maybe he won't last forever. If I —"

"Hush," said she. "Not against him! Not against *that* man, dear! I'd rather see you fight the devil, bat wings an' sulphur cloud, an' all!"

Jim Fantom looked helplessly around him. He could not help but feel the difference which existed between himself and Kendal. It was a danger from which he would not shrink, and yet he dreaded facing it.

"Wait, wait," he heard the girl saying to him. "Wait for good luck. And perhaps I'm all wrong!"

But he knew that she was burdened by a dread of the future, for as they sat at the supper table, though she made herself chat cheerfully enough, yet, in the pauses of the talk, he could feel her eyes upon him, cherishing him with pity and with fear.

She followed him to the threshold when he said good night. There she stood half in lamplight and half in moonshine and clung to him suddenly, with a tremor. But though she shook with fear and sorrow, yet her voice she kept steady.

"It's hard to let go of you, Jim," said she. "Because I feel as though once you're past my finger tips, tonight, I never may touch you again. Be careful, be careful!"

He smiled at this fear and said:

"Only tell me how Kendal acted, and what he said!"

"Nothing but what I've told you. He stood here at the door and wanted to know what I lacked here. That was all. Only it was his eye and his long, ugly face; it sort of made me sick. I felt as though he could get anything that he wanted. If he wanted me, that would be an end of things! I'm sorry that I spoke about it. I shouldn't have said a word. There was no reason to say a word, I know!"

He began to feel the same way about it, but when he had said good night and reached the edge of the clearing, he turned and looked back with a sudden qualm to see her at the open door, still, half lost in the dimness of the light from within and the light from without.

Cold sweat leaped on his face at the thought that he might never hear her voice again, but then he mastered the foolish emotion and hurried on through the woods.

He got to the house and had come in through the kitchen door when there was a sudden rush of hoofs outside, and Kendal burst in. He went through the kitchen like a storm.

"Where's Quay?" he flung at the cook.

"Right there in the dinin' room, havin' a good-night cup of coffee," said the "doctor."

Kendal fairly flung himself into the dining room.

"He's come! I've seen him!" he said.

Jim Fantom heard the chair of Quay screech as it was shoved back.

"Be quiet!" said the master of the valley. "Come in here with me. You're dreaming a dream. He wouldn't dare!"

And they passed hastily into the adjoining room.

CHAPTER THIRTY ONE

The cook looked askance at the face of Fantom, which was in a brown study.

"There's a thing worth knowin'," said the cook. "You take a pair of 'em like Quay and Kendal, to be a-scared of one man's face, that's a face worth knowin', eh?"

"I guess it would be," said the boy, and went slowly on into the dining room, through the hall, and up toward his own room.

Climbing the stairs, he could hear Kendal and Quay in high dispute, the voice of Quay an indistinguishable murmur, kept low and deep; the voice of Kendal rang sharp and high, with that peculiar nasal clangor which distinguished it from all the other voices of men. One thing he repeated many times:

"He gets it, or he gets me! He gets it, or he gets me!"

Fantom listened, sick at heart. He could guess well enough that Kendal was referring to the hunchback, and the thought that that deformed little man could drive the terrible Kendal into a panic was so unhuman, so amazing, that he could not believe his ears. Quay, too, was very excited.

But Fantom went on before he heard any more. He had no desire to play the eavesdropper; and his conscience was tormenting him because he had not given to Quay and Kendal a full warning that the cripple was in the valley.

In his room he found Chip Lander already preparing for bed.

The youngster was admiring the beauty of a newly purchased pair of spoon-handled spurs.

"You look at 'em, old timer," said he. "The flash of them spurs is gunna drop in the eyes of the girls, Jim. They'll be follerin' after me. Girls is like sheep, Jim. It's better to fill their eyes than to fill their ears. They're curious as kittens. If you dangle a string they'll come and grab for it. If they see the flash of these here spurs, they'll make a dive for to see them closer."

"If you wore a bell under your chin, that might make 'em look at you, too," suggested Fantom.

"Jim, I'm gunna find one soon," said Chip Lander. "If I gotta dress myself up like a flag an' go streamin' through the town, I'm gunna find a wife. The sight of your girl, Jim, was enough to head me for a house and lot. The minute I seen her, I begun to think of kids squallin' and rollin' about, and of Christmas Eve, an' mornin' papers, an' darnin' needles, an' garden patches, an' pet calves, an' tame bears, an' forty mile to dances, an' church on Sundays. I begun to think of those things the minute that I clapped eyes on her, because she sure has a household look, Jim."

"Aw, shut up," said Jim Fantom. "Leave her be. The minute you show yourself in town, you'll get you a wife for your pretty face, Chip."

"Don't she take on terrible bad, bein' left over there alone?"

"She's a lion-tamer, Chip. She can sling a gun with both hands. Sundays and holidays, she's gunna teach me how to shoot."

"I like the way you lie," said the other. "You do it so doggone easy, and plumb graceful. What's the ruction downstairs between the old man and Kendal?"

"I dunno."

"Some day the snake'll swaller the watch dog," said the youngster. "You watch and see. We're all waitin' for it. We know that it'll happen, one of these days, and then the Happy Valley'll turn into a hell-hole, right enough!"

There was a light knock at the door; it was opened an inch from the outside.

"Are you there, Fantom?" asked the voice of Quay.

It was softly spoken, and yet it caused something to thrill through the heart of the boy. He knew that his time had come, at last!

"Yes," said he, and stepped out into the hallway.

Quay looked at him quietly for a second or two. Then he held out in the open palm of his hand a small key made of brass.

"Somewhere in Kendal's room," said he, "there's a key that resembles this one. Take this along as a pattern, if you like. The teeth won't be the same in the other, of course. But take this along and try to find the other. I've tried a hundred times, and failed!"

He took time enough to smile with great good nature. Then he added:

"If you can find the key, I'm saved, and the valley's saved. If the key's not found, I'm lost, and the valley's lost. If you get it — or if not — be down in the living room in ten minutes. That's about your time limit. At the end of that time, Kendal will probably go to his room and you won't want him to find you there!"

The simplicity with which this was spoken gave it redoubled significance, for Quay talked with as little haste, in as matter-of-fact a manner as though he were chatting about the weather.

Only, toward the end, there was a slight bristling of his beard, as though the muscles about his mouth were straining.

Fantom took the key without a word and nodded. Quay turned his back, going down the hallway, humming to himself, while Fantom went in the opposite direction.

His heart was heavy, and cold as ice. He would not have dreamed that he could fear any man as now he knew that he feared the great Louis Kendal, but he was aware that if he paused in the execution of this mission, he would lose all heart to continue with it. He had to force himself straight on, now, or else give up in an increasing funk!

So he fought his way forward — as truly fighting as ever a man who leaned against a blizzard and dug his heels into the slippery snow crust under foot.

He stopped only to tie a bandana around each foot. In this manner he stifled the possibility of the spurs jingling, while his footfall was deadened. When he went on again, he was rather startled by the ease with which he could move silently.

So he reached the door of Kendal's room, at the southern end of the passage. It was locked! He turned back with a sigh of relief, but in a few paces he checked himself and set his jaw.

His life had been saved by Quay, and it was not in this easy manner that Quay expected him to give up this undertaking. Besides, if what Quay said was true, the fate of the entire valley depended upon the affair of the key. And Jo Dolan was in the valley, yonder in her cabin, now, washing the last of the dishes, glad of the crackling of the fire in the stove, listening dismally to the forest sounds outside. For all her courage, her heart was fluttering, and she thought of him as of a being in another world.

So he turned back again up the narrow hall, and tried the door at the right of Kendal's room. It too was locked, but that to the left gave under his hand with a faint groan. He entered and found an unoccupied chamber, cold and damp, the wind making a faint whistling sound as it entered through chinks around the window. He pushed the window open and leaned out.

From the watering trough, someone was

leading two horses back to the barn, whose door yawned wide, bright with the light of a lantern inside. There was no other thing in sight.

The window of Kendal's room was not far to his right, and it was possible to get to it by working along a narrow ledge that jutted beneath the window line, setting back the second story a few inches inside the lower one.

He slipped out at once, based his toes upon that narrow ledge, and took a finger hold upon the rough, curving surfaces of the logs. In this manner he came to the window of Kendal and looked about and beneath him.

A voice sounded loudly from the barn, where a man was cursing a horse, but nothing was in sight. So he tried the window; it was locked like the door!

However, window locks are rarely strong. He heaved with all his might, and, at the second pressure, with a slight sound of splintering wood, the lock broke loose. The sash rose sputtering from side to side noisily, in spite of the slowness with which he raised it. Yet it soon was wide open, and Fantom drew himself rapidly up and through the window.

Inside, he lighted a match, and from the match ignited a small lamp that stood on the table at the head of the bed.

Here in haste he remembered that the lighted square of the window could be seen from the outside, and he went back to draw the heavy shutters together. Next followed the survey of the room itself, as the flame strengthened in the throat of the lamp's chimney and threw a stronger light.

Something fluttered shoulder high, beside him. He turned with a gasp and saw a golden canary spreading its wings with a whir as it darted from side to side of its cage; then it dropped to a corner and lay there with wings outspread, as though exhausted by fear. He could see the pulse of the breast feathers as its heart fluttered in terror.

Somehow the sight of the poor creature's terror increased his own fear, until he found himself standing with gripped hands, and shortened breath as he stared around the room.

It was not such decoration as one would expect in a ranch house. To be sure the bed was a mere cot, covered with cheap blankets, and there was a still cheaper washstand in the corner, with a half-emptied bucket of water beside it and a granite basin on the top. But everywhere the walls were covered with weapons of all sorts.

At one end was a fan-shaped cluster of spears, all from Africa, and every one of a different pattern. Handbeaten, and shaped according to natural models, some of the spearblades were broader than the palm and thumb of a man's hand, thin-edged, useful to split an enemy's body or to strike with, as an ax, perhaps. They had the shape of a leaf, and, like a leaf, they were strengthened by a central stem, tapered from base to point. These were not of one exact pattern but varied as the leaves of trees vary. Intermingled among them were stabbing lances, with heads narrow as bayonets and sinister as rapiers; there were short-handled throwing spears with barbed points and various freakish patterns. Yet the fascinated eye of the boy touched upon each of these and dwelt an instant, as though from every one he learned something of the character and the inmost being of the man whose room he had invaded.

There were knives and swords around the rest of the wall, krises, Ghurka knives, stilettos that looked hardly more than needles on the wall, great head-swords from the East Indies, ceremonial weapons from India and Burma, straight, stiff-bladed poniards, delicate scimitars, curved like the golden disk of the new moon, and strange forms, such as Aztec daggers as broad in the blade as a man's hand, and no longer.

He searched the entire armory with keen interest, and, though he could not find the key attached to the point or the handle of any of these, yet he felt that he had learned an appreciable something about the great Louis Kendal.

CHAPTER THIRTY TWO

The clue to Kendal's nature with which he now felt that he was provided was that the man exulted above all things in the dealing of pain, so that all these grotesque and beautiful manners of giving death were delightful to him. It turned the place into a chamber of horrors.

He scanned the walls, next, looking for some crevice into which the key could be thrust. Then he examined the floor in the same way, but he knew that he was not making a faithful search, for all his nerves were jumping, his tongue was dry, he knew that the ten minutes had elapsed, and that the tall man might return while he was still at work.

There was a wardrobe in a corner. He opened it and found within a mackinaw of faded plaid, a tattered slicker, several pairs of trousers, worn shiny at the seat from friction against the saddle, two coats, and, on the floor of the cabinet, shoes and extra riding boots. He shook the boots and shoes, and listened for the rattle of the key. He plunged his hand hastily into pockets.

But the key was not there and he stood back with a breath of relief. At least, if he had not found the key, he had searched the place thoroughly! There was a last resource. A bit of matting lay before the washstand, and this he lifted, but the floor was naked underneath.

There was nothing more to do, and with a sigh he swung about and started for the lamp. In sixty seconds, God willing, he would be back in the adjoining chamber!

He came up so hastily that the little canary went into a greater frenzy than before, dashing from side to side of the cage, the wires of which chimed softly as it struck against them, then with a loudly clashing note.

The thought struck Fantom mid-step, and raised him to his toes.

In another instant he had the door of the cage open and the bird in his hand. His thumb struck what he wanted. Fitted close beneath the wing of the bird, harnessed to it with a thread delicately worked under the neck and body feathers, was a key!

One moment more and it was in his hand — the same sort of a thin-bladed little key as that which Quay had given to him as a pattern. Victory was his!

He restored the canary, which darted across the cage and clung to the opposite wires. The lamp he puffed out, parted the shutters and looked out.

Two men were sauntering from the barn toward the house. He dared not go out while they were there, but had to hang in agony at the window watching them.

He heard a distinct click behind him, and told himself that it was Kendal unlocking the door; so he whirled, gun in hand, ready to shoot. But the door did not open. When he looked out again, the two were idling at the watering trough, fascinated by the gleam of the water beneath the stars, as all human beings are. Then they went on, and disappeared into the kitchen door.

He was out the window at once. As he balanced on the ledge and pulled the window down, his feet lost their purchase, but he got a good hand hold on the sill and that saved him from the fall. He struggled up to the ledge again, but went along it with shaken nerves to the next window. Through this he crawled, and found himself at last safe, inside the chamber.

There he leaned against the wall for a moment and drew breath until his nerves steadied. After that, for he felt that he had exceeded his allotted time, he left the room and hurried down to the dining room beneath.

Two men whom he had not yet seen in the valley were there. They nodded carelessly at him and he waved to them. A moment later, out of the next door, came Kendal himself with Quay beside him. Controlled fury was in the face of the tall man and something like the cold of fear. Strain showed in the eyes of Quay, as well.

His glance found and clung to the face of young Jim Fantom, and the latter nodded almost imperceptibly. He saw the eyes of Quay widen with incredulous joy. Then the latter turned and put a hand on the shoulder of Kendal.

"You'll have everything that you wish," said

he, "but we'll wait till tomorrow morning!"

"Everything?" demanded Kendal sharply.

"Everything," reiterated Quay. "Let that end it, my old friend."

Kendal studied him, as if expecting a further explanation.

"It's more'n I expected!" he broke out suddenly. Then he added, "I'm gunna go out and walk some of the cobwebs out of my brain. Come along, the two of you!"

The pair trooped out after him, like obedient dogs at the heel. As they left, and the outer screen door swung shut with a noisy and metallic clangor, like the sound of Kendal's own voice complaining, Quay swung to Fantom with an outstretched hand; into the palm of it Fantom dropped the key.

As if it had been a thing of fire that burned his flesh, Quay caught it close to him, dropped it into his other hand, turned it.

"It's the same!" said he.

His eyes flashed with their strange, cold fire as he looked up to the boy.

"God bless the day when I found you," said he. "God bless the fool who came to kill you in Burned Hill and showed me your real self more clearly than a light falling on your face could have done! My lad, now everything is easy, I think, although your night's work is only beginning. Follow me!"

He led through the end door of the dining room, and through another, at the opening of which the damp, cold breath of a cellar rose into Fantom's face.

Quay took a small pocket lantern and with it lighted the winding steps which descended to a capacious cellar beneath the house. They passed through a wood store, another room filled with great heaps of beets, onions, potatoes, turnips, and long-rooted carrots. So they came to an end door, the last of the cellar, as it seemed, and before this, Quay paused. With one key he opened the top lock, and with another the lower. The door sagged softly, slowly open, with only onc deeply murmured groan midway in its swing.

It was as heavy as lead, and Fantom could see the reason for its weight in the shape of a half-inch slab of steel that reinforced the door on the inside. They passed through and stood before the one article of furniture which the room contained. This was a tall, narrow safe, propped against the wall, and, as it appeared, the old man looked sidewise at the boy, then nodded.

"You are about to see a treasure," said he. "For the sake of it, you may be tempted to murder me, lad, but I know your heart. You'll resist that temptation and fulfill my will, still. The year has hardly begun during which you're my man!"

"I am your man," said Fantom steadily. "You've given me my life; you've brought the girl to me. I'm your man to the end of the year, and after that."

"I believe you," said Quay. "Even if you were to find me liar, robber, and hypocrite revealed under your eyes, you would still keep your own honor and your word to me!"

Fantom stared at him.

"Yes," he said faintly. "But I'll never see that!"

Quay turned a shoulder on him and faced the safe again.

"You can do your thinking for yourself," said he. "You won't need an interpretation from me or from anybody else, when you see this!"

Like the door, the safe carried a double lock, and for the first he took the proper key from a vest pocket; for the second he used the one that Fantom had just secured from the room of Kendal.

At last the boy understood. For the opening and the closing of this safe, each man had one key, and it could not be touched by one without the other's consent, until at this instant both the keys were lodged in one hand.

The door swayed open. Inside, appeared a neat array of drawers of nickeled steel which Quay opened one after the other, swiftly, and laid them on the floor. Some were empty. Others contained what looked like small account or notebooks. Still others had their contents obscured by paper packages or leather wrappings.

One of these, the active and somewhat trembling hands of Quay unwrapped, and showed to the astonished eyes of Fantom four high stacks of greenbacks, closely wedged together!

Another was a bag of chamois, the neck of which he opened wide, and Fantom looked down into a weltering mass of light. Diamonds! Handfuls of them, stained here and there with the green of emeralds, and the red spots of rubies, like points of angry fire.

It was a vision of wealth undreamed of by the boy. But there were other packages which Quay was taking, and without a glance dropping them into the wide mouth of a saddlebag.

When he had finished, he faced Fantom, his beard quivering with the twitching of his lips.

"Now quick, quick!" said he. "Kendal is still taking the air!"

He laughed, a short, broken sound of exultation.

Then he led the way out of the room, closed and locked the doors behind him, and dropped into the boy's pocket all the four keys. Back to the dining room he went.

"Here!" said he, taking a quantity of cord from his pockets and a folded handkerchief. "Take these. Tie and gag me, without mercy. Pull the cords tight. Then go to the stable. Get the best horse you can find, and ride. Ride as if the devil were after you, as he's sure to be, before long. Take the road back toward Burned Hill. Outside the town, you'll find a small shack by the creek, with no one living there, a little cabin surrounded by poplars. Wait and watch there, or near there. I shall come within three days; or, after that, you can take the money, and it is yours!"

Sweat streamed down the face of Jim Fantom. He saw his dream dissipated, now. He saw the staring truth about the goodness and the benevolences of Quay. That greatness of heart which had made him gather in criminals to this valley had, in reality, been simply a mask under which he collected masters of crime who were used in all of their old talents under the keen direction of the partner, Kendal. This was the loot which they had gathered from a hundred robberies. What quantities of blood had been shed on this pillage he could not even guess!

"And the girl?" he asked hoarsely.

"The girl? The girl? What difference — ah, yes, the girl! Believe me, my lad, that the Happy Valley will be a naked valley as soon as this thing is known. Kendal will be gone on wings to follow you, and the others will stream after him, like bats. The women will follow. There will be left only the Chinamen and you, and the girl. Come back here to her, then. If I find you in the little shack — are you sure that you know the place?"

"Yes. I know it well. It was where McDonald Petrie lived."

"If I meet you there, I'll give you a deed of gift to the valley — to a thousand such valleys, if I owned 'em! Quick, quick! The devil will be back!"

CHAPTER THIRTY THREE

Fantom's hands worked fast, but his mind was fumbling in other directions. He was seeing the discovery by Kendal of the senior partner in this devilish business lying bound and gagged upon the floor, the fury of the pale-faced man, the frantic rage of the robbers themselves!

With lightning speed other pictures flowed through his brain. He remembered the conversation which he had overseen between Kendal and Rhiner. No doubt that Rhiner was asking for his own percentage of some recent robbery, and Kendal was putting him off.

The hunchback, too. He had encountered Kendal and made some demand of him which Kendal was helpless to resist. It was that demand which he had transferred on to Quay and which Quay had resisted until he made sure that the entire treasure would pass into his own hands through the agency of Fantom himself!

The whole story took on a new and wonderful light to Fantom. He could understand now why the eyes of Quay had seemed to him so deep, so filled with penetrating light. Penetrating they were, for they had looked through the body of Fantom to his very soul and there they had found a core of honesty upon which he could build in his fantastic scheme for the plundering of his associates in crime.

Quay had played his game, had saved Fantom's life from the posse's pursuit, had exerted himself to bring up to the valley the girl for whom the boy had formed his passion, and so had gathered him utterly and helplessly into the palm of his hand.

But she herself? Poor Jo in the cabin among the woods, what would be in her mind as she learned that her lover had fled from the valley without a word to her? Or was there prophecy in her sad feeling that they never would meet again?

And he said through stiffened lips, as his hands drew the cords tight:

"I'll do all this, but you on your side have to see her and tell her that, no matter what I've done, I'm coming back. That I love her. That nothing but death will keep me back from her. Do you hear?"

"I hear you. I'll tell her. Though God knows it's a way in which Kendal's suspicion can be fixed on me. His and all the rest! But when they close their hands and expect to find me under their fingers, they'll be closing on thin air, thin air!"

He chuckled softly as he said it, and, with an almost savage satisfaction, Fantom thrust the balled-up handkerchief between his teeth for a gag.

He left Quay helpless on the floor behind him, and, taking the saddlebag filled with the treasure, he left the house, only pausing for his rifle, and someone's slicker, which hung from a peg on the kitchen wall.

He draped the slicker over the bag, thrust open the kitchen door, and walked out into the night.

Straight before him, by the watering trough, he saw the tall form of Kendal, looking deformed even in the dull light of the stars. There he walked up and down with his shuffling stride, his two liege men trailing after him, still more like dogs at heel than men.

He was past them when Kendal's clanging, nasal tones arrested him.

"You, Fantom! Where are you going?"

A tension seemed to snap in Jim Fantom. He jerked around and snarled back:

"Shootin' owls. What else?"

Then he turned and pursued his way to the barn, in shuddering anticipation that the long, swift stride of Kendal would pursue and overtake him. But, as he reached the door of the barn and glanced back, he saw that they had not yet stirred to follow him. His brain swam with relief as he made sure of that, and he stumbled forward to find the right horse. Much depended upon that!

It seemed as though the answer were sent from heaven, for a lean, gray head was raised above the line of the stalls and he saw himself looking into a keen, small eye of fire.

When he stepped behind the horse, he found it was a tall gray mare which belonged to the great

Louis Kendal himself, a peerless animal, it was said in the valley, with the temper of a demon and the speed of the wind.

If she could blow him across the mountains beyond the reach of the followers who were to ride upon his traces, he would risk the outbreaks of her temper, he told himself. And instantly he had flounced the saddle upon her back. She grunted and swelled her stomach against the cinches. She sidestepped to crush him against the wall, and then tried to take off his arm with the snap of her teeth. An elbow in her jaw discouraged that idea; a knee wedged into her ribs made her let out her breath suddenly, and before it could be retaken, the cinches were jerked taut and the knot tied.

The bit of the bridle she firmly resisted, until he got thumb and forefinger into her mouth and pried down on the tender gums. At that she admitted the bit, but with a furious indignation, shaking her head, flattening her ears, looking back at him with eyes reddened by anger.

But he rejoiced in those signs. Let him convert all of her anger into power, and it would be well. Far better than some soft-tempered creature which would soon fail in the pinch!

The next matter of importance was how he could get her from the barn. There was a back door, but it led into a nest of corrals, and it would take much time to open the gates or lower the bars of these in order to get out

Yet there was no better way. He could not very

well go through the front door of the barn in the face of Kendal — on Kendal's own horse. So he backed the mare from her stall and started down the long aisle toward the rear door of the barn.

As he went, a horse neighed, and the mare tossed her head and whinnied in answer. But he reached the rear door of the barn and thrust it open as the voice of Kendal clanged from the front of the building:

"Hello! Hello!"

He drew the mare through the doorway with nervous hands.

"Hello, you — Fantom! What in hell are you doin' with Mischief?"

Fantom stepped back into the shadows which already had swallowed the mare.

He felt perfectly badgered and helpless. There was Kendal and two men with him; and behind him, between him and open country, appeared the cursed tangle of the corral fences.

"I'm takin' her out for a jog," he answered. "No harm in that, is there?"

"What'n hell you mean by touchin' my hoss, you fool?"

"Why, she sure needs a mite of exercise, Kendal," answered the boy in conciliating tones.

"Bring her back! Bring her back right pronto! I'm gunna give you a lesson in borrowin' the first hoss that you come to! Exercise? I'll exercise her, you blockhead! Take out Mischief, would you?"

He came stalking rapidly down the aisle of the barn, and panic turned the brain of Fantom dark. With a thrust of his left hand he slammed the door. Mischief, alarmed, wheeled and reared, but he followed the heave of the movement, and leaped onto her back, and found the stirrups.

For one instant, he looked down upon the fences from the height of her rearing, while he heard the ugly voice of Kendal shouting:

"Bill — Jerry! Come on the run! They's some hell-fire started. Scatter for the corral!"

And Fantom saw clearly what was before him. It was either jumping the fences or remaining behind to be slaughtered by the three experts. He dared not let them catch him, while the saddlebag was in his possession.

So he turned the mare's head toward that point where the range of the barriers seemed the thinnest, and urged her toward it at a full gallop.

Behind him, the door of the barn opened and the pale shaft of lantern light spilled toward him, as he put the mare at the jump.

"Are you gone crazy?" yelled Kendal.

Straight at the fence sped the tall mare, gathering speed and length in her stride, but at the last moment, she refused, twisting about with a catlike agility, in spite of her size, and racing back along the fence.

The Phantom, thrown from his seat, clung along her side, as he heard the roar of Kendal:

"I'll shoot you down, you idiot! Stop her, or you get it now!"

He could only wonder that Kendal had held his hand for so long. In the meantime, he had twitched back into the saddle, found both stirrups, and straightened the mare for the fence that rose ahead. It pitched up high. A five-foot jump, it looked to him, and doubly terrible in the darkness. Perhaps she could not jump at all — many a range horse never has learned the art!

But as they neared, this time, he felt her quarters sink and gather with a quivering tautness, and he knew that the mystery was at least in some part mastered by her. Up she rose, as a bird rises, at the same moment that the gun barked from Kendal's hand.

The bullet flew very wide. Not even the hum of it was in the ears of the fugitive, but the yell of Kendal and the sound of the shot had raised a nearer enemy.

One of the two who had been with the tall man had run about the rear side of the barn, in obedience to his master's command, and now Fantom saw a shadow step past the edge of the barn, and saw the glitter of a leveled gun.

Already he had switched the reins into his left hand, though another fence rose straight before him. Now, as the good mare pitched up at it with a grunt of effort, he slipped a Colt into his hand and fired at the menacing shadow.

There was an answering flash and roar from the ready gun of the other; but, as the mare soared and swung down clear on the other side of the barrier, from the tail of his eye Fantom saw the last gunman walk forward with outstretched hands, a pace or two, and then fall upon his face.

Another fence sprang toward them through the darkness, as it seemed to Fantom. She jumped it, in stride, as a bullet from behind knocked the hat from his head. It sailed forward; he caught it in mid-air, and sent Mischief gallantly on at the last barrier of all.

That also she cleared with ease, lightly, her ears now pricking as though she loved her work, and before him lay the open country, and the pale gleam of the lake and river beneath!

CHAPTER THIRTY FOUR

The brightness of dawn found him far away among the mountains. From the time when he left the house of Quay and hurdled the corral fences, and when the hoofs rang on the bridge, or scattered gravel on the valley road, or beat up the dust on the southern trail, he had had no sight and no sound of a pursuit behind him. The good gray mare had seen to that. She had flown over the level, trotted doggedly up the steeps, eased herself without a jar down the hard slopes.

So, in the rose of the day, he stopped at a brook and sloshed water over her legs, and massaged them with strong fingers, until a slight tremor disappeared from about her knees. He let her graze, then, for a little time, not standing still, but walking down the cañon with the girths of the saddle loosened.

She had made a grand effort; it had pinched her belly with fatigue and strain, but still there was strength in her. Indeed, he would have laid a handsome wager that the men from the Happy Valley would never overtake them, now, unless they possessed some means of getting a relay of fresh mounts beyond the southern edge of the valley. That might well be, but he doubted it. Though what the resources of Kendal might be outside the valley, he could not tell.

How could they even be sure of his trail, until the dawn-light enabled them to find the traces? He comforted himself with these reflections, remembering above all his last look down from the height.

The moon was just rising; the big trees were dark beneath it, the lake all silver-edged with ragged shadow, and the rivers were streaks of white. But no sound floated up to him; he saw no fire signals, which might have served as warnings to the allies of Kendal. And in the heart of that beauty and danger lay the cabin where Jo Dolan slept! So that picture reassured him for himself, but made him groan for the girl.

He thought of that as they wound through the rocky hills which went up on either side, with as monotonous a regularity as the rising and falling of waves — black and dreary waves, glinting with polished surfaces of rock.

The mare was grazing, stepping on, grazing again, and he followed half dreamily, with the fatigue of the ride beginning to creep into the marrow of his bones and numbing his brain.

Like sounds in a dream, then, he heard thunder in his rear. He looked back, vaguely wondering if clouds were sweeping up on the horizon behind him; but no clouds were there, and what wind stirred was cutting at his face.

It might have been the rumble of a small avalanche, he decided, but a moment later, he heard it again, and this time he knew — hoofs behind him, clattering and pounding!

In an instant he had jerked the girths tight and was in the saddle. He had barely brought her to a gallop when behind him he heard a long, pealing whoop, the Indian cry at the sight of game!

He looked back and saw the head of the pursuit spill out around a hill-shoulder, three men, leaning forward and flogging their mustangs; then, behind them, half a dozen others!

The good mare did not need to be told with whip or spur; she stretched away in her longest stride, at once; and the leap of the wind in Fantom's face told him that all was well. All was well for the moment, if only the riders behind him were not too freshly mounted!

They were out of sight now, with other hills between, and when they came in view again, four men, instead of three, were riding together in the lead, one of them a very tall man whose legs seemed dragging the ground on the small mustang he bestrode. There was something awkward and uncanny about him, even in the distance, and Fantom knew that it was Kendal!

Still the others spurred and whipped, while their horses kept resolutely to the same blinding pace.

The heart of Fantom sank. Yet the mare was holding them. How long, he could not tell, but it seemed to him that already Mischief was laboring in her gallop. Then before him he saw a steep rise of ground with no way around it, for the hills closed down on either side.

As they struck the slope it was as though a

bullet had passed through the brain of Mischief. She floundered, almost fell, and then staggered on with fumbling steps, her iron shoes ringing against the rocks.

She was ended. On level going she could have stretched away for long enough, perhaps, to withstand the challenge even of fresh mounts behind her; but this sudden and condensed effort of climbing was too much. She had gone down like a house of cards, and Jim Fantom knew there was an end to her as he came to the top of the slope.

They who followed knew, also. Their yells came barking on his ears, like the yelling of madmen, men mad for blood.

Once more he glanced back, to see that tall Louis Kendal had risen in the stirrups and, with head turned, was shouting instructions to his men. Perhaps he was bidding them hold their fire so that they could catch their prey alive, and so make of him a noble and a lasting example.

Fantom looked before him for shelter. There was none. Only small rocks and transparent shrubs stood about him, while the narrow valley wound away before his eyes.

Deep he sank the spurs. Mischief, with a stagger, came into a laboring gallop, but her ears were back, her stride floundered. She was managing no more than a trot, in speed, when the crest of the pursuing wave broke over the top of the slope behind them and poured after with a rush and a roar.

He turned in the saddle, unhousing his rifle as he did so. At that, they spread out to either side. To his amazement, they actually were reining in their horses! It was amazingly unlike Kendal to give up the game when the prey was at his hand.

Still more wonderful, the whole flight of the pursuers now wheeled about and fled before him, as though each man expected a bullet through his back.

Then a new sound burst on the ear of Jim Fantom, and, glancing ahead, he saw a burst of a dozen riders who had appeared as by magic from behind the foot of some hills. They were already upon him.

Sheriff Bud Cross rode in the center and in the lead; behind him or to either side came the others, grim-faced, tight-lipped. They rushed about him. A man was at his horse's head, another on either side, with the hard noses of Colts nudging his ribs.

"Hands up! Hands up, Fantom! Jerk up them hands, or we'll let light into you!"

Resistance was ridiculous. He had been thrown from one hand into another, and there was no escape. Therefore, he raised his arms slowly, and watched the sheriff with the rest of his men flying after the corps of Louis Kendal. He measured the speed of the horses, shook his head.

"You're right," said a familiar voice beside him. "They ain't gunna get the rest of the crooks; but we got you, Fantom, and we're gunna hold you till a rope stretches your neck for you."

He looked into the eyes of Tom Dollar, that old associate, that double traitor, and saw that Tom was laughing with a savage delight, while he thrust the nose of the gun harder into the ribs of his captive.

"Now lemme see you make your fast play, Fantom," urged Dollar. "You're faster'n lightning, they all say. You got something in your eyes that gents can't face. Well, here I am. I'm tryin' to face it. I seem to be managin'. Maybe Larry Phelan couldn't stand the gaff, but I can stand it. You hear me talk? I'm waitin' for you to do something, old son! Get yourself good and famous. What's the use of waitin' for the judge and the jury to hang you? Here's Judge Colt that'll give you a final opinion!"

"Let him be, Dollar," said one of the others. "Let him be, will you? He ain't got his hand in your pocket, has he?"

The face of Dollar wrinkled and turned pale, as though he remembered the fear which had driven him into disgrace from Burned Hill at the mere announcement that this man was approaching.

"He'd of liked to have his hand in my heart, tearing it," said Tom Dollar, "and you want me to be kind to him, maybe?"

"Leave him be. Leave him breathe. That's all. Here they come back already. That gang had fresh hosses, it looks like. They run you down pretty slick, Fantom, didn't they?"

"They'd of made him sick in another couple of minutes," said Tom Dollar exultingly, "but it's better this way. We can watch the crook this way when he comes up for murder. We can watch him hang, too. He'll look pretty on the end of a rope!"

He cackled with his pleasure. The whole body of the man writhed with his emotion, and Fantom could understand why. No doubt, for these days Tom Dollar had been in cringing fear that the bolt might fall upon him from the blue; so he had joined the posse in the desperate hope of getting mere protection from it. Certainly luck had played into his hands.

"I'll take his guns," said Dollar, unbuckling the gun-belt of the prisoner. "You fan him for a knife, Steve."

Steve obeyed. They had stripped Fantom of weapons when the sheriff returned from his futile burst after the others from the Happy Valley. One of the posse, riding on ahead, broke into a shrill laughter at the sight of Fantom, whose hands now were manacled together, and the man helpless. He turned his head and saw that the laughter came from little Sam Kruger.

"Well," crowed Sam Kruger, "and here's the hero back with his own home folks. We're mighty glad to see you, Jim! Shake on it! He won't shake hands. He don't see me, maybe. I'm too small. But I'll see you, Fantom. I'll see you hang, too, damn you!"

He shook his fist in the face of the other with an inexplicable malice. Here Sheriff Bud Cross rode in between.

"Back up, Kruger," he said in disgust. "What's Fantom ever done to you?"

"He's a murderer, ain't he?" barked Kruger. "Ain't he a damn murderer, I ask you? Are you gunna pet him and coo over him, maybe?"

"Back up!" repeated the sheriff. "You ain't pulling your weight on his wagon, anyway. Get out of my sight, and keep out. If his hands wasn't in irons, you'd all run up trees at the sight of him, and you know it."

He turned to Fantom with an apologetic gesture.

"You see how it is, Jim?" said he.

"Sure," said the prisoner. "But I see that I'm only a kind of a sheep, because sheep dogs have been enough to handle me!"

CHAPTER THIRTY FIVE

A score of led horses now came down the valley with four men in charge, and the sheriff gave quick directions.

"Some of you get to those hosses and change saddles. We're gunna go on after that gang of crooks. We're gunna follow their trail, and if it don't lead back to the Happy Valley, I'm a liar. Hurry up, now, and take care that black devil don't put his heels through the head of one of you!"

He pointed out a horse which did not need to be indicated. At that moment it bolted ahead against the lead rope, and spilled the string of animals of which it was one into a whirl of snorting, squealing confusion.

The others went obediently to do as they were bidden.

"Sendin' out a hoss like that — enough to spoil the whole job!" complained the sheriff. He turned back to his prisoner.

"Jim," said he, "why didn't you barge along north and get out of the country? Why not, when the goin' was so good up north, and the hangin' so sure down here?"

"I got two reasons," answered the captive, "an' the first one is enough. I didn't kill Larry Phelan!"

The eye of the sheriff was thoughtful and not unkind.

"Why, sure you didn't," said he. "They ain't any doubt that you didn't, I suppose, in your own mind. But the mind of the county don't figger that way, and I'm the county servant."

"Why," answered Fantom, "I don't hold no grudge, Bud. Not a mite ag'in you. You've done your duty. That's all. Only — to be run down by a crowd like that!"

"It takes all kinds of dogs to make a pack," philosophized the sheriff, "but I gotta say that I didn't pick that mean little snake, Sam Kruger. What's he got ag'in you, son? He furnished three fine hosses for this show. All for the sake of runnin' you down. An' how was I to know that one of his hosses — that black streak of deviltry over yonder — would cause so much trouble? I couldn't shut out a man from the party that put up as much good hoss flesh as that!"

"Kruger did all of that?" repeated the prisoner. "I dunno why it is, Bud. The fact is that I never stepped on his toes, that I know of. But you can't explain some things. Some folks hate as quick as a cactus stings. Little Kruger maybe is that way!"

"You mean what you say about Phelan?" broke in the sheriff.

"Mean it?"

"This ain't in court. I'll keep my mouth shut. But tell me if I've grabbed the man that didn't do the shootin'!"

Fantom smiled faintly.

"What for would I shoot a dog, Bud?"

"A dog?"

"Why, Larry Phelan showed yaller a mile wide, at the saloon, that same day. Why should I foller him up and murder him, I ask you? There in the saloon was my chance, if I'd wanted to take it. An' no murder, but a plain gunfight, with self-defense, an' all that kind of thing, and plenty of witnesses to prove that he came gunnin' for me."

"I never thought of that," admitted the sheriff, his head bowed.

He looked up quickly.

"You ain't a dead man yet, old son," said he. "An' when I get back from this job, wherever it leads me, I'll try to see that you get justice. But — prejudice is about two thirds of the battle, I'm afraid!"

"And I'm fresh from the pen," agreed Fantom.

"Ay, that goes pretty heavy ag'in you! I'm sorry, man, if you'll believe me?"

"I believe you dead easy."

He held out his hands in the irons and shook the right hand of the sheriff. The latter had removed his glove for that purpose. Now he said briskly:

"I wish you luck. An' you may have it. Keep your head up, an' keep on hopin'. So long, Fantom. Could I ask if they's anything in the Happy Valley that you could tell me about?"

"Nothing," he said, though he thought of poor Jo Dolan, and his heart swelled.

"So long," repeated Bud Cross. "I'll be seein' you inside of the week."

He was off his horse as he spoke, and soon throwing the saddle on the back of another which was led up to him. Then he mustered his forces.

"Here, you," said he. "We're ridin'. I can't take everybody. They's gotta be a guard left here with Jim Fantom. Dollar and Kruger, you stay here behind with him. D'you hear? Take care of him. I don't want no roughness. The rest of you, come with me and ride like hell. Maybe we'll get famous before this day turns dark!"

He turned in the saddle as the men swept off around him. The led horses were keen with spirit, anxious to go, tired of swallowing the dust of the riders, and they communicated their freshness to the men. There was a general whoop, and off they went, arrowlike, only the sheriff calling:

"Good luck — see you later, Fantom!"

Dust blew up behind the galloping horses, making a shaken veil too dense for the eye to penetrate, very soon; as it blew away, the riders had disappeared, leaving only the horse wranglers, who were getting their strings in order, and Fantom, with his two guards.

"We ain't good enough to ride with the rest of 'em," commented Tom Dollar savagely. "All we're good enough to do is to stay back here and watch this here — dead one!"

"He'll be dead before long!" said Kruger, nodding his head with a grin of satisfaction.

"Look here," said Jim Fantom. "Tell me why you got it in for me, Kruger. Not that it matters, but I'm sort of curious."

"No. It don't matter, anything that I think," said Kruger bitterly. "What am I but a runt? I ain't any Larry Phelan, the girls always would be sayin' behind my back. I ain't famous, like Jim Fantom. I got no good qualities; but I can keep my neck out of a noose and bullet outside of my skin, it seems! That's something. That's qualities enough for me!"

Fantom watched him with the interest he would have shown toward a strange beast or a queer insect.

"It's all right, man," said he. "I understand. It's all right. Go ahead and show your teeth!"

"Damn you!" panted Kruger, through his set teeth.

"The main thing, Sammy," broke in Tom Dollar, who had been watching this conversation with much interest, "is that we gotta pay a lot of attention an' take a lot of care of this here fellow, ain't it?"

"That's what the sheriff said," answered Kruger, looking hard at his companion, as though eager to read a hidden meaning in his words.

"That's what the sheriff said, all right. Well, then, the first thing is what hoss are we gunna put him on to ride him back to Burned Hill?"

"I dunno. Anything," said Kruger.

"Now, what kind of talk is that?" demanded
Dollar in mock horror. "As though we'd bring
back a man like Fantom into his home town on
any kind of a lookin' nag! What would the girls
think of him, if they seen the hero come back not
fixed up right on a fine hoss?"

"Sure," snarled Kruger. "What would they
think?"

"We gotta give him the finest hoss that we got
in the herd, don't we?"

"Yeah?" drawled Kruger, not following the
drift of his companion.

"And what's the finest one?"

"Why, I dunno. What are you drivin' at, son?"

"Is they a finer lookin' hoss in the outfit than
that black?"

"You mean that streak of darkness, yonder?
You mean that jumpin' thunderbolt?"

"Why, I'm thinkin' of the impression that he'll
make with our friend here on his back, goin' into
Burned Hill."

"Goin' *through* Burned Hill, you mean. He'd
go through it in two winks. That hoss could
jump over the mountains in about two kicks. He
flies, he don't run! What you mean, Tom
Dollar?"

"Why, I'm only thinkin' about the honor that
we'll be doing to the most prominent citizen of
Burned Hill. I'm thinkin' of the fine procession
hoss, that Darkness, yonder, would make. He

belongs to you. Would you loan him, Sammy?"

Suddenly the thought struck home in the heart and in the brain of Sam Kruger and his head tilted back in a chuckle.

"Loan him? I'll give him away for such a job as that. I foller your drift now, old son. Sure I do! Hey, you! Bring in Darkness, will you?"

They brought in Darkness, and Fantom, without complaint, looked over the most magnificent creature he ever had laid eyes upon. There is no beauty in man or in woman to compare with the beauty of the perfect horse, and Darkness was perfect. From his shoulders to his quarters, from his short, strong back to the whipcord drawn in his flanks, from hocks to knees, and the hammered iron of his lower legs, he was fleckless and flawless.

There was not a hair of white on all his body, or in his rippling mane, or his gracefully arched tail. Even standing there, when the wind touched his mane and tail, and he turned his head toward it, he seemed in floating motion.

But he was wrong. In the red, furious eye lay the answer. He was totally, hopelessly wrong, it seemed; and, as one of the other horses came near, he lashed out with both heels, backed up, and kicked again; then reared and struck at the man who was dragging on his reins.

"Who'll ride him?" said the wrangler. "You, Tom? Or you, Kruger?"

He looked with contempt at the little man, but Kruger answered:

"We got a champeen with us. He'll take a turn out of old Darkness."

"You gunna take the chance to set him loose on that hoss?" asked the wrangler.

"Hell, no! We'll have our ropes on him, won't we? We'll just set pretty and watch champeen Jim Fantom ride that hoss! In case he should get a fall, we'll shackle his feet under the belly of his hoss. Why not?"

The horse wrangler looked from one to another of them in manifest disgust.

"It's your business. It's your hoss, and you're guardin' the man, but it looks like dirty work to me, if you want my opinion."

"I *don't* want it," said Tom Dollar sharply. "Hosses is your business, not men!"

The wrangler flushed an ugly red. For an instant the heart of Fantom rose with the hope that he had found one who would prevent this cruelty, but the wrangler was not a man of action with guns, and Tom Dollar had a neat reputation with a six-shooter. The wrangler turned his back and walked haltingly off toward his string, like a man whose conscience bids him turn back again.

CHAPTER THIRTY SIX

They had to blindfold the black stallion, and when he felt the weight of Fantom, heaved up on his back, he crouched beneath it almost until his belly touched the ground. When he rose again, it was only half-way erect, his muscles quivering with readiness to leap away. In the meantime, a rope was passed beneath the girths, binding the feet of Fantom fast.

"There you are!" said Kruger, standing back with a sneer of malice. "It sure shows that we think a lot of your safety, Fantom, tyin' you into the saddle so's you can't possibly be thrown!"

But their real meaning was obvious enough. Such a devil as Darkness was reasonably sure to throw himself and roll to get the burden off his back; and if that happened, it was horrible and quick death for the fastened rider.

But Jim Fantom looked not at the two, and their faces strained with greedy satisfaction. He looked at the head of the stallion, the flattened ears, the shimmer of light that ran up the silky neck, as the big horse trembled with rage and with horror.

"He's *been* rode, once. Two years back," Kruger encouraged him. "Let him go, Tom!"

They were on their horses, each with a rope around the neck of the black, and now Dollar leaned and twitched the bandage from the head of Darkness. The answer was sudden and unexpected, for Darkness, like an uncaged panther, sprang at Dollar's horse and tried to take him by the throat.

The mustang whirled and fled for dear life, while Kruger was unable to get his own pony into position before the rope, that was fastened around the horn of his saddle with a single hitch, came taut, and, with the violence of the shock, horse and man toppled to the ground and rolled over and over.

Loudly screaming, Kruger, with terror and with pain, came lurching to his feet, and fled, blinded by fear, while the rope, falling out of its hitch, slipped free and darted like a snake after the flying stallion.

Tom Dollar shouted in turn. He looked back, and the flying danger was close behind him. He was mounted on a fine cutting horse, himself, and that horse dodged like a bird in the air when a heavy taloned hawk is dropping at it from above. So the horse dodged, but the stallion followed, catlike with venom and with speed.

A bullet might settle it. Tom Dollar drew his gun and fired, but the back of a dodging, swerving horse is no safe shooting platform, and the bullet missed its goal.

Hastily he undid the rope from the horn of his saddle and cast it free; and the stallion, as though it was only for this that he had fought, straightway left his prey and darted off through a gap in the hills.

There was a chorus of frightened and exasperated shouts from all who remained behind, at this. The horse wranglers were far behind, and none mounted. Frightened and half stunned, Sam Kruger hardly knew what had happened, and Tom Dollar was at least a hundred yards away before he could straighten his pony in pursuit.

It was like chasing a comet. The black horse went away with winged bounds. None of his viciousness was expressed in bucking on this day; it was as though he were striving to blow the weight from his back by the sheer speed of his gallop. With every bound, Tom Dollar, futilely discharging his revolver, was jerked away to the rear.

Enough danger remained in the saddle with Jim Fantom. Above all, those dangling ropes might at any moment be trodden upon, or tangle the powerful legs of the stallion. For that thing, no doubt, Tom Dollar and Kruger would be praying.

However, Fantom was not quite helpless. He could reach out with his manacled hands, and, taking the nooses, one by one, enlarge them and cast them over the head of the horse.

So that first danger was removed, only to be replaced by a second, for the shadow of a wood appeared in the valley before them, and into it the stallion rushed at full speed.

His purpose was instantly clear. It was not the

first time, apparently, that he had used such a ruse as this to displace a rider; and now he swerved right and left, beneath the lower branches, or shaved close to trunks, hoping to crush the leg of the rider.

A hundred deaths whirred past the face or over the head of Fantom, but still he swerved from side to side and ducked, half helpless though he was from the tightness with which he was bound to the saddle.

There was the possibility of some guidance through the one rein which had flown into his hand. Anxiously he waited for a chance to catch the other, as a dozen times it darted toward him like a whiplash and just eluded the frantic grasp of his hands.

The stallion reached a thicket of high brush. Through it he dashed with outstretched head; but for the rider it was a scourging of a thousand whipstrokes, and finally a blow that seemed to crush in his forehead.

How long he hung swaying, he could not tell, but at least he knew that the sun was high, when he recovered, and beating cruelly on the back of his head. The black stallion was grazing in a lovely meadow, ringed around with the dark woods, a meadow streaked and dotted with flowers.

When his rider straightened at last in the saddle, the big horse lifted his head, also, and looked back askance at Fantom, with an eye from which the red stain had disappeared. He pricked his ears with friendly curiosity, and then sniffed and stamped, as though annoyed by the sight and the smell of the blood which covered the face of the man.

Fantom raised his hands to the cuts with which his face was covered. He touched his forehead, and found there a great lump, but the bone of the skull had not been fractured. He was reeling with weakness, and with the blood which had run down into his head as he hung from the saddle, but nevertheless his brain cleared rapidly. Hope was the wind that blew it clear as crystal.

The fluttering of his heart grew steadier to a strong beat. Slipping his hands far down, he gathered in one rein, then the other, and knotted the ends. At that, he felt that two thirds of the battle had been gained, for the horse was now in his hands, gentled, obedient to his will.

It stepped freely out, with an easy, daisy-clipping stride, and moving its head a little from side to side, as though it were enjoying this day's journey and all the fresh beauty of the open country around it.

It eased the heart of the rider to feel the horse so beneath him, giving his strength and his intelligence freely to this new master of a few hours.

Behind him, he knew not even in what direction, lay the pursuit which now must be wandering on his trail; before him lay he equally knew not what, but at least some chance of freedom, if only he could loose his feet and his hands from the steel manacles that locked them together.

The meadow narrowed at the farther end, then suddenly expanded into farming fields, checked across with fences, spotted with cattle, and pale green here with growing crops, black or gray yonder with the summer fallowed ground.

Small houses stood in the distance, their chimneys smoking, and the whole atmosphere of peace and the stillness, the sacred stillness, carried his spirit suddenly back to the Happy Valley that seemed a thousand leagues, a thousand years behind him.

"Hello!" said a voice behind him.

He turned his head sharply and saw a ragged boy, barefooted, an old shotgun over the crook of his arm, a battered hat upon his head with tufts of straw-colored hair thrusting through the gaps.

"Hello!" said Jim Fantom, and suddenly he realized that he was helpless, even before this small boy! That gun over the crook of his arm was the decisive factor.

"Jiminy!" said the boy. "You been through it, all right!"

"I been through it," admitted Fantom.

"Jiminy!" gasped the boy. "Feet tied — and — and handcuffs! Who are you?"

The muzzle of the gun slowly swung around until it covered Fantom.

"I'm a fool," he said bitterly.

"Yeah?" asked the boy, his young eyes stern with questioning.

"I'm a fool," said Fantom. "I did this on a bet, an' I'll never collect enough to pay for what's happened to my head and face, let alone for the rest of the whangin' that I've got. Just cut this rope that's holdin' my feet, will you?"

"You did it on a bet, eh?" asked the boy, unconvinced. "Maybe you better come along and tell pop about that bet, and who you are."

"I'm Hugh Chatterton," said Fantom. "I'm from up the Black Mountains way."

"The deuce you are!"

"Yep."

He wondered, as he spoke, how far away the Black Mountains might be.

"When d'you leave 'em?" asked the boy.

"Why, I left this morning, early."

The boy gaped.

"I bet you left early," he agreed. "You must of left on the wind, too, because no hoss in the world would blow you here this fast! What sort of a bet did you have?"

"That I could ride this brute with my feet tied under him, and my hands shackled, like you see. He's near killed me."

Suddenly the eye of the boy lighted.

"That's Darkness. That's the fightin' hoss!" said he. "I seen him at the rodeo last fall. He sure punched holes in the sky. He dropped the gents that tried him all over the field. He sure is a wicked one!"

"He is," agreed Fantom.

"And —" the boy paused. "You rode him

out!" said he. "He looks plumb gentled, now!"

"He's easy goin', now. He worked himself out."

"Who are you?" asked the boy again.

"Chatterton."

"Chatterton, eh?"

He stepped closer, staring brightly, his eyes as cold and keen as the eyes of a hawk.

"Not Jim Fantom, by any chance of luck?" he suggested.

CHAPTER THIRTY SEVEN

To Fantom it was like the tolling of a doom bell in his ears. And it seemed to him that it was some twice-told tale that he, who had evaded the strength of grown men, and the skill of cunning fighters, should be captured at last by a child. He looked on the valley again. This, also, seemed a familiar scene.

"Well?" asked the boy, sharply.

"You're right," answered the other. "I'm Fantom."

"By Jiminy!"

"Take me on in. Your father will be glad to have me. They have a tidy little reward for my capture by this time, I guess!"

"They got twenty-five hundred posted. Maybe it's growed by this time," said the boy. "You're Fantom, are you?"

"Yes."

"Who put you on that hoss?"

"The sheriff's men. Kruger and Tom Dollar."

"Dollar — him that run away from you. And Kruger? Kruger?"

His voice rang with scorn.

"Them two caught you?"

"I ran into the whole posse."

"And the sheriff left you with them, and they stuck you up like that — and then you got away?"

"Yes. To bring twenty-five hundred to your old man. I guess you could use it, maybe?"

"Jiminy! Could we?" murmured the boy.

He rolled up his eyes, but the infinite possibilities surpassed his imaginings. He looked again at the helpless man before him.

"Dollar and Kruger!" he repeated, as though the names stuck in his throat. "Them two! They wanted to see you busted up more than a — than —"

"Then a hangman's rope. Yep. That's what they wanted."

"Phelan — what made you go and snipe at him?" asked the boy, his face turning stern. "I mean, after you'd showed him up at the saloon, that way?"

Fantom shrugged his shoulders.

"You just aimed to get even with him, eh?" asked the boy, his features still rigid.

"Son," said Fantom slowly, "after what happened in the saloon, what use was there in shootin' a dog?"

"Hey?" said the boy, startled.

"Some other man might have stepped in, old timer. He'd know that the blame would come my way."

"Never thought of that!" gasped the youngster. "Never thought of that, at all! Why, then —"

He paused, agape at a vast idea.

"Then they'd hang you for nothin'!"

"No," said Fantom honestly. "I've made my share of trouble for other folks."

"Hold on," said the boy. "Only — twenty-five hundred —"

Then, with a resolute shake of the head, he drew out a clasp knife, unfolded the blade, and stepped closer. There he paused again.

"Well," he said, "it's only square. *I* believe you, but I guess older folks wouldn't. Not with twenty-five hundred to make out of you! Pop, he'd give a leg for that much!"

The knife slashed the rope, and the feet of the rider were free! The boy stepped back with a sigh and a frown.

"There's still the hands," he said.

"You've done enough," said the other. "I want your name."

"Me? I'm Bud Loring."

"Bud, I wanta shake hands with you."

"Sure," said Bud, with a flashing grin.

They shook hands.

"Jiminy," said Bud, "to think of the guns that that hand has grabbed out of leather! Well, you come back with me, and I'll snake a file out of the blacksmith shop behind the house."

He led the way; Fantom drifted through the trees near by, sufficiently deep to be sheltered from observation, and so they came up behind a little dilapidated house with a crooked smoke-stack leaning above it, and the ground all around scratched hard and bare by wandering chickens that looked as starved and broken down as the house itself.

The boy disappeared into a shed behind the

house, and presently came back with a pair of files.

"These are the boss kind for steel," said he. "Dad's a good blacksmith and he keeps the right kind of tools!"

The right kind indeed they proved to be, biting into the hard metal of the manacles as though with a diamond edge. Still, the work took time, and the files had to be turned repeatedly to fresh edges as the teeth grew duller and the steel of the wrist bands grew hot. The first one, at last, was cut through in two places and the right hand of Fantom was free again.

The boy fell to work on the other, panting and sweating.

"You've had bad times?" said Fantom courteously.

"Pop got the rheumatism. He couldn't stand the work around the shop in Burned Hill. I mean, gettin' hot at the fire, and then cold at the anvil. He had to quit and come out here. He sold out and bought the junk left after the big Hollison house burned down. It used to stand right where the cottage does. But bigger. That low rock wall, that was part of the foundation. So's that pile of junk, here. I root around in it and get a lot of stuff out of it."

"Hollison? I've heard of 'em. I must of been in the penitentiary when that house burned down."

"Sure?"

The boy looked up at him with wide eyes, horror and respect in them for one who had endured so much in the world.

"You seen things, I bet," he murmured.

"Bud-die!" screamed a woman's voice from the cottage.

"Jiminy," said Bud. "It's lunch time, and ma'll give me a bad time of it, I guess!"

He writhed in anticipation.

"Go right on," said Fantom. "I'm goin' to give you something that'll make her glad you stayed away."

"Are you?"

"I am."

The boy worked furiously. One segment of the circle was penetrated. He commenced a second sawing.

"Bud!" yelped the summary voice.

He tilted back his head and a far-off voice issued from his lips.

"Com-ing!" he wailed.

"That'll hold her for a minute, I guess," he panted. "She sure will go after me, though."

The file squeaked and scraped. It had lost its first sharpness, but still it sawed down into the steel slowly, steadily.

"They've done wrong by you," broke out Bud, as he worked. "They've kicked you when you was down. They've done wrong!"

"You've made it right again," said Fantom, deeply touched.

"D'you mean that?" asked the boy.

"Ay. You've balanced my account for me. I'll never forget you, son."

"Thanks," said the boy.

"Is there anything that you could ask out of me, Bud?"

"Me? Well, of course there ain't anything that I'd dare to ask. But one of Jim Fantom's guns —"

"I haven't a weapon," said Fantom. "They fanned me and got everything."

"Hold on! You got bare hands, then."

"I've a horse that's better than a gun. It'll keep me away from trouble so's I won't have to fight."

"Ay. He's a jim-dandy, all right. But you without a gun — that'll go kind of hard, maybe?"

"Well, maybe it will! But we gotta learn how to dodge the bad corners, Bud, when a man lives like me, with a fist over his head, all of the time."

"I bet you do. You'll be goin' away, I guess? You'll try Mexico, I reckon?"

"Some place, some place," muttered Jim Fantom, "there's gunna be a happy turn to the road. I'll wait for that! I can't run away!"

"What keeps you?"

"Something a pile stronger than ropes and handcuffs, old timer."

"What would that be? Well, it's your own business, only I'd think that the outtrail would be the trail for you!"

"Would you?"

He fell silent. The heat from the friction of the file burned the skin of his wrist; then the teeth actually touched the flesh, and the handcuff broke off with a faintly ringing snap.

"Bud Loring, I'm gunna skin you!" cried the

voice of the mother from the cottage.

"She will, too," panted Bud, scrambling to his feet, for they had been sitting down on the ground, facing one another.

"Wait one minute," said Fantom, flexing his hands with indescribable joy in their freedom. "You've taken the handcuffs off my wrists. You've taken the rope from around my neck. Now I want to leave something with you to remember me by!"

He stepped to the loaded saddlebag and opened the mouth of it, wondering as he did so that when the saddle was changed from the gray mare, Mischief, to the back of Darkness, no one had thought to examine the baggage of the captive. But after all, there had been a swirl of haste and of commotion.

Into the bag he dipped, found jewels gritting under his finger tips, and drew out a small handful. From them he selected a few. He knew something of the cost of diamonds, for he had priced them in the old days of gay extravagance, when stolen money fled easily through his fingers.

Whatever he took now was, in a sense, stolen again from his sworn duty to Quay. But he did not hesitate. Quay himself was not so small-souled as to keep so strict an account with one who had made it possible for his messenger to keep on his way.

So he counted out ten jewels of some price. If he guessed correctly, the least of them was worth five hundred dollars, and regarding them in that light, when he thought of what the entire mass of the jewels in the saddlebag must represent, his brain whirled with the greatness of the sum.

"Here!" said he to the boy, and dropped them into his palm.

Bud Loring gaped, helpless with awe.

"Mind you!" said the man, with lessoning forefinger raised, "you were rootin' around in the Hollison junk heap, and this is what you found! Found 'em in a little heap, close together. Remember that! It's more than the twenty-five hundred that your father would have got as blood money for me. Maybe it'll give him a boost with his rheumatism and buy him some more land and a better cabin. So long, Bud. You'll make a mark on the face of the country when you've growed up!"

Bud was frozen with amazement. He could not speak. Only when Fantom was on the back of Darkness again did he hear a faint, piping cry. But Fantom rode on without turning his head.

CHAPTER THIRTY EIGHT

A sense of predestination came to Jim Fantom as he rode on his way. The danger from Kendal, the danger from the law, had both met upon him and the one, as it were, had cancelled the other. He could have laughed aloud as he thought of this, but there was still before him business so serious that he could not afford mirth.

He was drifting the black stallion back toward his own country, and with every mile he was coming closer and closer to a region where every man and child was apt to know him. Even Bud had known the intimate details, had recognized the very horse that he rode.

In a way, it was like the flight of a bird, hunted up from the ground by dogs, and struck at in the air by falcons. So Kendal and his power threw him adrift, and the law was striving to seize him as he fled.

There was one great advantage in pursuing the way to the cabin, which was that it lay in the head of the valley above Burned Hill, and he could keep to the cover of trees all the way down to it. He determined to try to get there before dusk, so as to cast about him and provide for a comfortable night for himself and his horse if possible. The next day they must be rested, in order to make the long march back to the Happy Valley!

All was confusion to him when he thought of it. The Happy Valley, half deserted by the inhabitants, half raided by the police, what would become of it? What furious fighting had taken place in it, even before this? For if the men of the valley chose to make a stand, only miracles could help the sheriff and his little band.

He swung, now, into the head of the rolling ground which swept down toward Burned Hill. Behind him were the mountains through which he must penetrate to get back to the Happy Valley, and below him began the stream which finally wandered down to the town itself. It was a feeble, muddy trickle, and it would swell, after many miles, only to such a size as made the swimming pool which he had known as a boy.

He dismounted beside it and bathed the wounds of his face. None of them were serious, but there were uncounted small abrasions of the skin, and his whole face was swollen. The cool water comforted him, and he was able to go on with greater peace of mind, down through the later heat of the afternoon, down through the scattered willows beside the growing stream, until the sun hung low on the edge of the sky.

It had lost its heat, and now the earth seemed to be giving up the warmth that had soaked into it during the day, for the air was as hot as ever, and utterly still. Over the water was a continual murmur of clouds of insects, making spots of dun-colored mist, and this sound seemed to grow in volume as the sun sank, and Fantom entered at last the pale sweep of poplars in which stood the shack where he was to meet Quay.

Probably that gentleman of many artifices would not arrive until the morning, at the earliest, so Fantom pressed on, eager to make his arrangements for the night.

Finally, he could see the cabin looming through the trees before him, and here he dismounted and proceeded cautiously ahead, until, at the edge of the clearing, he paused to look out on the place. Darkness stood as silent as his name, as unstirring, with lifted head and with pricked ears, but straight before him Fantom saw the goal of this journey.

It was Quay himself, sitting on the doorstep, with the broken door sagging in behind him. Against the jamb his back comfortably reclined, his hands were locked about one knee, and he puffed contentedly at a pipe.

There was such peace, such philosophy in that bearded face, and the man as a picture fitted so well into the hush of the riverside, that for the moment Fantom forgot all that he recently had learned, and felt toward Quay as he had felt after their first few meetings — but the realization of the truth came back to him at once.

To one side he saw a pair of slender-bodied, long-legged thoroughbreds. Their saddles were doubtless piled inside the shack, and now they grazed on hobbles, eager with hunger. That explained how Quay had come down from the valley so swiftly!

"And here you are, my boy?" said Quay, without raising his voice.

Fantom was drawn in some confusion from among the trees and approached his master with the saddlebag in his hand.

"Never stand too long to watch a sad sight," said Quay. "Such a sight as fallen principles, abandoned hopes, ruined efforts. Such a spectacle, for instance, as old Jonathan Quay; once a philanthropist and now a robber. A poor robber, Jim, whom you are about to turn into a robber baron!"

There was such a mingling of whimsicality and hypocrisy and frankness in this speech that Fantom, with the burden of his long journey falling from his shoulders at last, broke into laughter.

"Good!" said Quay, nodding. "If you can laugh like that, you'll continue to be an honest man!"

"Continue?" said Fantom.

"Why, of course. You never were anything else. The stage robbery — that was a child's prank. Some children break windows. You held up a stage, instead. I'll wager I can tell you the moment of that robbery which frightened you the most."

"Can you?" asked Fantom, wondering deeply that this man did not seize on the saddlebag at once and examine the contents to make sure that everything was there. "What was the minute I was most scared, then?"

"Not even the time when the leaders of the coach came into view; not even when the guns were cracking and bullets went into your poor body; but afterward, when you saw some of the loot, and realized that it was stolen stuff!"

"Yes," admitted the boy at once. "That was the time. That gave me a chill, all right."

He placed the saddlebag beside Jonathan Quay. The latter did not touch it, but looked earnestly up into the face of the other.

"You've been through troubles, Jim, I see. Had a fall?"

"Kendal nearly got me," said the boy, "but I ran into the sheriff's gang. They tied me on the back of a hoss; the hoss ran away from 'em; I got a boy to file off my handcuffs, and the posse didn't look at the saddlebag. That's how I happened to get here."

"Kendal — the sheriff — handcuffs —" murmured Quay. "And all in one day. Oh, Jonathan Quay," he went on, raising his head and speaking softly to himself, "if you had known in a younger day what you can do! One finger mark of genius in my brain, young man. The ability to see others, to recognize the hearts of men and what their minds and hands can do. So I saw you, and in one glance I was able to read your secret. I could know you for what you are, trust you, use you! And reward you, too, by heaven. Hold out your pockets. We'll fill them with some of this sparkling stuff —"

The boy held up his hand and stepped back.

"Come, come," said Quay.

He held out what looked like a pile of pale fire in the palm of a hand which he had dipped into the saddlebag.

"It will be only a taste, my boy," said Quay.

Fantom shook his head.

"A few days back," said he, "I'd of taken it and mighty glad to get it. But I can't take it now."

"Can't? Can't?" said Quay. "Don't be foolish, Jim. A good lad. A good honest lad, as I knew you from the first. But don't cut your throat for the pleasure of feeling your own pain!"

"I can't take it," repeated Fantom.

"Can you tell me why not? Stolen goods? Is that it? Jim, this stuff never could be traced back to owners. It's been pried out of the stickpins of a thousand miners, taken off the fingers and the wrists of women and from around their throats. For fifteen years this little saddlebag's load has been gathered patiently. A good many men have died to fill it; a good many have died to keep it from being filled. There's nothing big enough to be identified, I think. These jewels are the same as banknotes, but they take up even a smaller space. A share is due to you. A big share. Take it freely!"

"I don't want it," said Fantom suddenly, and from the heart.

"I want to believe you," said Quay patiently, "but I won't keep on offering."

"I'll tell you," said the boy. "There's Jo up yonder in the valley. What would she think?"

"Women," said Quay, "never hate evil that is doing them good. Particularly mothers, my son. Everything that helps to put clothes on the back of the child, give him a dignity of place, fill his pocket, is good for a mother. Believe me!"

Fantom swung his hand back toward the mountains.

"It ain't what I want," said he.

"And what do you want, my lad, if not what every other man wants? You want money, power!"

"I wanta live," said the boy, "not by a gun but by my hands. I wanta have the feel of an ax in my hands, and drop trees with it. I wanta see the ground turn up behind the plow whose handles I'm holdin', and watch the birds come whirlin' down behind to hunt for seeds and worms. I wanta plant and grow and harvest."

"Well, the call of the soil is a good call," said Quay, "though I don't quite understand a laborer's point of view. And your wife, Jim? What of her? Without servants —"

"Work won't hurt her!" said the boy. "We'll work together — me at the woods and the ground, her at the house. We'll work for each other. Them that have servants, they got no taste of life in their mouths. No clothes'll fit my wife so well as the ones she makes with her own hands; no food'll taste to me like what she cooks for me."

He waved his hand again toward the mountains.

"This here is my country," said he, "an' I'm gunna grow into it. It never is hard on a man that tackles it with his own bare hands, I guess. Anyway, that's the chance I'll take. And not money borrowed off of the stickpins and the rings and the bracelets and such of other people. That's the way I stand. I thank you just the same. But Jo and me, we wouldn't flourish none on that kind of planting!"

"Ah," said Quay, "it's like a voice out of my own past. I went up there to find such men as you and start them in life as you want to start. But then came Kendal and showed me how we could use the tools that had been gathered together. Well — I suppose that I regret my failure. But Kendal — he's beaten!"

He laughed a little, softly, brooding on his victory.

"Even Kendal can be beaten if there's a Quay to plan and a young Jim Fantom to act with me."

"What did Kendal say when he found you tied up?"

"Looked down at me and grinned. 'He wasted the time to tie you up, eh?' said he. You see, Kendal wouldn't have wasted such time. Death has the strongest ropes of all, in his estimation. And of course he's right! But I'll tell you something more, my lad. No man can be a successful criminal who hasn't once been honest. That's a thing which Kendal never tasted."

CHAPTER THIRTY NINE

Something crackled suddenly at the edge of the woods. It brought Jonathan Quay to his feet with a lurch, picking up a rifle that leaned beside him as he rose.

"It's my horse," said Fantom.

"Your horse — your horse," muttered Quay, with a deep gasp of breathing. "Well — for half a moment I thought that Kendal might have —"

"Kendal's far away," said Fantom. "I think that Bud Cross will keep him pretty busy today."

"Sit down," said Quay. "Everything that you say is good news to me. Sit down, and I'll write you a deed that ought to be legally binding."

He took out a notebook and began to write rapidly on a page of it:

"From the spring northeast of the foot of the lake in the Happy Valley," he said aloud, "one half mile toward the lake, to the three black stones called the Three Spades by the people of Happy Valley, and from that point south a half mile, or to the edge of the river, and following the river two miles —"

"Two miles?" murmured Fantom.

"From that point east along the river," repeated Quay as he wrote, "two miles or more to the cypresses —"

But the words drifted out of the mind of the

boy. He was seeing the place itself, a great domain of lofty trees, of clearings of rich black mould, of thickets where wild berries grew, of fair green meadows by the river, already spotted with cattle that browsed on the rich pasture, in the imagination of Jim Fantom. He saw the face of his wife at the cabin's door; he heard in his heart the voices of his children. Peace descended upon the soul of Jim Fantom, and he felt that all was well.

"And here you are," said Jonathan Quay. "You'll find the valley an empty thing. They'll sweep out of it. Perhaps except young Chip Lander. He's an honest boy in the making, I take it. Then there's the Chinamen. I don't know what will become of them. But probably they'll stay on their river holdings. They're peaceful fellows, and you can turn a penny by hauling their truck across the mountains to the nearest markets. Gradually, you can become a king up there, my lad. If you have the strength and the ambition, try to keep up the village. Keep the storehouses and the stores in repair, unless the devils have burned everything in their rage and their hatred of me —"

"Of you?" said the boy. "It's me they'll blame for everything."

"Not when I disappear. They'll understand, then, that I was the man who planned it. Kendal will understand and let the others know. My friend Louis Kendal."

He laughed again, and the sound of that

laughter soured the very brain of the boy. He was on the very verge of flinging back even the paper to Quay, but the latter said hastily:

"Be careful of that! Don't let it rub too much. It's indelible pencil, but it will rub and smear unless you're careful. You'll notice that I say in there: 'for value received!' Well, my boy, I've received the full value. You'd better bring your horse in and prepare to spend the night here, however."

"I'm startin' back," said Fantom, to whom the thought of spending any more time with Quay had become intolerable. "I can jog off to the edge of the high ground, tonight. I can break the neck of my trip back, before my hoss is wore out. I'll go along."

"We shake hands, then," said Quay. "We say good-by! A melancholy word to an old man, my lad. But one of these days, you shall hear from me again. Perhaps, when your hands are callused a little thicker, you'll change your mind about your needs. Young ideas are hard ideas, four square, with four sharp corners; but time rolls them and chips them and pounds them until they're round enough to go anywhere, at my time of life. Good-by, Jimmy. Good-by and take good luck with you. I've never met a better man. You may tell your wife that. It will mean something to her, because you'll find that no man is a devil to a woman, unless he's taken bread out of the mouths of her children. Good-by again!"

So Jim Fantom left him, took his horse at the edge of the clearing, and rode off up the river trail. At the end of the open, he looked back, and saw Quay waving. He waved in return, and turned his back on that face.

It was growing into the reddest time of the sunset, when the flame has left the sky and only smudges are here and there upon the clouds. Color in the sky, but darkness on the land, and breathings of moisture coming up from the soil by the water. The humming of the insects, too, was a perpetual soft hymn on his left hand, while Darkness glided on with a dainty step.

There was no need for a tight rein, even in this close going among the trees, for he picked his own way deftly, and kept to his course as though he had a compass in his mind's eye.

Fantom had gone on for some minutes, when he heard the distinct noise of a horse behind him, and pulled aside into a thicket. Presently, a rider jogged a big animal into view, coming rapidly up the river trail, weaving among the trees. When he was beside the place where Fantom had concealed himself, he checked his horse and looked around in search, as though he expected to be met at this place. The light was now too dull to enable Fantom to make out the fellow's features, but that was not necessary. The outline of his body plainly showed that it was the hunchback, again! And a sudden cold sense of predestined tragedy rushed over the boy.

"Fantom!" called the other softly.

He was startled until the very hair prickled on his head.

"Fantom!" called the cripple once more.

Jim Fantom rode out into the dusk.

"How in God's name did you know I was here?" he asked.

"I didn't have a bird to tell me," said the hunchback composedly. "Will you come back with me to the cabin?"

"To what cabin?"

"To the one where Quay was."

"Was?"

"Yes. I mean just that."

"He's gone already?"

"Yes."

"Is there anyone else there?"

"Not a soul."

"What do you want of me?"

"I want you to go back there and use your eyes. Then you're a free man, unless you care to talk to me about what you see."

"I've turned my back on that place," said Fantom uneasily. "I ain't goin' back again."

"All right," said the hunchback. "You're the one man, I think, who could do anything about it. But I can't force you to go back."

"I'll go," agreed Fantom suddenly, but his blood was ice, and why, he could not tell. It was as though the little man breathed out an atmosphere of dread.

He was already in the lead, trotting his horse rapidly among the trees, through the gathering darkness, and Fantom followed him back, with a beating heart, until they came out into the clearing.

There his first sight was of Quay sitting as before, at the doorway, his head slightly inclined as in thought, or in sleep, perhaps.

"I thought you said that Quay was gone," said Fantom, his voice harsh with suspicion.

Instead of answering by word of mouth, the hunchback turned his long, ugly face toward Fantom and gestured for him to make a closer investigation. There was something in the little man's silence, in the slowness of his gesture, that told Fantom what he would find.

Jonathan Quay sat at ease, his head bowed until the chin rested on his breast, and with open, dull eyes he looked into eternity. The handle of a knife thrust out from his breast above the heart!

Death had come instantly with that stroke. His left hand lay loosely upon the threshold, with the pipe still in the fingers, and the right hand lay in his lap. Quay was gone indeed, and beyond recalling, beyond pursuit. All his years of crime and scheming were robbed of their fruit, for the saddlebag was gone, and with it the whole of his labors on earth!

The boy turned back his horse to the hunchback, now barely discernible in the gloom.

"Do you know?" he asked.

"I saw!" said the hunchback.

"And?"

"I saw Quay sitting there. I saw you leave. I was wondering how I could get for myself from that saddlebag what is due to me, when my friend, Louis Kendal, appeared slipping down the side of the house. I wanted to yell. Rather lose everything than have it fall back into the hands of that shark. But the sight of Louis hunting isn't easy for the nerves to follow. I was upset, in short, and while I watched him, it was only a second as he turned the corner and came upon Quay.

"I saw the flash of the knife. It seemed as long as a sword. I saw it go home into Quay's body, and the old man's head jerked back once and then fell forward.

"Kendal picked up the saddlebag and slipped away into the woods he had come from. Then I went after you. I'd seen you say good-by to him. Of course, Kendal had, too. He'd been there, waiting."

"What drew him down?"

"I don't know how he knew. All I know is that I followed him like mad across the mountains after the sheriff came whirling up through the valley —"

"And what did Cross do?"

"Nothing. The word had gone around. There was an exodus in progress. Every team in the valley was harnessed to buckboards and wagons. Mules and horses, the little mustangs, and draft animals for the plough, they were all used. Whole families worked like mad. The Chinese came to help and they were paid by getting half the household furnishings which were left behind. They went to the store and gutted everything that was worth carrying away. Down in the cellars of the store there were heaps and heaps of all sorts of utensils and everything that the valley needed. They swarmed through, helping themselves. They carried out bales of blankets and tossed them onto their wagons; they brought out canned food of all sorts, clothes, tools, ammunition, rifles, revolvers, knives, spades, hatchets, the whole hardware of the store. Bundles of ax-handles, pitchforks, bristle on top of the loads.

"They roll out barrels of flour, sugar, salt pork, dried meat, and when they have heaped their wagons with all they will hold, they smash what remains with the ax-heads. They look at the storehouses, filled with good sweet hay, by thousands of tons, with flour, with oats, barley, wheat, with enough to feed all in the valley for many years.

"They cannot leave this behind. They are afraid to remain in the place. They will leave nothing behind. Suddenly Rhiner, or some other, gives the word. Half a dozen men kindle the fires, and they begin to leap and roar in the dark of the night. This happened all in the night, d'you see? After you had left, after the word had been passed around that Quay and Kendal also were gone! The whole village goes shooting up in flames that burn very well, because the logs that compose them had been well seasoned."

"But the men that followed me?"

"Some were riding with Kendal. But Kendal himself had given the word that the end had come, that their valley was now known, and the sort of people who were in it. They must root up and move away. They must find another Happy Valley. All who remained, remained to pack up what they could carry off with their horses, and the rest was broken and ruined."

"I hope they choke in the desert!" said the boy savagely.

It was growing completely dark; only the loom of the tree tops against the pale sky showed that utter night had not yet come.

"They may do worse than that. They'll be wrangling with one another, before long!"

"They burned the whole village?"

"They burned it all. Once the flames started rising, they went mad. They wouldn't leave one log standing on another. Some of them scattered here and there. They passed along the valley, and touched the torch to every cabin."

"To every one?" cried the boy in an agony.

"Even the Chinese huts went up in smoke. They gave the poor devils only a little time to huddle their few things together. Into their clumsy carts they heaped what they had, and had to start their trek out of the Happy Valley. The house of Quay went up in flames along with the rest. I saw it burn with a good deal of satisfaction. If only Quay and Kendal had been in the flame, I wouldn't have cared for the money they've lost me!"

"Every cabin?" echoed the boy, with a groan.

"Until they came to your place in the woods, where Chip Lander stopped 'em with a rifle, and shots over their heads."

CHAPTER FORTY

"Lander!" cried Jim Fantom. "Chip Lander. God bless him! I'll make him know how I feel about that! Man, man, you mean to say that no harm came to the house — or to her?"

"They piled around it like yelling Injuns. But Lander was inside. It was dawn, then. He was still carrying into the house some of the load of loot that he'd taken from the stores — his share of the plunder."

"Hold on. He'd taken the loot back from the store to *her* house?"

"Yes."

Sweat burst out on the forehead of Fantom. Then he explained, aloud:

"He had no house of his own. So he turned his share over to her!"

"Ay, exactly. He turned it over to her. He was still carrying things into the house when they same in a swarm, yelling like devils. He shot over their heads. I think he even grazed one of the men who tried to set fire to a shed outside the house. When they saw he was in earnest, they spilled back from the face of the map, and only over in a corner there then I started out of the valley. I had a good horse, and another on the lead. I looked back and saw the whole valley thick with smoke, because there wasn't much wind, and the smoke rolled up into a big, white tableland. Now and then through a rift there would be a sight of black ruins, and a welter of flames on them.

"Then down the south trail belched a rattle of horses. They were coming back, the riders from the Happy Valley, but without Kendal. Kendal was gone, they shouted to me, and went on in a whirl. Not far behind came the posse of the sheriff.

"They dipped down into the smoke, and that was the last of 'em. They didn't bother me. The law has no hold on me."

He laughed a little as he said that.

"But what will they find? That the clues and the traces that they hoped to find are blotted out. The valley's wiped from the face of the map, and only over in a corner there is the place of Jim Fantom, with a woman keeping it, and Chip Lander's rifle, as well. A brave lad, is Chip!"

Fantom was silent. Then he murmured through stiffened lips:

"Yes, brave, brave! Of course —"

His voice trailed away, for he was seeing vividly the picture of Chip playing the hero, striding from room to room, the wreaths of pungent smoke of gunpowder brushed aside by his swinging shoulders, and Chip laughing, making light of everything, a hero!

A hero with Jo to watch him, admire him, listen to the yelling of the crowd in the dull dawn-light outside, and contrast it with the cheerful voice of this brave youngster!

What would be the effect upon her?

She had loved him, to be true. But she might change. All women were capable of change. And she was intensely emotional, her nature leaped swiftly to a new goal. So, in a moment, as he had learned to love her, she had learned to love him. And here she found at the crisis that her betrothed lover was gone away, she did not know where, slipping off like a thief in the night and leaving a stranger to take his place with her as a guard!

Terrible fear flowed into the body of Jim Fantom.

"The valley's swept clean, then?" he asked.

"The valley's empty, by this time, I suppose. The sheriff won't find anything. The men, the women, the children, the horses, the cattle are gone. The Chinamen are plodding afterward, not knowing enough to tell the law how they have been wronged. It's an exodus to find another Promised Land, except that there's no Quay there to make them the promise or to show them how such things are built. Genius isn't found waiting at every crossroads! And Quay was a genius."

He was silent, and the boy as well, until Fantom murmured:

"I have to start on! One minute. How did you pick up the trail of Kendal?"

"Partly cleverness, partly guesswork, and the power of a pair of strong horses. I spotted him with my glass when he was miles off. I pulled up on him and shadowed him through the hills. And so we came here. That's all! Where are you going, young man?"

"Back to the Happy Valley."

"Then hurry, or Kendal will be there before you."

"Kendal? There again? What's there for him to find at the place?"

"A beautiful woman waiting," said the cripple, and laughed viciously in the darkness.

Fantom shook his head.

"Lander, Lander!" said he. "That's the man I fear. He's handsome. I've always feared him! He's been the hero, now. But Kendal? She'd laugh in his face!"

"No man or woman ever laughed at Kendal," said the other. "It isn't likely that she'll be the first to set the example. No, no, my boy. He'll go there to buy her if he can't persuade her."

"Buy her?"

"He'll spread the diamonds on the table before her and make them into a map of a beautiful life. I can see his long fingers arranging Paris and London, drawing out Italy for her. Kendal can do those things. He'd move an angel, if he chose!"

"I believe in her!" said the boy.

"Young man," said the other sternly, "Quay was a well-balanced, thoughtful, successful man, with his mind turned toward philanthropy. But Quay failed to stand against the temptations of that demi-devil, as the poet says. Quay went down. Will *you* be able to stand, d'you think?"

"Besides," muttered Fantom, terribly shaken, "he don't care about her. There's been no sign!"

"There *has* been a sign. There was a time the other day when, for the first time in his life, Kendal was helpless in the hand of another man. I was the man! I had a gun covering his heart, but that wasn't my power. I'd seen him prowling by the cabin; I'd seen the face of the girl; and something made me put the two things together. I suggested to Kendal that I'd drop in on her and tell her a few little stories of his early life. At that threat, Jim Fantom, he turned to water. His face was wet with perspiration. In another moment he'd capitulated. What he had taken fifteen years before from me, plus a handsome interest for the intervening years, and a little more — to make up for shock to my feelings, let's say, and loss of happiness in the meantime!"

He chuckled, and the chuckle was like a snarl.

"He promised all that I asked. Swore sacredly that I should have it all; and that would have been done, except that Quay stood in the way of the fulfillment, of course. Quay wanted everything, not taking out the little that I demanded. Quay had learned greed among all the other evil qualities that Kendal planted in him for the first time. However, Fantom, if Kendal thought enough of the girl to be helpless in my hand, do you think that he wouldn't use every gift that God poured into his clever, treacherous brain to take her in some way and to make her his?"

"I believe it, I believe it!" said the boy. "Then I start on, man, at once. Good-by. You've told me things that are worth ten years of life, or a thousand years of hell to me!"

"Wait," said the hunchback. "Suppose that I show you a way to save ten hours on the return to the valley?"

"Ten hours saved?"

"Ay, the way that Louis Kendal traveled down through the mountains. Trails that no other man knew, I suppose. By the same token, he's sure to beat you back — by ten hours!"

"God!" gasped Jim Fantom.

"But come with me, and I think that I can improve even over Kendal's trail. Besides, he doesn't know that we're following!"

"Save me ten hours," said Fantom, "and I'm your slave for my life."

Ten hours!

"Catch up those two horses of Quay, then," said the hunchback. "They'll be no further use to him. As a matter of fact, it's a white horse that he's riding now, and it's already arrived at the end of its journey, I suppose. That's a horse that's never in the stall, and every trip it makes with a crowded back. Yet it never grows tired."

He chuckled once more in his sinister manner, but the boy already was at work unhobbling the two horses of the dead man, and did not hear the last words of the other.

Straightway they were off, with the two animals upon the lead, and, brushing through the woods, they came into the open, rolling ground beyond the poplars and headed for the mountains that climbed above them.

The boy watched the hunchback. Obviously the man was not accustomed to so many hours in the saddle. He was continually twisting from one side to the other, striving to get into a more comfortable position, but that comfort he could never find.

Yet he did not wince from the journey. He never complained. The body of the boy himself, expert horseman though he was, turned leaden with the dreadful fatigue of this second journey, and he marveled at the manner in which his companion supported himself. But still the hunchback clung to his work, gripping the pommel of the saddle, often, and bowing his head with agony, but never uttering a word.

So they climbed by a swifter and straighter line through the highlands, so they worked through the long hours of the night, and, still in the darkness, they came to the edge of the valley and saw the first stone of dawn thrown, as the Persian says, into the bowl of night.

CHAPTER FORTY ONE

Rapidly the dawn-light spread, the eastern peaks taking the reflection from the opposite sky; and, as they went down the trail along the valley wall, they could see the whole picture beneath them, the river and the lake gradually flushing pink, with ripples of silver and with markings of gold. It was indeed, like a painted picture at that distance, looking as though a child with sooty finger tips had smudged it, for here and there where houses had stood were little dabs of black, and from some of them thin wisps of smoke stood up like white spears in the deathly quiet of that cold morning air. So they came down into the valley, riding hard.

They had changed saddles three times, during the night, and they changed again at the valley's brim, letting Quay's two horses run loose on the edge of the woods, and dashing down at full speed. The horse of the hunchback stumbled and plunged with utter exhaustion, but Darkness, with wonderful might still, was gliding on with a high head.

"An enemy's gift," said Fantom aloud, though he had not intended that the words should pass his lips.

The hunchback turned a face on which the dawn revealed unutterable exhaustion. His lips were pressed tight together and grinned back with overmastering resolution.

"A dead enemy!" said he.

"Hello!" exclaimed the boy, startled out of his own thoughts.

"You were speaking about the horse?"

"Yes."

"Kruger's in jail. He'll hang, young man, you'll be glad to know."

"Kruger in jail!"

"Kruger's in jail. That fall he got when he was yanked off his horse fractured his skull for him. The coward thought he was dyin', and confessed that he murdered Larry Phelan."

"Great God," cried Fantom, "am I a man free of the law, then?"

"As free," said the hunchback, "as any of us are, who have to keep our heads turned over our shoulders all the while, wondering what society and custom will do with its whip, and when our turn will come for a lashing. But free from the shadow of the jail, at least. There's no ghost of a gibbet at the end of your trail now, my friend."

"Why should Kruger — little Sammy Kruger — why should he kill Phelan, in the name of heaven?"

"Jealousy, I think they said. Jealousy over some girl — some boy's quarrel at a dance, and a little man's vengefulness, which never dies. I am myself a little man, you see!"

He grinned at his own remark, and the expression it gave to his face was ghastly in the extreme.

They had swept down to the floor of the valley, and now, they galloped, they looked back toward the top of the cliff — and instantly shrank small on their horses and drove them into the cover of the woods, for, at that instant, above them appeared the great Louis Kendal, swinging a tired horse down the slant trail for the valley beneath!

The boy looked at the hunchback, and the hunchback looked back at him, in pale excitement, and they sent their horses on at a brisk gait, avoiding the road, because there was danger that the dust they raised might not yet be settled when Kendal came along, and then he could be sure that others had passed before him down this road.

A burden of infinite weight fell upon the brain of Jim Fantom. In all things, the hunchback had proved a good prophet. How, then, if the gun of Kendal should win the battle which now surely was before them? What of poor Jo Dolan, gathered into the crafty hand of the monster?

They cut as a bird flies, across country, through narrow streams that dashed them cold and wet with spray, up banks, through towering woods which still kept the night in their cañons, and so at last they drew near to the clearing.

The hunchback saw it first. He pointed a long arm, and, following that direction with his glance, the boy saw a wavering arm of smoke that rose in the air above the trees.

They dismounted here and held brief consultation. It was best, they decided, to await the coming of Kendal on foot, and at the verge of the clearing. What happened then would be a matter of guns, and the empty holsters of the boy had been filled from those of the hunchback — good guns, new guns, that fitted nicely to his hand — and he swore to himself that, if only the leaden weariness would leave his hands and his eyes, he would at least kill Kendal, even if he should die himself in accomplishing that task. For the man filled him with an immense loathing, not as a dangerous man, but as a dangerous beast, with a reptile's poison in his touch.

They came softly close to the clearing, and, as they did so, heard the pounding of a horse coming up from the far side of the clearing. It startled them both, but it could not be Kendal. Even he had no witchcraft to fly so fast!

And so, reaching the edge of the screen of trees, they saw Chip Lander come trotting his horse into the clearing, and singing out as he came:

"Hey, Jo!"

The kitchen door flew open, and Jo Dolan stood there, waving and smiling.

"I never saw anything better than you, this morning," she told him. "I've been quakin' all night!"

"Not me," he answered. "I was as snug in that new lean-to as a wolf in a cave with his winter fur on. Doggone me, Jo, but I'm glad to see that you have breakfast started. I'm gunna do things to it!"

He threw the reins of his horse and swung down to the ground.

"Come in for hot water," said she.

"I need cold to wake me up," said he.

So he rolled up his sleeves and washed at the basin of the spring, while the girl disappeared indoors.

"You see?" said the hunchback, in a murmur. "They're not in love with one another, in spite of your fears."

"I don't know — I don't know!" said the boy. "You can't tell. You never can tell!"

Chip advanced, blinded and dripping with water, toward the kitchen door, through which a towel flew. He caught it from the air and climbed up the steps, drying himself.

"Shall we go in and tell them?"

"There's no time, probably," answered Fantom. "There's no time. Besides, it's my fight, now. It's my war with Kendal, an' not Chip's. He's done enough for me! He can't do this! An' Kendal would kill him out of hand, with no trouble."

He was kneading his fingers and wrists and then flexing his fingers to restore their suppleness, as Chip ran down the steps and gathered an armful of wood from the woodshed.

The girl followed into the open doorway.

"I dreamed it, too," said she.

"That he was safe?"

"Of course it'll come true," said Chip. "That'll be my luck."

"Oh, Chip," said she. "You don't wish any harm to him, do you?"

"Why shouldn't I?" said Chip cheerfully. "Isn't he in my way, Jo? Of course he is, confound him! An' I wish him a broke leg, anyway. Before he got well of that, I'd of chopped so much wood and raked so many leaves and planted so much potatoes for you, Jo, that you couldn't help paying a little attention to me!"

She leaned in the doorway, laughing down at him.

"I pay a lot of attention to you now," said she. "Dear Chip! What would ever of become of me, if it hadn't been for you?"

"The trouble with me," said Chip, pausing in thought, in spite of his armload of wood, "is that I've become a friend."

"Isn't that better than to be an enemy?"

"Not a mite! You take a friend, and a girl never gives a hang about him. Lot better to be an enemy. Look at Jim Fantom with you!"

"He wasn't my enemy. Not ever!"

"Sure he was. He was everybody's enemy when he come back to Burned Hill. Be honest. You told me yourself that you were so scared of him that your knees shook, and you had to be sassy to him to keep yourself together."

"I liked him right away," she answered.

"Sure you did. Because he'd killed a few men, here and there. Nothin' much to boast about, but just enough to flavor him. But after him, along comes me, and I didn't seem anything but

331

raw. What had I done but a couple of holdups and such? You couldn't expect a nice young girl to take no man-sized interest in me!"

"Come in with that wood," she commanded, "before the fire goes out. Oh, Chip, God wouldn't let nothin' happen to him!"

"God never has paid much attention to goin's on in Happy Valley," said Chip Lander, "and it's expectin' a lot to think that he'll start in now."

She pressed her hands against her face, shutting out a vision.

"Louis Kendal never will reach him. Say that for me, Chip!"

"Louis Kendal never will reach him, of course," said he. "Nobody in the world can ride like that Jim of ours. And didn't he grab the finest hoss in the valley, pretty near?"

"Oh, Chip, to think of him doin' such a thing! An' three men shootin' at him!"

"The devil takes care of his pets," observed the other. "I gotta say that for him. He never favored me, much. I always been a little too good for him. Three men didn't shoot at him very long. He plastered Steve Cumber for good and all. Steve'll never blow another safe. But tell me, Jo," he went on, as he climbed the steps toward the door. "Tell me this, will you?"

"What is it?"

"What'll I do bad enough to make you like me a little more?"

"I do like you. An' I love you, too, Chip dear. Of course I do!"

"Hell fire!" said Chip. "You love me like a brother, don't you? Well, I'm gunna go out and kill me a man or two, and then I'll be able to come back here and sun myself and sit around and there'll be nothin' but smiles. Two more notches on my guns, and I'd make Jim Fantom so doggone jealous he couldn't see!"

"Oh no," said she. "Jim's not that kind. There's no more jealousy in my Jim than in that mountain. He's so big!"

"I weigh ten pound more than him," asserted Chip, at the door at last.

"His heart is so big," said the girl. "He has such a great big heart!"

"I'm tired of talkin' about that Jim Fantom," said Chip. "It never seems to get me nowhere!"

They vanished through the door of the house as the hunchback gripped the arm of Fantom, looking straight before him to the farther side of the clearing. Fantom followed that direction with his own gaze, and there he saw leaning against a tree, the long and misshapen form of Louis Kendal himself!

CHAPTER FORTY TWO

It seemed to the boy, at first, that Kendal was looking straight toward him, but the next moment the other had left his tree and was moving with his usual long, clumsy, but really swift stride toward the house. Over his left shoulder was slung the saddlebag of treasure.

The very thing which the hunchback had promised was, it appeared, about to be performed.

With all his might, Fantom wished to step forth and confront the other, but his legs had turned stiff as ice, and trembled violently beneath him. He had not realized the hypnotic force of the man until he saw him again, face to face.

The clutch of the hunchback deepened in his arm.

"Walk out, walk out!" said he. "But put your hands on your hips. Laugh at him, if you can. Do something to break him down, Fantom! For God knows that, man to man and hand to hand, there's no one under this sky that can stand against him. He's got to doubt himself before he ever can be beat!"

The boy listened, and suddenly he knew that it was true. There was no better way to explain the unhuman force of Kendal than by under-

334

standing that he never had admitted to himself the possibility of failure. There was nothing but absolute surety in the man, like the surety of the lion that never has failed of a kill.

But to face down Louis Kendal? He shuddered at the thought. Yet every instant carried that potent danger closer and closer to the cabin, where the girl was now laughing with Chip Lander at breakfast. The clink of the dishes dimly could be heard. There they sat, cheerfully, Chip no doubt gay as could be, and she willing to be amused, no matter how heavy her heart might be with anxiety for her lover.

Then strength came to Jim Fantom. With one gliding step he was in front of the tree, his hands upon his hips, laughing!

Louis Kendal was quite turned away, and yet that swift animal eye saw the danger instantly and whirled toward it. The saddlebag was cast from his shoulder as he spun about, and his long fingers were gripping the butt of a Colt, slung low in a holster strapped about his thigh. He was half crouched, and a sneer contorted his long, pale face as he glared at Jim Fantom.

The laughter which Fantom had forced became real. He shook with a hysteria of fear. His head rocked back, and still he laughed, soundlessly, his hands upon his hips.

When the nervous frenzy passed, and when he could look again, he saw that Kendal had straightened and stood stiff with amazement. Actually he was agape, and then shut his teeth and his lips into a grim line.

Amazement of another sort struck through the brain of the boy. Kendal himself, the animal Kendal, had been shocked by that laughter which he had witnessed. The effect of that shock was still plainly visible, as though the lion itself, ranging the forest, had come upon an unknown monster, terrible through its strangeness.

Fantom could understand why. Even in his childhood, it was not likely that many men had so much as smiled at the pale, ugly face of Kendal! Then hope, and after it, strong courage rushed through the heart of Jim Fantom. His blood grew warm. Indeed, it was as though he never had felt the freezing grip of the man upon his arm.

"You've followed me here, boy, have you?" said Kendal suddenly. "You couldn't let one lesson do you?" And he started forward.

"Good!" said Fantom, nodding. "Get close enough to be sure of your shot."

Kendal halted as though he had been struck with a club.

"You little fool," said he. "Do I have to shoot you down here, where you dreamed of being happy? Go back into the woods, where we'll be out of sight of other folks!"

"Stay here, Kendal," said the boy. "I have a friend along that wants to see if Louis Kendal can be hit with bullets. I have a friend along that couldn't see you so good, if we went back into the dark of the woods."

The harsh voice of the hunchback broke in:

"Ay, Louis. Here I am. Here's your dear old Edgar, waiting to see you clutch at your chest and stagger like a drunkard. After you've died, I'll help myself from the saddlebag to what's due me."

The cripple had moved a distance to the side, during the first words that Fantom had interchanged with Kendal, but now he appeared in turn at the verge of the trees; and, at his voice, Kendal turned suddenly toward him, recollected himself, and whirled back toward the boy, as though realizing that he must not face from the greatest danger.

"You white-faced toad," said Kendal, "when I'm through with the kid, I'll handle you. I've kept my hands from you long enough. There'll be a finish to you now!"

"You'll never finish with him, Louis," said the other. "He's the end of your rope and the finish of your trail. He's the last news and the bad news, Louis. He's the master that every man has to meet!"

The mouth of Kendal snarled.

"Boy," said he to Fantom, "I'll do this much for you. I'll let you make the first pass for your gun, and may that start help you!"

Somehow, Fantom found the strength to smile, and he said not a word.

"Louis, Louis," said the hunchback. "Don't be a fool. Your master, Louis! You're talking to your master!"

"Talking about your life," added Fantom, "get out your gun and fill your hand. I'll tend to you then!"

The long, pale face of Kendal turned crimson; then it blotched with purple and white again. Even at that distance, the boy could see a tremor run through the tall body, the first tremor of doubt. No answer came.

"If you're afraid," said Fantom, his detestation of the man turning into confident strength, "come closer to make surer of your shot. Step up closer. I'm gunna wait here for you."

Kendal made half a step forward, and then drew back to his former position.

"You're drunk!" said he, speaking with difficulty.

Fantom smiled, and there was no effort in forcing it, now.

"The time's runnin' on, and your courage is leakin', Kendal," said he. "You'd better make your play, now. It'll be better now, than later."

He could hear the hiss of Kendal's intaken breath.

"Damn you!" whispered the tall man. "I'll —"

A form stepped into the doorway of the cottage, and a long, trailing scream of a woman rang over the clearing.

It shocked Jim Fantom; it drove Kendal desperate, and in his desperation he made his move. Incalculably swift was the whip of his hand and as the muzzle of the gun cleared the lip of the holster, it was exploding rapidly. A bullet plowed the ground at the feet of Fantom. Another hissed at his cheek.

Then, for the first time, he was able to fire. A blind shot he felt it to be, but it doubled Kendal suddenly to his knees. His gun fell as he dropped, and, reaching for it, he crumpled on his side and lay gasping. To his death day, Jim Fantom never would forget the way the man bit at the air, like a fish in water.

The voice of the hunchback was calling:

"Again, again! Shoot again, Jim Fantom! The devil's never dead until his eyes are shut."

But Fantom, gun poised, stood back against the tree and waited an instant, until he saw Jo Dolan running down the steps, and Chip Lander bursting past her, and springing into the lead.

Once more Kendal strove to gather his strength, but once more he failed, and this time rolled upon his back. Fantom, the girl, and Chip Lander met in a group about him, she falling on her knees and reaching to pull back his coat, for a huge crimson stain was rapidly spreading upon the breast of it.

He spoke, his usually clangorous voice now a husky whisper.

"There's no use," said he. "I'm going out. You've beat me, Edgar. Your damned voice and the sight of you was enough to freeze me. It wasn't the kid. It wasn't Fantom!"

He turned his head so that he could see Jim Fantom, and his lips wrinkled in a bestial snarl again.

"I should of finished you when I had you in my hand. I guessed it then. I know it now. But every man makes one mistake. Damn you, and may the devil bring you bad luck!"

The voice of Chip Lander broke in:

"They's no devil here now in the Happy Valley, Kendal. He's gone with you."

"Hush," said the girl. "He's gone!"

His eyes had closed, but after a moment they opened and he looked up at the sky.

"Edgar?" he whispered faintly.

The hunchback dropped on his knees beside the other.

"I never meant to keep it," murmured Kendal, "but when you found out, then I was forced out the door, so to speak. I never meant to rob you of the money. I had ways in mind of replacing it —"

The voice of the hunchback was suddenly touched with emotion.

"God knows that I forgive you!" said he. "Nothing but hate of you has kept me moving these fifteen years, but now that I see you this way, I forgive you, old man, with all my heart."

"She always guessed I'd go wrong," said Kendal, muttering.

"Who?"

"My aunt — your mother!"

He closed his eyes again.

The others had drawn back a little from the dying man, leaving the two cousins together.

"A fool of a kid!" cried Kendal suddenly. "A rat of a half-backed little cur like that to be the

340

ending of me! God help the man that stops to listen when there's guns in the air!"

His glance froze on vacancy. It seemed to Fantom that death had come, but suddenly Kendal smiled. His whole voice came back to him, ringing out with horrible loudness:

"Jonathan! Jonathan!"

With that, he died.

But yet it did not seem possible that the man whose strength had the valley and all of its people so long in his hand had now actually disappeared. The body itself, lank and deformed, still seemed able to spring to life.

Jo Dolan took the hand of Fantom and whispered, looking up to him with half frightened and half saddened eyes:

"Come away! The poor little man wants to be alone for a moment, I think!"

They stole off together. Chip Lander trailing after, and the hunchback remained crouched by the dead man, his hand on the cold hand of Kendal, his eyes on the faintly sneering face.

CHAPTER FORTY THREE

Sheriff Bud Cross had become a great man in his community and in his county. He could feel it on this bright, hot morning of the early summer when he left his house and sauntered down the street toward his office.

There was a difference in the manner of others as they greeted him. Their smiles were bright, but a little nervous. Men seemed anxious to put the best foot forward when in his presence. Women smiled at him, however, with an open delight. There is no shame in adoring a hero!

Children followed him, the boys imitating, half in fun and half in worship, his long and lumbering stride. For, like most cowpunchers, he was not entirely steady on his feet.

He understood what had made the great change. If he could not have guessed, the Burned Hill *Bugle* would have made him aware of the reason, for it attributed the scattering of the outlaws of the Happy Valley entirely to the work of the sheriff.

Rhiner, ex-murderer, having been caught, had confessed recent crimes which implicated many. The dead body of Quay, the hypocrite, had been found. Swift rumor said that Louis Kendal, of unsavory fame, revealed by Rhiner as the master mind, also was dead.

The glory for all of this fell upon the sheriff, and when he disclaimed credit, but placed it upon chance and the odd workings in the Happy Valley of a young man named Jim Fantom, Burned Hill shook its united head and smiled at such modesty. Had not even the real murderer of Larry Phelan confessed? And was he not at this moment in the jail, tremblingly awaiting his trial?

This, also, was mysteriously attributed to the agency of the sheriff, and therefore Bud Cross protested no longer but rather grimly set his teeth to wait for the reaction which he was sure would set in.

But he was glad when he could turn in from the street to his office, which was a little white-painted shack wedged in between two of Burned Hill's most important stores. He shut the gate in some haste, behind him, as though fearing that the youngsters who trailed behind him might squeeze through. And so he came to his office door and inserted the key in the lock.

As he pushed the door open, the sheriff became aware of a taint of cigarette smoke in the air — not stale, but fresh! Instantly his hand was on the butt of a revolver, and slowly he thrust the door wide.

His suspicions were at least in part justified. There were armed men in the room, two of them. One was Chip Lander, and the other was Jim Fantom. But they were smiling in a friendly fashion at the sheriff, and in a farther corner of the room sat beautiful Jo Dolan, smiling also.

The sheriff released the handle of his Colt in haste and slammed the door behind him.

"Well," said he, "I can't say that I was expectin' you folks, but I'm glad that you made yourself at home!"

Chip Lander pointed toward a window, still ajar.

"We came in the side door," said he. "We arrived pretty early, an' we figgered that it would be better to avoid the crowd. We want a marriage license, Sheriff."

"I ain't the justice of peace," the sheriff pointed out.

"But you can take the price that we pay for the license," said Chip Lander.

"I don't see why I should. What's behind all of this grinning, folks?"

Young Jim Fantom stood up.

"Because we're not payin' in cash," said he.

He slung a deep saddlebag over the crook of his arm and poured forth upon the table a flood of glittering jewels, of diamonds, rubies, emeralds, sapphires, and several thick packages of banknotes.

Some of the gems rolled off the table and glittered on the floor, but they lay unregarded.

The sheriff stared, entranced.

"The Happy Valley loot!" he said beneath his breath.

"It's the whole layout," said Fantom, "except for some stuff that went to a man that helped me run down Kendal. If it hadn't been for that, we never would of got this! He took around forty thousand dollars' worth, but you can see that they's somethin' left!"

The sheriff approached the treasure with a slowed and awful step.

"Fantom," he said presently, "you've give me a lot of hard riding, but now it seems to me as though it was only a short trail. But a lot of this will come back to you. They ain't half of it that will ever be claimed."

Fantom shook his head.

"It don't look like money to me," said he.

"It is, though," said the sheriff. "What's the matter with you, man?"

"Why, I can see nothin' but guns, when I look at it. Guns in leather, guns comin' out on the jump, guns spittin' fire, guns shootin' into the dust, guns shootin' into men, an' the men fallin' to this side and to that. Men lyin' bitin' at the air," concluded Jim Fantom. His face grew pale. "I don't want nothin' connected with this pile of loot. I've had dirty hands, an' I want to rub 'em clean with hard work. Me and Jo, here!"

The sheriff looked from one to the other.

"Is Chip the witness?" he asked.

"Naw. I'm the chief mourner," said Chip good-naturedly, "in this here company."

"Is it a company?" asked the sheriff.

"Sure," said Chip. "It's a company. Fantom is the boss; his girl is gunna be the straw boss, and I'll be the working gang. I'm gunna be teamster and hoss wrangler and cowpuncher, and all that Fantom will have to do will be to cut down trees, an' cut 'em up, an' clear ground, an' plow an' harrow an' sow an' reap an' thresh an' a few little things like that. We're all started for an easy life!"

The sheriff looked at them with glistening eyes.

"The Happy Valley?" said he.

"Sure. Where else?"

"I'd leave everything for such a chance," said Bud Cross. "But the doggone luck keeps me tied down to the town!"

He looked sadly out the window at the single street of Burned Hill. To the sheriff it seemed as though existence were walled in between the double row of house-fronts. He could not see, at that moment, the greatness of the mountains beyond, but he felt that somewhere among them new lives were beginning and happiness would be taken out of the soil and out of the air.

"You stay here," said he. "I'll go out an' get the justice an' the minister, too. But you stay here, because you'd likely draw a crowd."

He started for the door.

"Wait a minute," broke in Chip. "I'll go along."

"You better stay here," said the sheriff.

"No," said Chip, "because it's a kind of a small room, an' I hate to crowd it."

So he went grinning through the door at the sheriff's heels.

The two lovers remained alone, looking at one

another with frightened eyes. They thought neither of the past nor of the days to come, but only of the treasure of that moment, greater than the heart could hold.

The employees of G.K. Hall hope you have enjoyed this Large Print book. All our Large Print titles are designed for easy reading, and all our books are made to last. Other G.K. Hall books are available at your library, through selected bookstores, or directly from us.

For information about titles, please call:

(800) 223-1244
   or
(800) 223-6121

To share your comments, please write:

Publisher
G.K. Hall & Co.
P.O. Box 159
Thorndike, ME 04986